EIGHTEEN
in 1942

**Destined For War From the
Day They Were Born**

EIGHTEEN
in 1942

Destined For War From the
Day They Were Born

K.J. McCall

Published by

 JJ PUBLISHERS, LLC

Printed in the United States of America

Cover and Book Design by Jeffery M. Hall, www.iongdw.com

Author photo by Denny and Donna Bingaman

Library of Congress Control Number: 2014950085

ISBN: 978-0-9845589-2-6

*In memory of my father, World War II veteran,
and quiet wellspring of integrity and good sense.*

February, 1945
Berga, Germany

.... black-uniformed SS troops guarded the gate with German Shepherds tugging on leashes, emaciated kitchen-workers scurried to fill the cans fast enough to avoid punishment, foundering inmates shivered in their prison-issue pajamas. Once there were lynchings! Right in front of them, right out in the open! Bodies hanging like laundry from ropes thrown over a beam in the courtyard as the GIs stood in the kitchen waiting area. Like the rest, Corbin turned away. He didn't want to see, feared what the SS would do if they caught him looking. All he wanted to do was separate himself from that horrible place ....

ONE

September, 1941
Judson, Pennsylvania

O n this day as every other thus far in his seventeen years, Corbin O'Connell was safe and full of breakfast. But the time would come when he'd trade everything for a bit of food and no longer expect to reach the age of twenty-one. Life to him even now seemed unfair. Out of bed every morning at five except when he got up earlier, countless hours in the fields to work the family farm. Secretly, he hoped for a war; getting drafted would mean a noble escape and there'd be nothing his father could say.

His greater burden though was of the heart, caught-up in love the way he was with Daisy Hall. Thoughts of her took up all the space in his mind. The very sight of her made him ache. But his best friend, John, a rich man's son, had already staked that claim.

More to the moment was worry over his temperamental truck – a valid worry since it often chose times like this to act up. Corbin set the plumed hat down and draped his band uniform across the passenger seat, careful not to crumple the ironing job his mother had just labored over. He held his breath as he tried the ignition, raised an eyebrow in surprise at the steady idle. And he wondered going out the dusty dirt road whether he'd make it the five miles to town before the old thing died.

It was the beginning of another September in Judson Pennsylvania, another school year, another fall. Stretched high across Main Street a sturdy banner hailed:

JUDSON LABOR DAY PARADE, 1941
SPONSORED BY OTTINGER INDUSTRIES

Eager crowds had gathered at the curbs under a blue-bowl sky. Nearly everybody was involved some way in this hour of local pageantry that had taken months to prepare. In keeping with tradition, the Veterans of Foreign Wars were the ones to start things off, their gouty commander in a Cadillac convertible while the rest hoofed behind him sweating in wool uniforms from the Great War. Men on the sidewalk removed their hats. An occasional one saluted.

The Judson High School Marching Band followed in stark contrast, resplendent in gold and white. They radiated pure energy as they rhythm-stepped to their own music, sunlight glinting so much off the brass instruments that onlookers had to shield their eyes. While friends on the sidelines hurled playful taunts, Corbin O'Connell and John Ottinger marched along next to each other – both of them seniors, both of them trumpeters, both of them dreaming of Daisy Hall. People in town viewed the two inseparable, side-by-side in any alphabetical line and together by choice the rest of the time.

For the seniors it would be a year of lasts: the last homecoming, last gridiron game, last spring dance. It would be their last time, too, for marching in the Labor Day Parade this way as part of the Judson youth. Later, they'd be relegated by time and another war to the cadre of yesteryear heroes ahead of them, except for the ones added to the name plaque in Memorial Park.

It took the band nearly thirty minutes to reach the reviewing stand where the mayor and other VIPs lounged in comfort out of the sun. As the drum major lifted his baton, forty teen-aged heads snapped to the right. And on the down stroke, forty instruments erupted in a rousing Sousa march.

John aligned his eyes with the platform and found his father. They made brief eye contact and the father smiled. John would have smiled, too, had his lips not been wrapped around a mouthpiece. He knew he was lucky – the automatic respect of his peers, a sewn-up future – all because he was an Ottinger. Not to mention one day marrying the prettiest girl in town.

Corbin pushed his own images of Daisy aside to focus on his playing. Next to her, music in general and the trumpet in particular mattered most to him – the reason he played better than anyone else. His future had not yet taken shape. From the depths of his teenage wisdom, any chance at happiness involved leaving town, so getting out of Judson was his only clear plan.

A block or so behind them, Daisy waved at the cheering crowd with a white-gloved hand. Queen of the Peach Festival back in August, she glided now atop a flower-draped Chamber-of-Commerce float, seated on a stool hidden by her voluminous skirt. On a bend in the road she caught sight of the marching band, stole glances in its direction to search out the trumpeters. Despite a nagging guilt she let her eyes travel over

John to rest on Corbin, and allowed them to stay there for the whole of that brief clear view.

Not far away, from a prime spot on the curb, Velma Hix had anchored her eyes on Corbin as well, with a look that could be described only as predatory. If the two young women tried to read each other's thoughts, Daisy would correctly guess Velma's but not the other way round.

Soon, far-reaching events would complicate these tangles of youth. Though America was still at peace with the world, Adolf Hitler had provoked a reluctant Europe into war. When he absorbed Austria and occupied Czechoslovakia in 1938, they'd hoped he would quit there. When he invaded Poland in 1939 defying threats by the British and French, they deemed it a brazen attempt to seize the continent. When he invaded Western Europe in 1940 and attacked the Soviet Union in 1941, they judged him a dangerous megalomaniac trying to take over the world.

In some ways the folk in Judson felt removed from all that, separated from it as they were by the vastness of the Atlantic Ocean. But the first peacetime mandatory registration in U.S. history had taken place in 1940; a few Judson boys had already been drafted as a result.

In another three months apathy will vanish, heavy thoughts shifting to the forefront.

The parade will be shorter in 1942.

There will be no parade at all in 1943.

By that time the streets of Judson will be nearly empty of young men, some never to return.

T W O

Corbin took a cigarette from the band of his work hat and cupped a protective hand around a match flame to light it. An ominous sky threatened from the farm's north edge, a line of tall hickories swaying as one. He pounded the last fence post further into the ground, nailed three rows of barbed wire in place as dark clouds materialized overhead. A cool drop smacked his arm. Above the encroaching wind he heard the gallop of a horse and seconds later spotted Daisy Hall on the adjacent bridle path as she rounded the bend a little too fast, trying to beat the storm. A flicker of longing came and went in his eyes.

Through a downpour he paused to admire the repaired fence, then gathered his tools with urgency as lightning lit up the sky. He opened the truck door and whistled for the family Border Collie who came at a run and leaped in flinging rain. Corbin shoved the dog's head with rough affection, adding a cab clean-up to the list of chores that somehow had to get done before tonight.

On the back porch he dried himself and the animal with an old towel, removed mud-caked boots and entered the kitchen in his socks.

"Lordy son, it's about time," his mother said from the stove. "I was ready to let this supper burn to come and fetch you."

"I was near done so I had to finish."

Opal took a milk bottle from the icebox and handed it to twelve-year-old Jimmy to fill the glasses.

Corbin slid into his chair and reached across to tousle Jimmy's head. "Hey, squirt," he said.

"Don't stir up his hair at the table, son," Opal said, "it'll land in the food."

"Where's Wilbur?" Corbin asked. "Haven't seen him since breakfast."

"Gone to the Porter farm. I set him back a plate."

Corbin took a glass from his brother, drank the milk down in a single tilt and gestured for more. "Did he take old Thorny?"

Opal nodded. "If that bull does its job we'll have a nice stud fee, come winter."

The click of a cane on the wood floor announced Gilford O'Connell's labored trek across the living room. It was a good sound after a back-breaking fall last April and a summer spent in bed. With a shakiness that caused his family to gasp he crossed the threshold and eased down on a chair.

"Pasture fence is fixed, Pop," Corbin said.

"Good, then you and Jimmy can pick the rest of those Winesaps after supper."

With anger on his face Corbin opened his mouth to speak but Opal clamped a hand down on his arm. "Homecoming is tonight, Gil, the Winesaps can wait. Say the blessing so we can eat this food while it's hot."

Corbin attacked the evening meal he took for granted, slathering butter on four of his mother's biscuits. He consumed three with a bowl of beef stew; the last he doused with honey and ate for dessert alongside a berry cobbler. Everyone knew Opal O'Connell was the finest cook in Bucks County. A stack of blue ribbons proved it, won over years of entering contests at county fairs. She kept them in a tissue-lined Whitman's Sampler in the china cabinet intending to paste them in an album one snowy day.

Gil pushed his empty bowl aside and struggled to a stand. In a deliberate gesture he reached for his pocket watch, clicked it open to study the time. "Then, you boys need to wrap up those apples early next week."

"Yes, sir."

"But not Monday. After school you ought to help with the hay. Wilbur's about got it done, so you should be able to finish in one good afternoon."

Wilbur's about got it done, the words were music. Corbin hated bringing in the hay. He often imagined how awful things would be without Wilbur Dowd, who lived in an apartment above the dairy, employed as a farmhand for room and meals and ten dollars a week. They had taken him on during the Depression and the man was still there. He'd worked for simple room-and-board back then and happy to get it after staggering half-starved into Judson from New York City in 1931. Opal kept his clothes clean, set him a place at the table, nursed him when he was sick. They all assumed after this much time that he would never leave.

He'd better not leave. The farm was a load for two people, often too much for three. In Corbin's opinion they needed to hire a second Wilbur rather than rely so much on him his senior year. A summer of farm work was one thing – a necessity with his father laid up. But it was quite another for them to expect more from him now than a few hours a week. Corbin feared his willingness to work the farm all summer had been taken by his father as a commitment for life. Although, when it came to his future, there'd always been a gulf between his father's vision and his own.

On a regular basis, Corbin fantasized about making it big in New York. Wilbur often spoke harshly of the city he'd run from, saying it would be damned foolish for anyone to trade the oasis here for the misery there. But Wilbur was remembering a Depression-worn city. It was different now. Corbin had seen enough in recent movie house newsreels to know that. Broadway was pulsing once again in its old glory, weakened but never beaten. And the jazz world's best musicians ruled 52nd Street. Dreaming of the city, Corbin faithfully performed tonguing exercises in the truck, closed himself off in his room at every chance to practice scales and fool around with lip buzzing. But there was so little time for that anymore.

At the supper table Gil liked to share his crop knowledge. He'd seemed especially intent on it over the summer, perhaps because he could do nothing else. "You'll see things different one day," he always said, following with the proverbial, "There's nothing more important than the land." Corbin saw no point to all the lectures since crop knowledge would be useless in the city. Gil saw no point to all the trumpet practice since a horn would be useless on the farm. At times, they appeared to know little of each other. Neither was much of a talker and when they did talk it was mainly to disagree.

The farm seemed to be the only subject discussed in the house, unless it was the threat of war. Corbin often asked a leading question to steer his father there and away from more lessons on productive corn fields or the finer points of fertilizing with manure. Most the time the tactic worked. For weeks now their table talk had been of a similar theme – whether America would join the fight or whether she wouldn't, whether she should or shouldn't.

In those early days of October with a hint of autumn in the air, the war news was difficult to miss. Across the Atlantic, most of Europe was suffocating under Nazi control. In every occupied city Hitler's troops hung their imposing Swastikas from buildings, enforced draconian edicts against the Jews. Shocking newsreels even showed them parading unchallenged through the streets of Paris. And across the Pacific, Japan was feuding with the United States and Britain over an oil boycott, which posed another worry on a different front.

Judson folk reacted with skepticism to headlines about Hitler; the man seemed too brazen to be real. Reports might be exaggerated, some thought, to soften isolationist opposition to the war. Opal was in the isolationist camp. Where else should she be – the mother of two sons, the eldest nearly eighteen? In her opinion Gil should take the same stand; they were his sons, too. But he would never be isolationist. No man in Judson was isolationist.

Gil had assured her, however, that neither son would go to war. They'd get an occupational deferment just as he had in the last war. He was a farmer then, from a family of farmers, and farming had been as essential as bullets. The way he saw it they were still a family of farmers and farming would always be essential as long as armies needed to eat. Corbin hadn't sided with either parent in the isolationist debate or heard their talks of deferment. His thoughts of war were naive and basic: it was fine with him and he planned to go.

———— ⁓⁓ ————

Opal stood in the doorway of Corbin's bedroom, watching his image in the dresser mirror as he knotted his tie. She smiled with pride at how handsome he was – all lean, brown and muscular from a summer in the fields. "It's crooked," she said. "Here, let me straighten it." He gave in to the mothering and turned to face her. "I heard the Raiders won against Mayfield today."

"Yep."

"Good, it's always nice to win on Homecoming weekend. Who are you taking tonight, son?"

"Velma Hix."

She finished with the tie and gave his shoulder a pat. "Been seeing a lot of her lately. Why don't you go out with another girl once in a while?"

"Like who?"

"I don't know ... wish you could find somebody as decent as Cleona Bell."

He rolled his eyes, picked up a shoe and rubbed it with a cloth.

"She's a good one, tending to her sick mother all summer that way. Hardly seems fair to carry such a burden at her age."

Corbin blinked at her, wondering whether she saw any similarities between Cleona's burden and his.

"Donnie Dunn seemed to like her. Wasn't she his girl before he ran off to the Navy?"

He pondered the question a moment, unsure of the answer. "I guess," he said. Donnie had been hanging around with Cleona for years, but who knew what went on between them. A few months ago Donnie had abruptly left school and joined the Navy, lying about his age at seventeen. Everybody in town had been shocked by that stunt, apart from Corbin, and perhaps Cleona, who knew Donnie did it to escape his rigid Army-sergeant father.

"The two were naturally drawn together I suppose, neither quite fitting in," Opal said. She fished in a drawer for a pair of black socks and held them out. "Well, beauty isn't everything but I can't expect you to see that at your age. Cleona could stand to lose a few pounds though ... no denying that." Opal studied her own image in the mirror, planted hands on her waist to evaluate the slender frame that hadn't changed in twenty years. She leaned in to study her face, ran fingers under her eyes. Definite changes there. She sighed and turned away. "Did your dad give you any money?"

"No," Corbin said with an edge of annoyance.

Opal pulled a wrinkled five-dollar bill from a pocket and handed it to him. "Try not to be too hard on him, Corby. I know it's been rough for you this summer but imagine what it must be like for him, not being able to support his family. That's hard on a man." She dusted the end of the dresser absentmindedly with a corner of her apron, lifted the scarf a bit to wipe under it. "Is Velma really what you want in a girl?" At last, what she really wanted to say.

Corbin picked up the other shoe to shine it. "Velma and me ... we just want to have fun."

"That's what *you* want, but what does *she* want? A girl like Velma will try all sorts of tricks to hook a good-looking boy like you. She might let you do things."

If I'm lucky, Corbin thought.

"Has she?"

"Has she what?"

"Let you do things."

"No Momma, she hasn't let me do things." *Not yet, anyway*.

"It's the girl's job to control how far things go. If Velma doesn't do her job, you'll have to do it."

"Don't worry so much, I can handle it."

"I sure hope so. You could get into trouble with her."

THREE

Velma Hix edged a stocking up her right leg and fastened it front and back to her garter belt, then did the same thing with the left, leading with her knuckles to cut down on the chance of snags. There'd be no replacing them now, not the silk kind anyway. Back in August when trouble first surfaced with Japan, newspapers had warned of the impending silk shortage and any female old enough to spend money bought every pair she could find and afford. Velma had clawed her way to the counter of Digby's Department Store and managed to come away with an extravagant three pairs – all the same shade, nestled in pink tissue in a flat pink box. Those hose had cost her a whole week's pay.

To earn her own money she waitressed at the Star Diner three nights a week and Saturdays, and spent it all on clothes. Her father disapproved expecting her to chip in for expenses at home, but he'd see things differently when Corbin O'Connell proposed.

Velma knew the other girls envied her. While they swooned from afar over Cary Grant, Corbin reigned as local heartthrob. She figured every girl in town pined after him, except perhaps Daisy Hall. For one thing, it was hard to improve on black hair and Irish-blue eyes. And on top of that he was so darned chivalrous: he not only opened a door at school for a girl but put a hand on her back as if it were tricky to enter and exit; he not only opened the truck door for a girl but helped her in and out as though she might otherwise get hurt; he not only switched to the street-side in town to protect a girl from reckless drivers, but placed a hand on her waist to gently nudge her over. Such treatment made Velma feel like the most highly-prized creature in the world. Though she sometimes wondered whether, in all this chivalry, Corbin had simply found a legitimate excuse to get his hands on her. Not that she minded; he could manhandle her like that anytime.

Without even trying he was able to make a girl fall in love with him. Completely. Permanently. For Velma, after just one date, it was goodbye heart. Yet he seemed unaware of his magnetism, which added even more to the appeal. He seemed vain about his hair though, she had noticed. Rarely without a comb, he tended to use it often – raking it through that conspicuous head of hair with an ever-so-slight tilt to the head, like a model posing.

In front of a mirror, Velma slipped a new frock over her head and smoothed it down. She checked to be sure her stocking seams were straight, stood there to admire her image. The dress hugged her hips, flared to the knee and swayed delightfully when she moved. It had cost her $16.50 at Digby's, an outrageous sum for a bit of red rayon she could practically fit in her purse.

Velma had seen Daisy Hall at Digby's that day, shopping with her mother for a Homecoming dress. The Halls were always putting on airs, it seemed to Velma, as if they were in the same league as the Ottinger's rather than owners of a grocery store. It was the largest in Judson and right there on Main Street, but still.....

Everyone had oohed and aahed when Daisy stepped out of the changing room in a long moss-green, frothy-looking thing. This annoyed Velma since nobody had oohed or aahed at her. It even made her hesitate about the dress she chose.

Scrutinizing her image now, Velma hesitated again. All the other girls would likely be in long dresses tonight. She took a pivot step and twirled. On the other hand, skirts to the floor restricted a person to a lumbering jitterbug while her dress was perfect for fast footwork and turns. She smiled at her reflection and decided it was worth a fashion blunder to be the only girl to show her legs – assurance that every male in the room would be stealing glances at her.

Velma had a reputation for being "fast", and did not understand why. She *had* gone all the way with a blond college sophomore from Drexel, but just the one time and nobody in town ever found out. She intended to let Corbin do it at some point; she'd let him tonight if she thought it would get him to the altar. But there was the thing about men wanting a virgin for a wife. That's what everybody said anyway and she couldn't prove them wrong; the college boy had never once called since that night under the bleachers.

Reflecting on the summer escapade, she wondered why she did it and decided it had been simple curiosity. Afterward, she failed to understand what all the fuss was about. She didn't look any different, feel any different. Sex wasn't a one-time thing for goodness sakes; all her equipment was still there. Men were so silly to demand purity in a wife, and walking contradictions, too. They spent hours in a vehicle trying to get a girl to do it while requiring a wife to be virginal. A girl who had done it was damaged goods, even to the one who'd done the damage. So, basically, the girl a man did it with would never be the girl he married. Was that fair?

Well, all wasn't lost. She'd simply start over – forget about the college boy, save herself for Corbin, prove it by fending him off. A few liberties wouldn't hurt though, to remind him of what he was missing.

Did the other girls allow liberties? Maybe it was something they giggled and rolled their eyes about over cherry sodas at the diner. Velma often longed to be part of that group crowded six and seven in a booth, especially at times like this when shared confidences might actually help. But beyond that, spending time with them seemed like fraternizing with the enemy and she trusted her own instincts the most when it came to men. After all, it was she having dates with Corbin every Saturday, she going to the Homecoming dance with him now.

Let the others be reserved; she'd be flashy. She was certain Corbin liked her that way. Let the others wear those dainty cotton dresses; she'd stand alone as Judson's sweater girl. Let the others hide demurely under tents of mossy green; she'd steal the show tonight in ruby red.

FOUR

The seniors dominated Homecoming, underclassmen quietly observing in the shadows where they belonged. Together they had transformed the Judson High School gymnasium into a crepe paper paradise, impressive though a little overdone. Round battered lunch tables had been commandeered into elegant service draped in heavy white linen to the floor. The Pinky Yeagher Orchestra of Philadelphia, hired by the Booster Club with funds from George Ottinger, filled the decorated stage.

Heavy in brass, the orchestra intrigued Corbin. So much so that when a young trumpeter stood up to play lead in a snappy arrangement of *In the Mood*, he motioned for a football-playing junior to dance with Velma. This left him free to study the musician – a guy named Paul he later found out. Corbin envied him. Style somewhat choppy to the practiced ear, timing off a hair with the drummer, but already playing lead trumpet in a professional orchestra at the age of twenty-two.

Paul turned out to be the ambitious type – Pinky Yeagher just a stepping-stone for him. His sights were set on Tommy Dorsey, even had an audition the following week. The trumpeter handed out advice like a sage: Corbin ought to practice practice practice, immerse himself in Dorsey recordings, and study the man in person if he could. The advice lit a fire. Corbin wanted to leave the dance right then and go to the record store.

Velma pretended to dislike dancing with a dopey junior but she didn't really mind. Corbin could better admire her from the sidelines, better witness the other guys' gawking. She was truly annoyed though when Corbin danced with Daisy. Twice. And he even danced with Cleona – because Daisy asked him to, no doubt. Why else would he dance with somebody too fat and ugly to get her own date?

Velma saw the way Corbin stared at Daisy from the corner of an eye thinking nobody noticed. And she saw the way they danced all cozied up like a couple. Velma would have feared Daisy as dangerous competition had the popular girl not already been paired up with the only son of the richest man in town. Daisy got all the breaks, was always the main attraction. Peach Queen, for instance. And at the Halloween Ball last year when she dressed as Snow White and everybody declared her a perfect likeness. Well, what if she did look like Snow White? What was so great about that?

Tonight was no different. Velma had to hide her resentment when they called Daisy up to be crowned Homecoming Queen, an honor bestowed at the pep rally and bonfire the night before. In a sense, this dance was as much a celebration of Daisy's victory as the Raiders' win over Mayfield. Everybody watched her – guys with longing, girls with envy – as she floated to the stage like a film star in a cloud of chiffon. John escorted her and shared the spotlight as unofficial Homecoming King, basking in the glow from the achievements of somebody else.

When the orchestra stopped at midnight it brought everything to a close. Corbin drove Velma to Linden Lake and parked on a grassy knoll. The Ottinger's rolling five-acre estate glowed like a carnival across the water, even at this late hour. Countless white lights blazed into the night and shimmered again on the lake, snuffing out all the stars in the sky. The truck still smelled like wet dog despite Corbin's earlier attempts. Images of Daisy appeared before him, her billowy chiffon spread out all over the cracked seat. It was an absurd, impossible picture against the grandness across the lake – so clearly the more suitable setting for her. He reached for Velma then with an urgency she misread, and the two maneuvered there at cross-purposes for thirty minutes or so – Corbin trying to get somewhere, Velma determined to stop him, at least for a while.

In contrast, John drove Daisy straight home in his new Desoto and ushered her into the house. She half-expected him to be annoyed but apparently not. In his typically gentle manner he removed her cape, draped it across the hall table, took hold of her shoulders and kissed her. "I was proud of you tonight," he said, "proud that you're my girl. You *are* my girl, right?" He asked it with a lilt in his voice, never for a moment really questioning, while his eager eyes sought affirmation, never for a moment really doubting.

Daisy patted his arm and offered an automatic, "Of course."

He kissed her hand then, and said goodnight. That's how it always went. He never tried anything else, not even a second kiss. Sometimes, she wished he *would* venture further. Perhaps new-found ardor would rise up in her if she saw more of it in him.

She floated up the stairs and escaped to her bedroom, suspended in an evening afterglow. Hugging herself she twirled around the room. What a heady thing to be so openly admired. Girls knew when they were pretty; Daisy knew it by the age of eight. She soon began to associate her looks with preferential treatment but, to her credit, never thought of it as a personal victory – or worse, something to exploit. Yet times like tonight, well, they were exhilarating. And addictive, she feared, sensing even now a desire for more. She slid carefully out of her dress, encased it in a protective bag and hung it in the back of the closet with the Peach Queen gown and others.

Much had been spent on her collection of fancy dresses, often more than her father could afford. Fortunately, this year was shaping up better than any in over a decade and business was booming for Charlie Hall. During the Depression the store had nearly folded a dozen times.

Daisy stood in front of the mirror in her underwear and stared at the reflection with detached self-appraisal. There wasn't an inch of her she could not show off with pride if she'd wanted to flaunt it like Velma Hix. In a way, Daisy felt sorry for Velma. What must it be like to be raised without a mother? And Velma's father was evidently putty in his daughter's hands. This, according to Daisy's mother.

She heard a soft tap and said, "Come in," without bothering to cover up. Julia Hall opened the door and stood there wrapped in a faded satin robe that had once been grand. If Daisy wanted to know what she'd look like at forty, she needed only to study her mother. Minus the years they might have been twins – the same dark hair and perfect face, the same shapely legs.

"Your father was tired so I told him I'd wait up," Julia said. She always said this, as if her husband usually interrupted Daisy's reverie at this hour, though he had never done it once.

The father's approach was to wait until morning. He'd plant a kiss on her cheek and ask, "How's my Petunia, did you have a good time?" That's what he called her, Petunia. He'd whisper the question as though it were a secret and he expected a secret answer – a truthful answer only he would hear. And, prepared for it or not, he always got the truth. He and Wally, Daisy's twin brother.

"Is Daddy all right?" Daisy asked. "He looked kinda droopy earlier."

"It was bedlam in the store today. Now that people have a little money, they want to eat, I guess. And your brother had to leave to get ready for the dance."

"I've told you and Daddy a million times that I can help out in the store sometimes, especially on Saturdays. I can certainly work next Saturday–"

"Nothing doing. A future Ottinger should not be seen working behind a counter."

"Oh, Mother."

"Your father hopes to branch out next year and open a second store ... and maybe another one later. That's Wally's future, all of it will be his one day. Your future is planned, too. You'll finish high school in June, go to college in September, and marry John after graduation." Julia closed the subject by slicing the air with her hands.

"Is Wally home yet?" Daisy asked.

"Came in just ahead of you ... said you were the belle of the ball. Did you have a good time?"

"Oh, it was wonderful!" Daisy twirled on her toes with her arms in the air.

The older beauty laughed. "Homecoming Queen ... quite an honor," she said, recalling her own victory with a wistful sigh. "Was John proud of you?"

"Yes, of course."

"I saw Fern Ottinger in town this evening and she was so pleased. One would think her own daughter was crowned instead of a future daughter-in-law." She glanced around the room. "Where's your dress?"

"In there," Daisy said, pointing.

"Should really go to the cleaners before it's hung away. Here, I'll take it." Julia fished the dress from the closet and draped it over an arm. "Was Cleona at the dance tonight, dear?"

"Yes."

"Really? Did she have a date?"

"No."

"Then, who was she with?"

"With me ... with us."

"What did John think of that? He's liable to get tired of Cleona hanging around now that Donnie's gone."

"John didn't mind ... nobody minded. I didn't want her to miss the dance, Mother. Would it have been better if she had missed it?"

"No, of course not."

Daisy went to the bathroom and came back ten minutes later, clean-faced and wearing pajamas. Her mother was still there, straightening the collection of cosmetics on the dressing table.

"Did you dance with Corbin tonight?"

"Yes."

"How many times?"

"Uh, once." *Two songs though, back to back.*

"Fast or slow?"

"Slow."

"What did John think about that? Did it bother him?"

"Not as much as it bothers you."

"Well, it's just that ... I *know* my daughter when it comes to Corbin O'Connell. You had a crush on him when you were eight years old and for some years afterward."

It was true, except it wasn't just a crush. She'd loved Corbin since her eighth birthday party when he punched a bully in the nose for pulling up her dress. Hidden away in her jewelry box was half a wrapper from a stick of gum they'd shared when she was twelve, treasured to this day because it had been in his pocket. Even now she had no intention of parting with it.

"I'm not altogether certain you're over him yet." Julia looked at her daughter with her head in a slant, waiting for a response she didn't get. "*Are* you over him?"

"Yes, Mother."

"I certainly hope so. Corbin is from a good, hardworking family. Wally speaks highly of him. And I can understand what girls see in him. That crackle in his eyes ... I've seen it. There's something intense about him that makes him seem, well ... almost dangerous."

It was true. He often looked at Daisy like he was undressing her with those eyes and openly admiring what he saw. And he *did* seem dangerous at times, as though he'd be hard to control if he weren't so innately polite. That was the thing: he could melt a girl's heart one minute with his gentlemanly manners, then send a jolt through her the next with his electrifying stare.

"But he lives on a farm, dear," her mother went on. "That's his future ... that's his level. Do you want to spend your life on a farm?"

"Mother, how can you possibly know what his future will be? Or his 'level'?"

"He's dating Velma Hix. That should tell you something." She folded down Daisy's bedcovers and fluffed the pillow, a look of pride on her face from scoring a point. "Honey, you've already made such a splendid catch with John. I'd just hate to see you mess things up, that's all."

"Gosh, why all this talk about messing things up?" Daisy slid into bed and permitted herself to be tucked in, beginning to envy Velma's lack of motherly guidance.

"Because it's easy for a girl to be thrown by a pair of crackling eyes, my dear."

It was true – everything her mother said was true. Dancing with Corbin tonight, right from the opening bars of *Moonlight Serenade*, all she could think about was his chest pressed against her, his arm wrapped around her, his hand warm on her waist. She had mourned in advance its inevitable end. Then almost as though the orchestra leader sensed it, he phased into a dreamy rendition of *I'll Be Seeing You* without a decipherable break. And during the next three or four minutes, she became so welded to him that she feared sagging to the floor when the music stopped and he stepped away.

Just thinking about it now made her weak. She turned on her side and curled into a ball, remembering every moment when she should have been trying to forget. It did not take long though to isolate the most serious symptom, the real proof her mother was right about everything: while they were dancing she had a fleeting thought that others might notice and criticize, but it wasn't until later that she cared.

FIVE

George Ottinger pretty much owned the town square – the Star Diner, the Ott Building (a three-story office building), and half the Judson Hotel. He owned the Monarch Theatre, too, on the corner of Main and Fairview, and Ottinger Motors on North Hilton. The east end of Judson, beyond the railroad station, looked like a manufacturing town. Factory after factory sprawled on land along the tracks – ironworks, textiles, leather, a cannery – nearly all of it Ottinger Industries.

He had shut it all down during the Depression to keep from going broke. Except for the cannery, which he continued to run at full capacity, spreading the jobs as far as possible by holding employees at half time. Everyone had agreed it made sense to choose the cannery since any money earned would be spent on food. Judson folk considered it their right to pass judgment on Ottinger, just as it was with the president, the governor and the mayor. Though not an elected official he seemed like one to them, and if he had chosen to seek office he'd have won.

The town had fared better than most during the Depression, thanks to the cannery and the local outdoors. Nearly every man hunted and fished, and until late in the decade when wildlife became scarce, many a meal was brought to the table from Bucks County woods and streams.

The O'Connells had always been able to hunt on their own property, going for turkey before Thanksgiving and deer afterward. There were dozens of good spots to find plentiful game – some a short walk from the house, others an hour's hike or more away. Gil had gradually passed down all his hunting skills to Corbin, and nearly as much of it to John. It seemed to him that human traits were magnified while hunting, and in a boy one could almost see the later man.

It was all there in Corbin at ten – the keen eye and steady hand, the will to succeed, the tendency toward impatience and impulse. Whenever the young Corbin missed a shot he'd pulled the trigger too fast, without first finding that moment of stillness in which to take aim. Even now he tended to rush it. Corbin could be the best shot in the county if he'd only learn to slow down.

The young John had shown fine dexterity, yet tended to hang back and let others take the shot. Though it could have been simple disinterest, Gil had wondered back then if it meant something more. Now, after years of observation, he suspected a contentment with mediocrity in John, as if in light of the father's achievement, nothing was required of the son. He wanted to put a stop to this drift toward complacency, making him wonder whether George Ottinger saw traits in Corbin he'd like to squelch.

It bothered Gil more than he let on to miss hunting this year with the boys – another blow to his pride because of that clumsy fall from a ladder. Such a crucial time, too, with Jimmy being twelve, the year a boy often evolved into a true and independent hunter.

Gil liked to say he'd bagged the Thanksgiving turkey every year on his own four hundred acres, but it wasn't quite true. In 1928 he had aimed too low, peppered the breast of a fine fifteen-pounder that Opal then refused to fix. Two days before Thanksgiving she had sneaked into Hall's Market and brought home the last turkey left in the store – a tiny eight-pounder more the size of a chicken she'd serve. But it sufficed, with only Gil and four-year-old Corbin to feed that year. It seemed strange to Opal now, thinking back on it. Ever since then there'd been a crowd for Thanksgiving – sometimes so many that she'd served in two shifts with every chair filled and still had eaters standing around. This year there'd be eleven.

She ordered a nice twenty-pounder from the market to take the pressure off Corbin, since any hunting done this year would fall to him. But he liked hunting as much as he disliked farming, and took it as an affront. "You won't need any store-bought bird so you might just as well cancel it," he said, displaying a male pride that reminded Opal of Gil. "Jimmy and I are gonna scout on Friday just like always. John's spending the night just like always and we'll be out Saturday before daybreak, just like always. We'll bring you a turkey ... you can count on that." Corbin sounded so much like his father that Opal had to turn to the sink and swish a hand through a pan of dishwater so he wouldn't see her smile.

But she worried about the boys out alone. "I don't want them wandering far from home without you," she told Gil.

"Don't make sissies out of them now Opal," Gil said, patting her shoulder. "Corbin will be old enough to be drafted in a few months ... not that he *will* be drafted," he rushed on, watching her eyes cloud. "He'll get a deferment like I told you before, but the point is ... he'll soon be old enough, so you mustn't fret about a little hunting trip on our own property." Still, when the subject of possible spots came up, Gil suggested the creek ravine, an easy twenty-minute walk from the house. "We haven't hunted there in a good four or five years. It should be prime," he said.

So it was, on the Friday before Thanksgiving, the O'Connell brothers stood at the crest of the hill on the west side of the ravine. Corbin took a moment to gaze across at Rocky Knob. With the leaves off the bordering maples he could see it – the highest place on the farm, the highest place for miles. Not all that high compared to the mountainous west but high enough in this land of rolling hills. And not all that rocky either, just one giant rock jutting out of the ground from a deep shelf of ancient Pennsylvania limestone, smooth and flat as a tabletop.

The cold and the sun fought to dominate the crisp afternoon, the sun warm enough at this hour for Corbin to unbutton his coat. "With winter coming, turkeys don't care about breeding," he told Jimmy. "Their minds are on roosting sites and food and water, preferably not far apart." Corbin pointed down the ravine. "Somewhere down near the creek, turkeys are roosting at night in those pines. Pop said we can almost count on it. And this side of the ravine is more likely since it's east-facing and gets the first sun ... turkeys like the sun. If we can find signs of a roost, we'll be in good shape for tomorrow. I figure we've got about two hours 'til dusk."

They hiked down the hill through thick pine growth until they neared the creek, which ran through the ravine and out again, sliced the farm in half flowing behind the barn, between fields, along the driveway and under the main road as it snaked south. The sun had not yet disappeared behind the crest but it was dark under the pines. Low branches sagged on the ground. The brothers had to crouch and crawl to search for signs.

"Look ... see these droppings?" Corbin was on his knees holding a branch aside. "These spirals here are from a hen. Find some that are straighter ... gobbler droppings are straight."

"Hey, over here," Jimmy said from not far away.

Corbin joined him and studied the ground. "Those are gobbler droppings all right, and they're fresh. And look at the square-tipped feathers ... they're from a tom. Yeah boy, a gobbler has definitely been roosting in this tree, lately I'd say." He looked across the creek and pointed. "See that boulder over there? If we set up tomorrow beside that boulder, we should have a clear view of any bird that roosts in these trees tonight and drinks in the creek at sun-up." He patted Jimmy on the back. "Let's get out of here. They'll be looking to roost soon because turkeys don't like moving around after dusk."

"Neither do I," Jimmy said.

They started their trek back up the hill, chasing what was left of the sun. Halfway up they were breathing hard; the climb had them sweating in their coats. When they got to the top they were both winded but kept moving. Every step taken in daylight would be one less to take in the dark.

"Momma's probably getting supper ready by now," Jimmy said. "We're having ham."

"Biscuits?"

"Yep, with fresh apple butter, I'll bet. She was putting some up today."

"Good, I'm starved."

"I think I saw turnips in a pot on the stove, though." Jimmy chuckled at the face his brother made and nudged his arm.

"That's okay, I could live on biscuits and apple butter. John will be glad ... about the apple butter, I mean. By the way, I saw you looking at his sister last Sunday at church. Are you sweet on her?"

Jimmy didn't answer.

Corbin snatched his brother's hat and ruffled his hair. "Don't blame you if you *are* sweet on her. She's a cute little thing."

After supper, John and Corbin took Daisy and Velma to a movie at the Monarch. They tended to do this frequently, double-dating on a Friday night. The foursome always sat on the right, five rows from the back, men wisely placed between the two distant females. And there was never any necking; they actually watched what was on the screen.

Tonight was no exception. They found their seats in the dark theatre in time for the first newsreel: dreary footage of exploding villages, snowy battlefields littered with twisted metal and frozen soldiers in Germany's relentless attack on the Soviet Union. Though the images caused moviegoers to grimace, the reality seemed remote. At least it wasn't the streets of London being bombed by Hitler's Luftwaffe anymore.

The second newsreel proved more sobering: up on the screen, larger than life, Hitler ranted to a crowd of thousands that the Jews were subhuman, the Aryan race superior, and he had been chosen to lead them to "rule the world for a thousand years." His frenzied throng stared at him in trance-like adoration and erupted in glassy-eyed chants of "Sieg Heil! Sieg Heil!" An unseen announcer with a deep serious voice broke in to say the Axis Power alliance of Germany, Japan and Italy shared a common goal: to take over the world and divide it amongst them like an apple. Then Hitler, as if to prove the point, declared with pounding fists their united contempt for Americans – timid undisciplined scum under the influence of Negroes and Jews, no match for his Aryan armies.

This was stupefying! This was personal! The heretofore silent theatre hummed like a beehive, angry voices tossing comments into the dark. "Someone has to stop this maniac," Corbin chimed in. A baritone voice behind him crowed, "Damned right, O'Connell. Damned right!"

The film they came to see, *You're in the Army Now*, was light fare after the newsreels – an old-school cavalry officer uniformed in tin hat and leggings riding a horse into battle. Though all done for comedy, it wasn't far from the truth. The United States was working day and night to replace horses with tanks, tattered World War I wool uniforms with modern ones, and turn-of-the-century guns with M1 rifles.

Later, John set his valise on the floor in Corbin's room, kicked off his shoes and plopped down on the spare bed. He thought of the bed as his bed, the room as his room, nearly as comfortable there as he was at home. "Hey, wanna go to the Eagles game on December 7th?"

"But, they're playing the Redskins at Griffith Stadium that week ..." Corbin snapped his head around, alert. "You're going to Washington?"

"Yeah, you want to come?"

Did he want to come – what a question. A football game, and in Washington, to boot. "Sure I want to come. Just you and Pop Ott?" Corbin and George Ottinger shared a passion for football, bigger fans than John would ever be. Corbin had wanted to play for the high school and the coach tried to recruit him, but since practice always started in August the harvest invariably got in the way.

"Yeah, we'll take the train down on Saturday and make a weekend of it. Only thing is ... Dad has a meeting there on Monday morning so we'll have to miss school. Is that okay?"

"Of course it's okay." Corbin peeled off his sweater and tossed it on a chair." It'll be the last game of the year for the Eagles, with their dismal season."

John studied Corbin in his undershirt, envying his friend's muscled arms and sculptured chest. "Can you keep a secret?" he asked.

"What is it?"

"Dad's working on a big contract with the government. That's why he's going to Washington."

"Why all the secrecy?"

"It'll mean converting the shoe factory from shoes to Army boots."

Corbin frowned. "Will the people lose their jobs?" he asked, thinking of his uncle who worked there.

"No, they'll just make combat boots instead."

"Where will everybody get shoes, then?"

"We aren't the only factory making shoes. And even if we were it would be tough luck, what with the war effort."

"So the factory might make the very boots we'll wear one day. Does Pop Ott think we'll get into the war?"

"Yeah, especially now, with this contract."

"What if we do get in? You'll go won't you?"

"If I have to ... if I'm drafted, I mean." John didn't expect to be drafted, though. He'd get an occupational deferment; his father would see to that.

Corbin sank down on his own bed. "I'm not waiting to be drafted. I'll enlist at the first hornblow,"

"Yeah, I figured. You *want* to go."

"Of course I do. All the guys want to go. We've got to help Churchill put a stop to that crazy Hitler. You saw the newsreel. He'll be coming after us next ... him and his Aryan armies." Corbin said the last with a sneer.

"I'll go if I have to, like I said, but I'm not itching to enlist the way you are. After college I'm going to marry Daisy and start working with Dad."

Corbin jammed a fist into his pillow at the mention of Daisy's name. "I'll enlist even if there isn't a war. I'm getting out of Judson one way or another, and once I'm gone I'm not coming back."

"Where will you go?"

"City somewhere ... maybe New York or New Orleans."

"Well, we might not be in Judson forever either. Maybe I'll run for office. Dad thinks I should. That could mean a move to the state capitol ... or even Washington. I could buy one of those big houses down there, Daisy would love that." He looked at Corbin for confirmation. "She'd love that, wouldn't she Corb?"

"Sure John, Daisy would love it."

<hr />

Opal had not yet lit the fire in the stove so the kitchen was cold at five in the morning. Corbin set three glasses out on the table and poured milk into them, made quick sandwiches from leftover ham and a half-dozen biscuits. He heard the floorboards creak as his mother stirred upstairs. "Jimmy, light the stove so Momma won't need to," he said. Rufus scratched at the door and John let him out.

The three scarfed down the make-do breakfast, donned boots and hunting jackets and stepped out on the porch, each armed with a shotgun and turkey load. Corbin pointed a finger at Rufus and said, "No ... you have to stay, boy."

It was late enough that the stars had faded, yet still early enough to hear the owls. Aided by slats of light from the barn where Wilbur was milking, they cut quickly through the family vegetable garden, boots crunching on withered plants covered with frost. After that the going was slow as they disappeared into the dark. They had to rely mostly on memory to angle around the upper field where scattered pumpkins they could barely see lay shriveled and broken. It was a different route from the one the brothers had taken the afternoon before, in order to approach the ravine on the east side this time.

When they reached the crest of the hill their eyes had adjusted enough to descend. They made fast work of locating the boulder and took positions near it on the ground. It was perfectly still now, too late for owls, too early for day birds. The only noise was the muffled run of the creek. They often gained a fresh perspective out there away from every man-made thing – perhaps what they valued most about hunting, though not old enough or wise enough yet to know it. As sunlight crept up behind them it turned the black sky to gray and soon revealed their position's assets: clumps of scraggly bushes to hide behind, tall evergreens towering in the rear to break up their outlines, clear view of the creek and the trees on the other side. "This should be a real good spot," Corbin whispered. "It won't be long now. Who's taking the first shot? You want it, John?"

"Naah, you go ahead."

Corbin nudged Jimmy's shoulder. "You want to take it?"

"Uh, okay ...."

"Just remember to aim for the beard and you'll blow its head off."

The morning birds soon started – first one, then another, then a symphony. Every eye picked up movement as a twitchy cottontail appeared. A doe ventured out and crept to the creek to drink, followed by another. The hunters stiffened and then relaxed; they weren't there for deer.

The first sign of a turkey came at full light in the substantial rustling of pine branches they could see and hear across the rocky creek bed. A hen stepped out of the brush and proceeded with caution. The deer glanced up, then went back to drinking with a disinterest no human felt. Two other hens appeared in the clearing.

Long seconds passed, enough to make them wonder if three hens were all they'd see. They caught sight then of another bird through low-hanging pine branches as it came into view bit by bit. It was a tom, a big one, with a red beard that must have been a foot long. Corbin gripped Jimmy's arm and leaned in. "Take time to aim. You've got all the time in the world," he whispered. "And remember ... aim for the beard."

Jimmy leveled the bead on the gobbler's beard and followed with his gun as the bird strutted to the creek. Just as the impatient side of Corbin began to think his brother would never fire, Jimmy cracked off a shot. The forest exploded. Animals vanished. A heavy branch flew from a tree down the way as the gunshot echoed in the distance. At the creekside a headless turkey flopped in the shallow water sending spurts of blood downstream. Against the sudden stillness, the sight and sound seemed magnified.

The other two whooped up and down, the need for quiet gone. "Look at that! You blew its head clean off!" Corbin howled while Jimmy stood stunned with his shotgun still aimed. Corbin took it and set it aside to wrap him in arms. "Wait'll Pop sees, and Momma, too. No need now for that store-bought thing. Great hunting, great hunting! Wait'll Pop sees." Corbin detected sorrow on Jimmy's face, and guilt, but a few congratulatory pats on the back seemed to knock them away.

They packed up and headed home with the prize. Nobody said much during the climb, especially Jimmy who lagged behind shouldering his kill. Corbin glanced at John hiking beside him with a carefree gait, the strap of his gun case resting securely on a shoulder. That gun case – cordovan leather, soft as butter. No other Judson hunter owned such a thing, and it must have been mostly for show since John hadn't even bothered to uncase his gun. It had gone from shoulder to ground and back to shoulder, all the while packed away.

About halfway to the top Corbin reached for the turkey. "Here, let me have it. You take a breather." He gripped the bird by its feet and swung it over a shoulder.

"How much do you figure he weighs?" Jimmy asked.

"Twenty-five ... maybe more."

When they crested the hill, Jimmy asked, "Want me to take him now, Corb?"

"Not yet but don't worry ... you'll be the one to carry him in. It's your prize, after all." Though the quick and easy hunt made Corbin happy he soon realized it would mean an afternoon of chores. Not for John, though. John would not find work waiting when he got home, today or any day. There were so many things to envy about John – enough to damage a friendship if Corbin were the type.

SIX

The Capitol Limited left Philadelphia at 2:43 p.m. on Saturday December 6 and arrived at Union Station on schedule at 5:25. George Ottinger flicked a wrist at a porter who wheeled their luggage to a waiting taxicab and loaded it for a hefty fifty-cent tip. It had been dark in Washington for nearly an hour, the sights of the city ablaze. Out the window the U.S. Capitol seemed close enough to touch, and further away the Washington Monument glimmered in the night sky. As they headed up Massachusetts Avenue, Corbin recalled John's words about living in the city with Daisy, and as the grand estates appeared one after the other he found it depressingly easy to imagine.

Ten minutes into the ride the taxi passed through wrought iron gates into the courtyard of the Carlton Hotel – built from limestone in the Beaux Arts style to impersonate an Italian Renaissance palace. The driver circled around an illuminated pink marble fountain to the front portico where eager bellhops flocked.

They checked into absurdly luxurious accommodations. Corbin counted four telephones in the suite he and John shared. The bathroom even had one, making him wonder who he'd ever talk to sitting in there. It had been a big deal just to get the single telephone at home, installed two years ago on the kitchen wall.

At eight o'clock they ventured down to the lobby for dinner. It was an impressive lobby, furniture imported from Italy mixed with American and British antiques, arranged in comfortable groupings on expensive Orientals. Potted palms leaned against stone pillars of Tuscan origin. Corbin traveled the wide expanse with his eyes and stopped short at a sign on a pedestal: *The Tommy Dorsey Orchestra featuring Frank Sinatra, tonight at the Carlton Night Club.*

John followed the saucer-eyed stare. "Hey, Tommy Dorsey! Maybe we can see the show. What do you think, Dad?"

"Perhaps, but one thing at a time. Let's eat first."

The hotel restaurant was an elegant affair – gleaming chandeliers, tall arched windows, vermillion drapes. It seemed all the more elegant being simply named *The Grill.* George Ottinger was clearly well-known there, chatting like an old friend with the tuxedoed Maitre d' who ushered them to one of the better tables, then looked doubtful when asked about the show. He mumbled something about it being sold out for weeks, but Ottinger casually handed him a fold of money anyway and said, "See what you can do."

A restaurant of this caliber was typical with the Ottingers, so Corbin approached it with the same casual air of belonging they displayed. But the prospect of seeing Tommy Dorsey was another matter, a chance he'd been dreaming of and hoped to work toward. Yet here it was, dangling in front of him tonight – so close at hand yet not guaranteed, resting in the whim of an unseen stranger. Corbin reached over and clamped a hand on Ottinger's arm. "I appreciate this, Pop Ott," he said, "no matter how it turns out."

After dinner the father retired to his eighth-floor suite. Corbin and John took a short walk around the corner to the Carlton Night Club. They had to push through a surprising crush of young women waiting to steal a glimpse of Frank Sinatra – Billboard Magazine's Male Vocalist of the Year, and the cause of repeated pandemonium at New York's Paramount Theatre. John was armed with a note from the Maitre d' and another fold of money stuffed in an envelope, with instructions to give them to Maurice.

The money bought them standing room against the back wall for the ten o'clock show. The exclusive club, perhaps the most luxurious part of the luxurious hotel, boasted interior walls, chairs and carpet that appeared to have been dipped in the same odd shade of purple, a color Corbin had never seen. It was all the rage now, this grayish, pinkish plum – *mauve* to the interior design set.

Tommy Dorsey gave the crowd what they wanted from the start: Frank Sinatra's rendition of Cole Porter's *Night and Day*. Dorsey led with empty hands, the famous trombone nowhere in sight during this showcase for voice and strings. Corbin's first reaction was an instant emotional high – a mixture of joy, enthusiasm, desire. He wanted to be up there with the rest in all their precision, showmanship and ease. He wanted to audition for the man this very night and wondered how far the Ottinger influence could stretch – whether another note and money envelope could make it happen. Corbin thought of Paul, the trumpeter with Pinky Yeagher. A quick search of the faces onstage said Paul wasn't there.

They followed with *Let's Get Away From it All*. Corbin missed when Dorsey picked up his instrument but somehow it was in his hands. The band leader soloed with an effortless grace, producing a chain of silvery tones that had become his signature sound. He had mastered breath control like nobody else, making an actual art of taking in oxygen as he sailed through the piece without a visible breath.

At that moment Corbin wanted to pack up, quit school his senior year, leave his family in the lurch and move to New York City. Anything for a chance at this life, a chance to learn from such a master. He'd heard all these songs on his record player at home but listening from now on would be different. Listening would bring it all back.

An owlish man with round spectacles and a trumpet in his hand stood up to lead a snappy number. Corbin recognized Ziggy Elman from pictures he'd seen. The man's playing was as bright as his instrument, strong and unrestricted yet every note enunciated and sharp. Corbin watched with complete absorption, barely breathing himself as he took it all in. This was how he wanted to play, how he hoped to sound! He shook his head in amazement wondering if others in the audience knew Ziggy was as much a master of his craft as Dorsey and Sinatra were of theirs. The burst of applause at the end said they knew. Part of Dorsey's brilliance, then, was an ability to gather the best: Ziggy had played for years with Benny Goodman, drummer Buddy Rich with Artie Shaw. No doubt, every musician onstage had executed his own sterling ascent to reach this summit.

Paul wasn't up there because he wasn't good enough. Simple as that. Corbin suddenly felt foolish. Who was he kidding? He wasn't even fit yet for Pinky Yeager, much less Tommy Dorsey, and with so little time to practice he might never be ready. He'd be stuck on the farm picking apples and mending fences forever. His earlier elation disappeared, replaced all at once with anger and self-pity that would have worried Gil O'Connell, had he known.

———～～～———

December 7, 1941

By noon, Ezra Knox had already delivered a half-dozen telegrams and returned to his apartment behind the Judson Western Union Telegraph Office. It was busy for a Sunday. He switched the radio on to let it warm up, lit the pilot light in the stove, turned burners on under a clean frying pan and the coffee pot left from breakfast. From pantry and icebox he pulled fixings for lunch and built himself a sandwich of doubled-up cheese and a thick slice of ham. When the coffee heated he poured it into a cup, stopping short to avoid the last few drops thick with grounds. He set the empty pot in the sink, flipped the sandwich neatly to the other side with a pancake turner. The radio came to life with a crackle and hum. He played with the knob until he found the strongest signal for the Columbia Broadcasting System.

Over an advertisement for Chevrolet the teleprinter buzzed. Ezra turned off the stove, left the sandwich there and took the coffee with him to the front. Another military officer called back into service – this one for Harold Sturgill, Captain, U.S. Navy, retired, ordering him to report to the Office of Chief of Naval Operations in Washington, D.C. on January 5. It was the same everywhere – the armed services begging retired officers to reenlist in their hurried efforts toward readiness. Judson had a cadre of such men and Ezra knew them all. Some were members of the local draft board, of which he was head.

He mounted the gummed tape onto a blank telegram form and slid it into an envelope with a sigh, grateful for being too old to go back in. So there was an advantage after all to aging. He tossed Harry's envelope in the empty cigar box on the counter until after lunch. Nothing so urgent that it couldn't wait until then.

At 2:25 p.m. the big one came: API FLASH, WASHINGTON – WH SAYS JAPS BOMB PEARL HARBOR. Reading it, Ezra became the first in Judson to learn of the attack but he did not remain exclusive bearer for long. At 2:30, Harry Sturgill got another telegram: JAP ATTACK PACIFIC. EXPEDITE. REPORT TUESDAY.

At 2:31 p.m., news anchor John Daly came on the air for his regularly scheduled *The World Today*, and opened with, "The Japanese attacked Pearl Harbor, Hawaii by air, President Roosevelt has just announced. The attack also was made on all naval and military activities on the principal island of Oahu." Daly mispronounced Oahu but nobody commented on it that day. Hardly anybody had ever heard of the island. The same was true of Pearl Harbor – a place few had heard of before December 7 and afterward few would forget.

By the two o'clock kickoff at Griffith Stadium the Japanese were already bombing the U.S. fleet. Since nobody in the stadium knew it yet, they still cared about brawny men tussling over an odd-shaped ball made from pigskin. Press-box reporters soon got word of the attack but Redskins president George Preston Marshall demanded they sit on it because it might disrupt the game. So Griffith Stadium, for the next 150 minutes, remained an island of pre-war ignorance while the rest of America careened.

But the aggressive reach of the scrambling military soon broke through, erupting in an unprecedented number of stadium broadcasts that smelled of big news: *Admiral William Blandy is asked to report to his office at once; if Philippines Commissioner Joaquin Elizalde is in the stadium he is urged to contact his office immediately; would FBI Assistant Director Edward Tamm please come to the press box.*

Players on the sidelines stared at each other, questioning. Onlookers did the same as they blew on their hands and tried to keep warm. They all suspected something but few imagined an attack so disastrously bold. While the Redskins and Eagles traded leads, more military heavy-weights and the D.C. police superintendent were called out of the stands. Yet the game went on. Twenty-seven thousand fans cheered plays or cursed calls, still believing the outcome was everything while husbands, sons and brothers were already dead or dying five time zones away.

Washington walked off with a win at the end of it. Short-lived news. Perspectives changed as crowds exiting through turnstiles read screaming headlines pitched by newsboys. Players who opposed each other moments ago would soon fight on the same side, and reporters would cover the play-by-play of that more serious game.

At lunchtime Monday, President Franklin Roosevelt went before a joint session of Congress to ask for a declaration of war between the United States and the Japanese Empire. John and Corbin listened on a hotel radio. After the ten-minute speech, all across the land, war became the subject of every headline, topic of every conversation, focus of every thought.

The train out of Washington later in the day reflected a nationwide surge in troop movements. In every car, the richness and continuity of plush burgundy-red seats were lost in a medley of Navy whites, Army olive drabs, Marine greens. Servicemen displayed high spirits as if they were on holiday. Flirty young women admired them. Civilian men respected them and swore to join up as soon as they got home. Cozy couples held hands discussing whether to marry now or wait. Romantic sensibilities had been heightened by war and uniforms in just one day.

As the Capitol Limited picked up speed it was a microcosm of America coast to coast. Worry was born in women with husbands and sons – a nagging worry that would prove long term. And when an old Chinese couple stood up and hurried off the train in Baltimore, people glared at them thinking they were Japanese and therefore the enemy.

Corbin watched a half-dozen sailors lift seabags from overhead racks and exit the train laughing. He envied them their freedom so much that he decided to enlist immediately, brave the war at seventeen rather than wait until graduation in June. The whole thing might be over by then. Donnie Dunn hadn't waited; he had run off with no warning to join the peacetime

Navy, volunteered for duty in the quiet Philippines to avoid the threat of Europe. Well, he'd surely be in the thick of things now, braving the war at seventeen whether he wanted to or not.

In Philadelphia they transferred to the 614, which ran through Judson on its way to New York. They managed to get two facing seats at the end of a car in the less-crowded train. Corbin watched the signs of the city disappear out the window. "I've decided to enlist when I get home," he announced on impulse, mind abuzz with his newly-formed plan. Two pairs of eyes stared at him. "I'll finish school later," he added, addressing the most likely objection. The words hung there alone for a long few seconds, advancing to absurdity in the silence.

The father gave a slow blink. "You will do no such thing. You'll graduate first and ... then decide." His voice was firm yet devoid of emotion; he might have been ordering breakfast from a callow waiter. "You're underage, your family needs you at home, so we'll hear no more about it." This, from a man who rarely took a bossy stand, even with his own son. He had punched the words directly at Corbin but slanted his gaze toward John at the end, apparently saying it for the benefit of both in case impulsive patriotism proved contagious.

Corbin lapsed into embarrassed silence. He suddenly *felt* underage, ashamed to have needed a reminder of family obligations. He nodded his head, traded meaningful looks with the older Ottinger who gave a tolerant smile and looked away. Gil O'Connell would have been grateful for this had he known, since the clipped and certain words delayed his son's enlistment plans.

As they sped through flat farmland Corbin took up his window watch again. Nothing to look at but fields and sky, nothing to study but cows. He caught sight of a low-flying plane in the blue expanse, the sun glaring off it so much that Corbin had to shield his eyes and squint. It was hard to tell the size of it – whether it was a small one in the local sky or a big one farther away. The body of the plane appeared to have a big red circle. He rubbed dust from the window with an index finger to improve the view. It looked like a Jap plane. Maybe a scout plane or even a bomber – that circle the distinct Japanese *rising sun*. He pulled his eyes away and looked around. Wasn't anybody else seeing this? He almost called out. Then common sense took over and he felt silly. Why would the Japs care about farmland in Bucks County, Pa? But he needn't have felt silly. Imaginary enemy planes were being spotted now from California to New York, even in unlikely Kansas and Iowa.

By the time they arrived home, President Roosevelt had already signed the Declaration of War with Japan. Three days later, Germany and Italy declared war on the United States and Congress responded in kind, plunging America into another world conflict after just twenty-three years of peace.

SEVEN

J udson saw its own rash of quick enlistments from boys who did not have to go. And they already had boys in the Pacific. Though most were over the age of twenty-one, everybody still thought of them as boys. Especially now with each in such danger and so far from home. Right from the start the town adopted a no-news-is-good-news philosophy. Then the first *we regret to inform you* telegram arrived forcing Ezra Knox, witnessed from many windows, to trudge three blocks to Irvin Street in freezing rain and hand it to Elvira Morgan so she'd know her son had been killed on the USS Oklahoma.

Elsewhere, New York City Mayor Fiorello La Guardia predicted that the war would come straight to the Big Apple, straight into the neighborhoods, which left the people in Judson fearing the streets of their town might be blown to bits. Their own mayor drew cheers when he proposed formation of a home guard made up of experienced local hunters. They were proud of their hunters, and if anybody could protect the town from invasion it would be hunters turned soldiers.

Along the Atlantic coast, searchlights wagged across the night skies on the lookout for enemy planes, and people with binoculars kept watch on the beaches in search of German submarines. Adding to the threat of Germany – if Japan were to conquer the Pacific, the Atlantic could be next as a target. Judson's Home Guard joined others to patrol the banks of the

Delaware River just a few miles away, in case nautical sabo-
teurs from either enemy managed to slither up undetected
from the ocean.

The newly-formed local Office of Civil Defense ordered
people to hang blackout curtains at windows and close them
each night before turning on lamps. Such precautions eased
the tension for some and increased it for others. Julia Hall
considered it all a nuisance, took part solely out of fear of
embarrassing reprisal. But for Daisy, evenings in dim candle-
light proved a soothing sacrifice. And, like telling ghost stories
round a campfire in days gone by, a tingling sense of danger
came with sitting in the dark, heightened now by the real danger a blackout implied.

The Christmas season occupied minds with the soothing
balm of tradition, and as 1941 calendars were torn from walls
and replaced with ones for 1942, the new year brought with
it a sort of adjustment that settled silently over the landscape
with the January snows, extinguished fears of enemy attacks
and added starch to backbones.

Attitudes had shifted after Pearl Harbor. Everyone now
seemed to support the effort to rearm, and the few who didn't
did not say. In an unparalleled attempt to produce war materiel in a hurry, the makers of automobiles, commercial aircraft
and luxury liners became builders of tanks, bombers and
battleships.

A new challenge then surfaced to find enough supplies.
Rubber, for instance. It took half a ton to build a B-17 bomber, and twice that for every Sherman tank. Yet the main source
of raw rubber was the Dutch East Indies, which the Japanese
Empire now controlled. President Roosevelt called on the

country to contribute scrap rubber for the cause, so Judson responded by setting up a collection point the following Saturday in Memorial Park. Impressive piles of useless tires, raingear and leaky garden hoses appeared by the end of the day, and rubber drives became a regular Saturday thing, but each week the piles grew smaller since people had only so much of that stuff lying around. And when it came to tires, the idea of what was useless soon changed when the government rationed them, too, and each man decided to hang onto an extra in case one on his own vehicle reached an even more useless stage.

Similar pleas were made for scrap iron and steel. People were asked also to cut down on home heating fuels and curtail unnecessary use of gasoline. But voluntary gas rationing proved ineffective, so mandatory gas rationing began, along with a nationwide maximum *Victory Speed*, which was set to thirty-five. It was just as much, though, about the shortage of rubber; if people drove their vehicles less and at lesser speed, their tires would last longer. At least that was the hope.

When it came to essentials, rationing combined with price controls seemed the best way to ensure everyone's fair share. Fair shares varied, though. For gasoline the average family got an "A" sticker for their windshield, limiting them to four gallons a week. Police and clergy got a "B" sticker for eight gallons a week. But farmers, essential to the war effort, got a coveted "E" sticker – an unlimited supply. There was a string attached, however, in the form of relentless paperwork, which Gil O'Connell begrudgingly hacked through as he fussed at Corbin for driving the truck all the time.

Soon after gas rationing, the same thing happened with sugar and coffee. Ships delivering imported items like these before the war were now too busy transporting troops, armaments and supplies.

Corbin turned eighteen in March – old enough to be drafted in June but still too young to vote or buy a beer. The age range for draft eligibility had widened in February to ages 20 through 44, requiring Wilbur Dowd at 38 to register. Just a formality in his case though, since he worked on a farm. But others were drafted and many enlisted, swelling the ranks of men in uniform until every street in Judson had sent at least one.

Then another registration in April for ages 45 to 64. This group dutifully visited their draft boards and enjoyed every minute of it knowing nobody expected them to serve. Even Franklin Roosevelt went, allegedly sliding his signed draft card into a pocket of his wallet like everybody else. In Judson it meant the entire local draft board, along with a few others including Gil O'Connell.

Gil drove the truck himself for this trip to town, limped into the draft board office without his cane and stood in line. Afterward he found a bench to sit on and sent Ezra pointed looks.

"Something I can do for you, Gil?" Ezra asked when the door closed behind the last man.

Gil pushed himself off the bench, limped to Ezra's desk and eased into a chair. "No time for beating around the bush, I need Corbin on the farm."

"I know you do."

"He just turned eighteen."

"I know he did."

"Doesn't that mean he'll be caught up in the next registration?"

"Afraid so, the one on June 30. Getting them right out of school with that one."

Gil peered around the empty room, leaned forward and lowered his voice as if the place were full of spies. "He needs a deferment. When he comes in here to register, you need to make sure his record shows deferment on account of farming."

"I can do that, Gil. Corbin certainly qualifies for occupational deferment."

"Don't wait for him to ask for it because he never will. Just give it to him." Gil flinched in pain and shifted in the chair. "He won't like it much."

"I know he won't."

"He'll probably try to enlist."

"He'll be denied. I just had a similar talk with George. He believes John qualifies for deferment since he'll be working in the summer to help meet those military contract deadlines."

"I'm not asking for any special treatment, Ezra ... understand that. Farming is an essential occupation, always has been, and I need Corbin here. The O'Connell farm will do its part for the war effort by producing food for the military, and that's every bit as important as what George is doing supplying combat boots and such."

"Of course it is."

"Corbin'll be able to hold his head up and be proud ... he just needs time to realize that."

"I hear you. Farming ... military supply contracts ... they all qualify for occupational deferment. Personally, I believe both boys can serve their country just as well from here, but I'll tell you the same thing I told George. I can't stop either of them from enlisting in the Navy or the Marines, and if they're going to enlist anyway it might just as well be with the Army."

For Ezra, telegram traffic had doubled since the war began, most of it non-military, just ordinary traffic resulting from more production, more consumption, more troop movements, more commerce, more marriages, more shipments, more travel. The only official telegrams from the War Department were pretty much the dreaded kind, which so far had been few.

But the war news? All bad in the spring of 1942. Hitler more than ever was the undisputed master of the continent, occupying most of Europe while he bludgeoned the British and the Soviet Union in an endless two-front war. Despite that, no U.S. Army troops had been sent to fight over there. Still in rigorous training, they just weren't ready yet.

In the Philippines, thousands of allied troops were stranded where General MacArthur left them – out of the reach of rescue on the Bataan Peninsula. The folk at home were disbelieving. The military couldn't just abandon the boys there! But the public had been kept in the dark about the ship shortage after Pearl Harbor; in truth there *were* no ships for such an errand, the remaining few too busy fighting the enemy. The stranded troops that managed to live surrendered, and just as many were lost on Corregidor when the Japanese landed there and took over.

Bataan and Corregidor – such strange-sounding names. Though the defeats occurred on mosquito-infested islands a half-globe away, they affected nearly every town in America. For Judson it meant five reports of fatalities in five days – five succinct messages rapped out in rhythmic, relentless redundance that had to be mounted on official Western Union Telegram forms and delivered. Most were followed by a letter from a commanding officer with statements like *Johnny died a hero, Johnny was a credit to his country, Johnny received a Purple Heart*. Plus the often-used soother, *Johnny didn't suffer* – so often a falsehood.

Every parent, every wife harbored a nightmare scene they played over and over – the one where they answered an innocent knock to be handed a tan-colored envelope. Their scenes might have varied a bit on the details but poor Ezra had a role in all of them, waiting sad-eyed and stone-faced to give them the telegram and walk away without a word. The real thing wasn't much different. Ezra *was* waiting when they answered the knock, and he did not speak. But as he held out the envelope his eyes told everything, somehow even conveying the seriousness of it – whether *wounded* or *missing* or *killed*.

Into old age, Ezra would blame those five telegrams for making him Judson's walking symbol of dread. Friends afraid to look him in the eye, fear on faces he'd known his whole life – in the diner, on the street, even at church on Sundays as though he might actually be callous enough to deliver a War

Department telegram there. The irony hit hard; as head man for both the local draft board and Western Union, he was one day shoving the sons of friends into war, and later delivering news of their deaths.

———— ✺ ————

As the farm's busiest time approached, Gil fretted daily that his impulsive son would enlist. But Corbin was too busy to think about it, what with schoolwork and fieldwork and Saturday nights spent trying to make progress with Velma. Not to mention the greasy jobs required by his exasperating truck – most recently to take the carburetor apart, clean the jets and piece the thing together again on a late Saturday afternoon.

The days grew longer and every available hour had to be spent shoveling manure for new planting, digging root vegetables from the winter before. Corbin and Jimmy were often in the fields right up until dark, hauling out beets and turnips by the bushel to pack them in burlap sacks layered with newspaper where they'd keep for months, invade the supper table all year long. Corbin especially resented work involving beets and turnips. Where was the incentive? He didn't like them, nobody liked them as far as he knew. Except maybe Wilbur but Wilbur didn't count, being an eager eater of anything Opal set down. Potatoes would always be Corbin's choice – white or sweet, baked, mashed or fried – it mattered not. Potatoes seemed the favorite of all members of this Irish family, so it seemed absurd to waste time and the space in a field when they could just as easily grow more potatoes instead.

Demands of the farm heated up as the weather grew warmer, forcing Corbin to give up trumpet practice altogether to study for exams. Then, the burden of getting an education ended abruptly in mid-June when the class of 1942 graduated on the front lawn of the high school under a perfect sky. Opal and Gil, to commemorate what they perceived as their son's entry into adulthood, presented Corbin with Rocky Knob, their treasured best, proudly handing him the official deed to make it legal.

"When the time comes and you marry," Gil said, "we'll build you a little house up there on your pick of spots."

"Overlooking the creek ravine would be a fine place," Opal added. "You could clear out some of those maples to open the view."

Rocky Knob – Corbin's spot to think, his spot to escape. Sometimes he even took his trumpet up there to practice in privacy, or what felt to him like privacy, though there wasn't much private about brass notes that traveled miles. On one hand it was easy to be grateful. They had just given him Rocky Knob, his favorite place in the world, alluring in any season. Yet all this talk of houses seemed more a lure than alluring and he couldn't help seeing it as just another chain to home.

The day after graduation Wally Hall enlisted in the Marines. His mother was aghast. "I don't understand why you're doing this now. You should wait until you're called instead of volunteering to be killed at eighteen."

Two weeks later the others stood in line together once again – this time to register for the draft. John was pliable and content with his occupational deferment. Corbin, however, responded as his father predicted. "What's that mean?" he asked with suspicion.

"It means you're excused," Ezra said.

"I don't want to be excused."

"Well, you are, at least for now. Farming is an essential occupation."

"Wait a minute! I should have something to say about this."

"Don't argue with the Army, Corbin. You can learn that lesson right now. Don't argue with the Army."

"Pop has been talking to you, hasn't he? You're in cahoots with Pop! Well, I'm eighteen now and I can enlist if I want. If you won't let me do it here I'll just drive over to Doylestown and join the Navy."

Ezra gripped his arm and barked, "You need to calm down, boy!" Then he leaned in with a sober stare, whispered in a conspiratorial tone, "You can't run off in the middle of summer. Wait 'til after the harvest ... then you can go."

Corbin nodded after a moment and kept nodding on his way out the door.

Ezra watched him go, relieved he backed down so easily. He only hoped the boy hadn't simply appeased him before heading to a Navy recruiter.

But Corbin wasn't serious; anger had merely gotten the best of him back there. Still nodding, he digested Ezra's little lecture as he sauntered to the truck. Everybody was always telling him he couldn't leave but nobody had ever hinted the prohibition would end. Yet here was Ezra, head of the draft board and practically his father's best friend, giving him the green light for the fall. *Wait 'til after the harvest. Then you can go.* The words carried great implication. This was progress, this was a breakthrough. He could enlist in the fall! Only a few more months – one more growing season. *I can do that,* Corbin thought, happier than he'd been in a long time. He could tolerate pretty much anything if it had a foreseeable end.

EIGHT

As nationwide war production ramped up with the summer heat, George Ottinger contracted with the military to produce C rations, restricting his cannery to that alone. It had been an easy decision. Besides being lucrative the contracts guaranteed a supply of metals unavailable otherwise. The message was clear: can for the military or don't can at all.

Ottinger in turn doubled his dealings with local farmers for a larger supply of their goods. He arranged in advance for Gil's entire fruit and vegetable crop as well as beef and pork, and promised solid contracts for 1943 as long as the war held out.

Gil hired another farmhand, a thirty-year-old drifter classified unfit for military duty because of a missing inner ear. There was no telling how long he'd stay but Opal put him up in the shed, set another place at the table and hoped for the best. Gil also hired six high school sophomores for the summer and assigned Corbin to be a kind of foreman in order to clear, till and plant more vegetables in additional pastureland.

Summer soon became routine and predictable. Weekdays for Corbin meant rising and retiring with the sun – no time to question contentment or plan the future. Saturdays, he worked in the fields until five. Saturday night was date night, when he went to a movie or a dance with Velma. No matter where they went, evenings always ended at Linden Lake, and by the time the corn was chest-high he had managed to routinely get her blouse off, but that was all. After a while the Saturday nights ran together, one no different from another, identical as rows of corn in the field.

Corbin and his trumpet managed to spend a piece of every Sunday on Rocky Knob. Gil complained that the noise might upset the farm but the hens kept laying, the milk cows kept producing and the tractor didn't seem fazed by it in the least. To get there Corbin had to cross the creek on a log footbridge and climb a hill too steep for anything but grazing. The top was the reward – an expansive gentle knoll separated from the world by banks of swaying trees; the giant rock a convenient table or seat, surface to stand on to see afar, or even a bed on which to lie at night and gaze at the stars. This time of year the dense line of maples tended to block every view but in the autumn, after the leaves blew off the trees, he could stand on the rock and see way across the ravine, clear into the next county. Big dreams always followed him up that private hill – performing on 52nd Street with Tommy Dorsey; Daisy in shorts and a halter top sunning on the rock beside him – both just fantasies, conflicting and unattainable.

Sunday was church day and a day of rest, Opal said. Corbin would have skipped the church part to sleep the morning away, except to do so would forfeit his only time on the Knob. Apparently sleeping late was not the same as resting. Resting meant a free afternoon to engage in a pursuit of one's choice, for which trumpeting qualified. But churching and resting had to be paired together; if he skipped Mass in the morning he had to work in the afternoon.

At least he got to see Daisy on Sundays, and without Velma who seldom went to Mass. But John was always there. Corbin had been seeing less of Daisy since school ended, although she'd recently taken to riding by the farm more often, enough for him to wonder whether she did it to see him. There were other trails – north fork, meadow trail, quarry loop – yet nearly every afternoon she took the south fork that ran along the farm's east fields. Corbin toiled in those fields most mornings but moved to the garden closer to the house after lunch. Too far away to allow more than a wave, which was probably best being caked with sweat and grit. He got so he watched for her anyway just to follow her with his eyes across the wide expanse of beans and tomatoes until she disappeared behind the towering corn. Then he'd turn to the last row and begin counting – up to thirty or forty depending on her speed – until he caught a splash of color flickering through the trees.

On a particularly sultry morning her timing must have been off. Corbin and his crew of sophomores were hoeing corn in the east field for the third and final time, the job everyone dreaded. The crop stood head-high by that point and nothing was worse than toiling between tight rows where no breeze could blow. Saddleback caterpillars had become a menace by then as well, with poisonous hairs that stung on contact triggering red welts that burned like a bee sting for a day.

As the sun approached the center of the sky, Corbin tore out of the corn. "Damn it all to hell!" he bellowed loud enough for the workers to hear, three welts already popping on his arms. He unbuttoned his shirt and peeled it off, wiped sweat from his forehead with it and draped it over the fence.

That's when he heard it – the *chink* horseshoes make meeting solid ground. He looked down at himself and prayed, "Please, not Daisy." Surely it wasn't. She had been riding in the afternoon, and her horse liked to gallop on the bend, slow to a trot on the turn. This horse moved at a smoother gait, like a canter. Not a gallop, too slow for a gallop; not a trot, too fast for trot. Definitely a canter. Just in case, he yanked off his hat in a panic and ran a comb through his hair, following with the palm of his hand. He grabbed the shirt and used it to mop his neck and forehead again.

She came into view about that time, slowed her mount to a walk and stopped in front of him.

"Be glad there's a fence between us. I smell like a field hand," he said, deciding to make a joke of it.

She'd rarely seen him without a shirt. In quite a reversal of roles she studied him in open appraisal: tan shoulders and flat stomach, brawny thighs fighting against their fabric covering, a young man with no love for farming who worked at it nonetheless, day after day. The overall effect was intoxicating. She adjusted her seat in the saddle and pulled her eyes away. "I must look a mess myself. This hair ... it's all in a tangle now. But it's too hot for a hat."

"It's a scorcher all right."

"Wasn't too bad back there in the shade." Daisy pointed over her shoulder to the line of trees she'd just ridden under. "Much cooler here than in town, I can tell you. You're so lucky, Corbin, having this farm." To keep from staring at him she raised her chin to appreciatively look around, though all she could really see from there were rows of corn.

"Lucky?"

"Yes, lucky. I know you don't see it that way, but you just don't realize what you've got. What is it ... 400 acres?"

"Something like that."

"You can grow your own food without depending on anyone. Think how well your family fared during the Depression. I'd much rather be on the growing end of things than the selling end."

"I prefer the eating end myself."

Daisy laughed and shifted in the saddle again. "I hear about your mother's cooking from John. Well ... you've got to go through all this to get there," she said, waving her arm in an expansive arc.

"Yeah, that's the problem. Boy, it's blasted hot in the sun. Aren't you hot sitting up there?" Corbin took his shirt, mopped his face again, ran a hand through his hair. "Can you stop a minute? We could get water from the well and cool off in the dairy."

"I'd like that."

As he yelled to the crew to take a lunch break he slipped into his shirt. Then he hopped the fence and reached up to help her down. She'd been dismounting since the age of ten, yet she swung a leg over to face him and permitted his hands on her waist. Well, it wasn't a question of permitting; she loved it when Corbin did stuff like that. And in the time it took to do it she thought only of his hands. He held her in midair longer than necessary before easing her to the ground.

Corbin took the reins and led the animal as they skirted the cornfield and headed for the house. "Have you ever had our well water? On a day like today, nothing tastes better than water from the well. It's so cold it'll make your teeth hurt, even this time of year. And the dairy ..."

Opal watched them tie the horse to a shade tree beside the water trough and stroll to the old well on the stone walkway leading to the dairy. Corbin cranked the bucket down to below the water level and up again, sank the dipper into the full bucket and held it out to Daisy.

Opal appeared on the porch with a glass in her hand. "Lordy, son, don't make her drink from that. Daisy honey, you don't want to drink from that old dipper. Pour some in here. I hardly ever use this well anymore, not since we brought plumbing into the house. The men still use it though ... and it's sure a day for cold well water, isn't it?"

Daisy took the glass and drank from it. "Gosh, that's good," she said.

"It's hot as blazes in the house, but come in and freshen up if you've a mind to."

"Thanks, I'm okay for now."

"Go in the dairy, then, and cool off."

Before the days of iceboxes, the dairy had been the place to store milk, butter and cheese. Hence the name. Opal still kept her surplus in there in tubs of well water. Most of the year the dairy was like a walk-in icebox the size of her living room. Both the house and the dairy had been there a hundred years, the house built of whitewashed clapboard, the dairy walls of fieldstone. Double walls of fieldstone actually, with a four-inch gap between. And it was that gap of nothing but air that made all the difference, allowing the dairy to be a naive and disinterested bystander when it came to the weather. The inside temperature rarely climbed above sixty-five in summer or fell below forty in winter, as long as the door stayed closed.

Corbin unlatched the door, placed a hand on the small of Daisy's back to usher her in. Out of a sense of decorum he propped the door open with an old Sears and Roebuck catalog, breaking a strict family rule. The floor was stone except for the back section of hard-packed dirt. Sacks of potatoes and the dreaded root vegetables were kept there in holes dug decades ago and lined each season with fresh newspaper. A dry place and cold year-round without freezing. On shelves that lined the walls almost to the ceiling, Opal stored rows of fruit and vegetable-filled Mason jars neatly labeled and organized – the product of her own little canning industry. The bottom shelf held apple crates, nearly empty now until the fall harvest.

"It's wonderful in here," Daisy said, looking around.

"Have a seat." Corbin pointed to the stool his mother stood on to reach the higher shelves. He sprawled on the floor in front of her and leaned against a row of crates. "This dairy is the best thing about the farm, except for Rocky Knob."

"Yet you couldn't name two places anymore different. So cozy and protected in here, so open and expansive up there."

"Yeah, you can see the whole farm from Rocky Knob. And the sky seems bigger. I remember John and me spending Sunday afternoons stretched out on the rock, searching for animals in the clouds. He always managed to find Battle-ax Baxter, too, with her hawk nose and jutted-out chin."

"Miss Baxter, our sixth-grade teacher?"

"Yeah."

Chuckling, Daisy pulled a handkerchief from a pocket and dabbed at her forehead. "I'm trying to identify what it smells like in here."

"It's apples ... apples and earth." Corbin reached in a crate and found two apples still decent enough to eat. He rubbed them on his jeans and handed the better one to her. "There aren't too many things that can beat the smell of earth."

"And the apples add a sweet element, don't they?"

"Yeah, even rotting apples don't smell that bad. It's Jimmy's job to sniff out bad ones before they ruin a crate. There are no bad smells in here ... no bad anything." Corbin had always loved the dairy – the smell, the order, the warmth in winter and chill in summer, the pleasant childhood memories. And on a more subtle level, it had been an oasis of plenty in a deprived land during the Depression. "You know ... this place was a fort, hideout and clubhouse for John and me growing up. On hot summer nights we brought quilts and pillows in here and slept right on the cold floor. We even formed a blood-brother pact on a rainy day in August when we were ten. We pledged 'blood brothers for life,'" Corbin said, laughing. "We were serious, too, enough to seal it by slicing a finger."

"I know, John told me. It means a lot to him even now. He often says how much your friendship means, how much you've always done for him."

"What's he talking about? I haven't done anything for him. It's always been the other way around."

"Nonsense. What about all those times in school when you made sure he got picked for dodge ball?"

Corbin's eyebrows came together in denial.

"You know it's true. If a team wanted you, they had to pick John, too. Everybody knew that. John has many good qualities but sports isn't one of them."

"They picked him because they liked him, and he was rich."

"No, they picked him because of you." Daisy bit into her apple and chewed. "It's amazing how cool it is in here. Hot as it is outside, it's almost too cool."

"Do you want to leave?"

Daisy gave him a soft look and shook her head. For the second time that day she allowed herself to stare at him – black hair misbehaving into wet curls on his forehead, sweaty work shirt the color of his eyes. She loved him in a blue shirt. He returned her stare until she had to drag her eyes to the shelves above his head, a sudden mutual fervor threatening to sabotage this innocent stopover.

Corbin cleared his throat and searched for something to say. "Believe it or not, we always preferred this dairy over John's fort. Remember that big tree fort Pop Ott built in the back yard of their old house?"

Daisy nodded and smiled. Corbin evidently appreciated *some* things about the farm, despite his protests. "It feels so safe in here," she said. "Even the war seems far away."

"The war *is* far away. It's way across an ocean and I'm stuck here hoeing corn for the summer."

"At least what you're doing is related to the war effort. Look at me. All I do is ride, swim in John's pool, play the piano every day. Mother says they are proper summer activities for a future Ottinger ... she's against my getting a job. She says there's no point in working now since I won't be in the future. What do you think, Corbin?"

"I think you should do what you want."

"Wish it were that easy."

"It'll soon be a moot point anyway won't it, since you're going to college in the fall?"

The plan was for Daisy to attend Sweet Briar, a women's college with a big price. "Yes, Mother's insistent about that, too. She wanted me to attend college with John but since he's going to a men's school she hand-picked Sweet Briar as the next best thing ... only sixty miles from Hampton-Sydney."

"If you could do anything you want, what would it be?" He asked the question innocently at first, related to what she'd said, but before it left his mouth he meant something different and imagined her saying, *I would be with you*, or some such thing.

She could tell what he was thinking by his face and gave him another soft look to let him know she knew. But she just said, "If I could do anything, I'd work for the war effort."

"Then that's what you should do," he said, reeling himself back in. "It's what I'm going to do. I'm enlisting after the harvest, with or without parent approval."

He had not touched her and he didn't intend to, though even in this brief time together a stronger bond had developed – an undeniable bond. He felt so right with her, so content, yet no real chance existed for them. A giant chasm had somehow formed, crowded with people who'd be disapproving or hurt. It was as much a dilemma for him as it was for her, burdened as he was with his own issues of loyalty and trust. John was his best friend and, even if Daisy were right about the dodge ball, John had still done so much more for him. Then there was Pop Ott to think about; he deserved loyalty in tons. The Ottingers had seen to it Corbin went to football games, as well as that golden chance to watch Tommy Dorsey perform. They had taken him on family vacations in the summer – to Atlantic City, Charleston and even Miami once. If it hadn't been for them, Corbin's traveling would have been limited to state fairs and livestock auctions. So the door labeled *Corbin and Daisy* had already been slammed shut.

NINE

For two years, military posters mounted everywhere had been urging men to enlist. In newsreels, recruits carrying suitcases hugged sweethearts and climbed happily onto trains. Lately, posters challenged women to support the war effort; newsreels showed female assembly lines in airplane factories. Two girls from the recent graduating class left town to work in such a factory and three others got jobs at the Ottinger Cannery. All this while Daisy perfected a selection of Chopin etudes. The last straw for her though was Cleona Bell.

It was no surprise to anyone when Cleona's mother died. The town quietly gathered to bury the woman on a morning in a summer storm. But Cleona surprised everyone when she suddenly closed up the house, climbed on a southbound train and headed for Baltimore with the idea of working in a factory.

Daisy saw Cleona off with best wishes and an artificial smile. On one hand she was happy for Cleona; the girl certainly deserved a fresh start. Yet for the first time in a long friendship, Daisy envied her. Baltimore sounded far more interesting than Sweet Briar, and Cleona was about to do something that mattered, something for the war effort, with nobody to tell her she should not. Daisy's envy made her feel like a worm; Cleona had shown only happiness for her constant good fortune. Which brought up an interesting question: had Cleona ever faked a smile to camouflage her envy?

The whole thing lessened Daisy's pity for Cleona, even produced a kind of respect. The girl had decided by herself what to do and then did it – a bold move for someone who must have felt quite alone. In contrast, Daisy had legions of people, most of them in opposition to anything other than college she wanted to do. She felt sure Wally would have sanctioned her independence if he hadn't joined the Marines, but all she had now of her brother was use of his '37 Plymouth.

Inspired by Cleona, and without telling anyone, Daisy sat at her desk on a morning in mid-August and wrote a letter in her best hand to the Sweet Briar admissions office to inform them she would not be attending in the fall. Then she dressed in an outfit she would wear to church, paid a visit to her future father-in-law and threatened to follow Cleona if he did not give her a job. Daisy's mother tried to forbid her but soon succumbed when she failed – anything to keep her daughter out of a Baltimore factory. John wasn't sure what to think at first, then decided he approved after hearing Corbin say he liked her spunk.

John left for college on a sticky morning in early September. He stood on the train station platform with an arm draped possessively around Daisy, sleek and expensive in a new linen suit probably worth more than Corbin's truck. John would rather have stayed home to attend a local college, had waited until the last possible moment to leave. But Ottinger men had always gone to Hampton-Sydney and he'd already veered once from tradition by choosing Judson High School over a private Catholic school. For the first time, he was taking a separate path from his best friend. "I'd rather not go. Don't tell them I said that," he whispered, nodding at his parents, "but I would honestly rather not go."

His mopey attitude annoyed Corbin. John had the girl, the money, the freedom – yet he acted as though he were headed to the reform school in Philadelphia. "Come on, snap out of it, you should be happy," Corbin said, giving John's free arm a whack. "This is an opportunity. If it were me, I'd already be gone."

John seemed to perk up at that. Somehow Corbin could always perk him up. When the last call for boarding was given and the last goodbyes said, it was only Corbin standing with John at the open door. "I'll probably miss you as much as anyone," John said. "Seems odd going our separate ways."

"Don't think of it as separate ways. Think of it just as ... a little side trip."

"Yeah, that's good, a little side trip. And I'll be back before we know it, right?" John stepped into the train as it made a jerky move forward. "Take care of my girl while I'm gone, okay?"

"Sure John, I'll take care of your girl."

"Blood brothers for life! See you at Thanksgiving," John yelled from the moving train.

Daisy soon formulated a new and satisfying routine centered around her shoe factory job, working six days a week, three in the afternoon until eleven. Each morning after breakfast she put on her jodhpurs and rode the south fork, which placed her along the O'Connell fence around ten. Work in that field had pretty much finished but Corbin was soon thinking up reasons to be over there. It was always a short visit and they stayed in their own territories – she on her horse, he perched on the fence.

They saw each other at Mass on Sundays, walking out together down the wide front steps and out on the lawn to chat for a moment like any two high school friends. There was only one problem with Sundays: they advertised so obviously that Corbin was there and John was gone.

Julia Hall had observed every detail of these little strolls, watching Corbin linger each week in his pew and step into the crowded aisle at just the right time. She wanted to say something but didn't dare. Daisy had shown such defiance over the job and, though specks of defiance had surfaced before, this display had been of a new order and Julia had no wish to invoke it again. She was finding herself in unknown territory as a mother – a defiant daughter of eighteen being harder to handle than a sulky daughter of twelve.

Opal had observed the Sunday routine as well, along with a few other things. The days of nagging her older son to get up for church seemed to be over; lately, he'd been dressed and out of the house ahead of the rest. And he seemed eager to be in an already-harvested field when there wasn't a need. She had known of his playground crush on Daisy and believed it might have developed into something more if not for John. It was understandable why John was now viewed the better catch but Opal believed in her heart that Corbin would one day be the better man. If he had decided to test his chances while John was away, so be it. No reason why John should *always* have the best of things, why he should have an open uncontested field for a girl like Daisy. If, without the constant display of Ottinger privilege, her son's qualities won the girl over, so be it. John would be hurt but he'd get over it.

For Corbin though, he had no real plan to win Daisy over. She was John's girl, John was his best friend, and that was that. But there was such temptation now, opportunities to see her alone more frequent and hard to resist. They inched toward each other in a gradual way through unsynchronized maneuvers designed to increase the chance of meeting. Their efforts were all completely independent – no stealthy passing of notes or clandestine planning. Neither did they discuss their seemingly insignificant adjustments to daily routine, and both avoided honest self-assessment of the purpose. Yet they operated as smoothly toward a common goal as the workings of Gil's Swiss-made pocket watch.

At the end of a rainy week in October, Corbin came home with chills and a fever that turned out to be Influenza. His mother wrapped a hot brick in flannel cut from Jimmy's old pajamas and placed it under the covers at the foot of his bed. Corbin slept days and nights away while a seasonal wind rattled the windows, dried up the rain and blew all the leaves off the trees. Opal coddled him like she did when he was a boy – frequent trips up the stairs to offer chicken broth or hot lemon tea, smoothing the hair from his forehead to check his temperature and plant a kiss.

On a bright morning nearly a week later he awoke with the sun in his face and a clearer head. He rolled over to escape the glare and, tangled in bedcovers, dozed a few minutes more. Soon, images of Daisy surfaced. How many times had he missed her? Twisting around, he looked at the clock: 10:05. Probably missed her again. He kicked off the covers and dashed to the window. Now, with the corn down and the leaves gone he had a clear view of the fence and the trail next to it, even the trails beyond the hickories. A half-dozen deer caught his eye and he zeroed in on them, knowing they'd scatter from a horse and rider.

Opal found him on the window seat in his underwear and handed him a cup of steaming tea. He took it wishing it were coffee.

"What are you doing out of bed?" she asked.

"Uh ... just looking."

"I'd have thought you'd seen enough of those fields for a while."

"Look different from up here."

She turned away to straighten the bedcovers so she could smile. "Aren't you cold sitting there?"

Corbin shook his head. "It's warm in the sun."

"Think you could eat a little?" she asked.

"I don't know ... got any coffee?"

"Sure I do! I'll be right back." A good sign, him asking for coffee. She left the room with a spring in her step and returned moments later with a tray. With the coffee, she'd brought a plate with a dollop of scrambled egg and a hot biscuit. Wasn't much, but no point overwhelming him right off. Until now he'd rejected any offer of food, yet this time he allowed the tray to be set in front of him. "Eat it while it's hot," she said. He picked up the biscuit and stared at it while Opal watched, working her own mouth a bit to encourage him. He nibbled at it at first, then realizing he was hungry, devoured it and the egg in three bites. She snatched the empty plate and went back for more, this time adding ham and a side of apple butter.

By early afternoon Corbin felt well enough to be fidgety. He hadn't seen Daisy in over a week. Impulsively, he dressed and drove into town hoping to see her on her way to work, in order to explain. Explain what? He owed no explanation; they'd had no plans to meet. But still, he tried to find her until her shift started at three. He even drove into the industry complex, a reckless thing to do. What if Pop Ott had seen him? In friendly unsuspicious inquiry the man might have asked why he was there, and Corbin could've created suspicion floundering for a valid excuse. In an afterthought he picked Jimmy up from school and drove him home. It pleased the younger brother so much it made the older feel guilty.

Determined to see Daisy when her shift ended at eleven, Corbin drove to town again after the family went to bed. His timing was better this time – cruising down Grant Street in front of her house just as she stepped out of Wally's Plymouth.

"I see you're feeling better," Daisy said.

"Good, so you knew. I didn't want you to think I just didn't show up .... in case you rode by ..."

"Your mother told Daddy and he told me. The infallible Judson grapevine."

It would have been dark enough to see the stars had it not been for the streetlamp she stood under. The country had gone soft on blackouts and air-raid drills after nearly a year without any bombs or invading armies. Corbin tilted his head to study her in her overalls and short winter jacket, head scarf tied in a topknot like Aunt Jemima. Her cheek had a smudge of something that looked like grease. She was so adorable he could hardly stand to look at her because looking only made him want to touch.

"Gosh, I must look a sight." She yanked off the scarf letting her hair tumble like an ebony waterfall.

"First time I've ever seen you with grease on your face." He gave her a white-toothed smile.

"Oh, gosh." She found a handkerchief and wiped the wrong cheek.

"Here, let me get it with mine." He dragged a freshly-laundered one out of his pocket. "This is clean ... except for the axle grease I just removed from the driveshaft," he teased, nodding at his truck. With the crackling eyes that worried Daisy's mother, Corbin stepped in to wipe away the smudge. "Good thing for the streetlamp. Wouldn't have seen the grease without it ... probably wouldn't even have seen you."

She suddenly felt conspicuous and backed out of the light.

"No need to hide. We're not doing anything wrong." But he followed her.

"The grapevine could work to our disadvantage here."

"Maybe. You looked adorable by the way, with grease on your face."

"I did?"

"Let's put it like this ... there's no fence between us here so I suggest you stay at least three feet from me. Otherwise ..." With catlike exaggeration he crept toward her in the dark.

She giggled in transparent delight, scooted into her yard and closed him out with the gate. Anyone still awake in a nearby house would have heard them laughing.

"See you tomorrow, like always? Might snow though," he said.

"Sure, see you tomorrow, even if it does snow. It'll be my last morning ride for a while."

"Why's that?"

"I'm quitting the factory to work in the market with Daddy starting next week. It'll be day work ...."

"Sounds reasonable, you working in the market. Wonder you didn't do it in the first place."

"Mother wouldn't let me then, but she's given her consent now for some reason. Preferable to the shoe factory, I guess. Aren't parents odd sometimes, the ideas they get about what's best?"

"Yep. Pop knows I don't want to be a farmer, yet he keeps pushing."

"Your father and my mother. Do you ever wonder if they're right?"

"Nope."

"Wish I could be so sure." The gate latch creaked as she fiddled with it. "Corbin?" Her voice was almost a whisper.

"Yeah?"

"It's nice when we talk like this, isn't it?"

"Uh-huh."

"See you tomorrow, then?"

"I'll be out there," he said, for the first time acknowledging a plan. On the sidewalk under the streetlamp he found her handkerchief where she must have dropped it, a creamy white square with a cluster of tiny purple flowers embroidered on a corner. He picked it up and waved it in her direction but she'd already gone in. With a foxy side glance he clutched it in his fist and, sniffing it, decided to keep it. He took the lavender-scented handkerchief to bed that night and several nights afterward. Then he tucked it in with an old wrapper from gum they'd shared when they were twelve, saved all this time in a box of trumpet mouthpieces.

He began to show up at Hall's Market more often. Opal became adept at manufacturing reasons to go: one day for vanilla extract; another to check the current cost in dollars and ration stamps of a pound of sugar; another to actually purchase her monthly allotment, which she promptly hid in an old potato chip can for Thanksgiving pies. Corbin soon learned to avoid the market in the morning when Julia Hall was there to throw darts at him with her eyes. And she was as good as Opal at manufacturing reasons – hers designed to busy Daisy elsewhere.

Gil continued to pick at Corbin for driving the truck to town so he switched to a bike. Then bicycles, too, became irreplaceable because of the metal; bicycle tires, because of the rubber. And their half-mile dirt road pulverized the tires, which Corbin had to patch and re-patch.

But all in all, the autumn of 1942 was blissful. Daisy and Corbin joined a committee to support the USO, spent hours sprucing up the armory for traveling servicemen. Never had the two spent so much time together, free from the physical presence of John and Velma.

The O'Connells went turkey hunting as usual the Saturday before Thanksgiving, the first time Corbin could remember that John didn't go. Gil went and brought down a fine twenty-pounder. Everything considered, it was a happy time for Gil, able to work the farm again and hunt with his boys like a father should. But what pleased him most was the way his eldest son had seemingly settled into life without any move to enlist.

John's return for Thanksgiving jolted Corbin back to reality. He found it hard to step aside after having Daisy to himself the better part of three months, and it was harder now to watch them together, jealousy and resentment his new-found companions. Things grew blissful again when John returned to college, yet he'd left a deeper shadow behind, looming ever-present and proprietary.

For Corbin, the weeks until Christmas meant a bittersweet trip from pleasure to pain. Opal saw it and understood. His daily encounters with Daisy, enough to please him in October and November, seemed unsatisfactory now. Nothing of consequence ever got said. What he wanted to say he knew not, but prattling on about USO decorations, the scarcity of coffee or the price per pound of butter seemed a waste of precious time while days disappeared on the calendar.

On the cold clear evening of a full moon two days before John's return, Corbin drove to town compelled by a need to see Daisy one more time, talk to her one more time while he could still pretend a chance. He knew it was fiction, knew seeing her in his determined irrational mood was probably a bad idea. Yet he did it anyway, the want of her now surpassing any bonds of boyhood friendship.

He parked and waited for her to walk home from the market. When she saw him she smiled as she shivered in her heavy coat, hands in her pockets. She spoke first, something meaningless and safe in that breezy tone, the hallmark of their relationship. He did not banter back as she expected but his eyes said much, filled as they were with stormy passion. Caught off-guard she halted in mid-stride. This was not to be one of their customary chats; it would be something more and they were going to have it under a streetlamp. She instinctively side-stepped out of the light.

He followed, put hands on her shoulders and pushed her further into shadow. "Day after day I have kept my distance, but I can't keep pretending nothing's happened. There isn't enough time."

"Don't ... please don't do this."

"Why do you act like there's nothing between us?" He shook her shoulders in frustration. "Sometimes you look at me and I think you're finally going to let me admit the truth, but before I have a chance ... you start pretending again that we're just friends, pretending we have nothing important to say."

"Corbin, don't. What we have now is all we can ever have ... you know that." Her eyes were unreadable in the moonlight but frowning eyebrows cut clear lines. "Don't you see? If we acknowledge that it's more, we have to stop."

He turned away in hurt surprise, ran hands through his hair and turned back, the lines of his face chiseled in granite. "But it *is* more. Don't you think it's time we acknowledge it?"

Caught up in the heated moment, neither felt the chill. She pulled her hands from her pockets and gestured broadly. "I have racked my brain thinking up safe things to say so we wouldn't cross the line. I thought you understood."

He softened. "I do understand." He stepped in to search her face and caress her cold cheek. "I feel bad about John, too, but –"

"I was afraid this day would come." She stared at him with injured eyes. "You've ruined everything now, don't you see? What we've had the last few weeks has been wonderful, and now it's over ... it's all over. We can't do it anymore." She pulled away from him and ran to the house. He couldn't be sure, but he thought she was crying. He'd never seen the adult Daisy cry before.

At the armory dance the following night, poor Velma tried to make Corbin jealous by flirting with a cute Navy seaman. Corbin barely noticed, too absorbed with whether to approach Daisy or leave her alone.

Daisy solved it by following him into the storeroom when he went in there for extra cups. "I'm sorry about last night," she said. "It wasn't fair to accuse you of ruining everything. The truth is ... it had to end soon anyway. And it was my fault for indulging in it, encouraging it ..."

"Do you love John?" A risky thing to ask but it seemed a fair question.

She shifted her eyes. "He's so trusting of me ... so trusting of you. He writes about you all the time in letters. 'Corbin is the best,' he always says, 'nobody has a better friend than Corb.'

And everybody expects us to marry ... my parents, his parents, people in town."

"I don't give a damn about them."

"But, what about John? He's never done a single wrong thing to either of us."

"I know, but you're the girl I love and that's never gonna change. Seems like a lot to sacrifice for a friend. There ... I've said it." Corbin sighed and leaned against the shelves. "He's always had the best of everything – the biggest house, new cars, trips to Europe, college, freedom to do what he pleased. None of that ever really bothered me though because, well ... it's his birthright, and he's been such a good friend ... my best friend. But when he gets the girl I love? That bothers me, it bothers me a lot. Especially if she loves me."

"I just don't want to hurt him."

"Guess I'm a smaller person than you are. To have you I'm willing to hurt him." Corbin crammed hands in his pockets and gave her a sober stare. "Do you love him?"

"I care for him. I care for him very much."

"That isn't the same thing. I'll tell you what I think ..." He shoved the door closed and crowded her to the wall. "I think you love me."

She put both hands on his chest and pushed against him. "If we give into this we limit ourselves to two choices. We either hide in the shadows like we're doing now, or we hurt him. And I can't bear to hurt him ... please don't make me hurt him. I'd rather be miserable myself."

Her words sobered him. He stepped back. "Well damn it, I refuse to hide like a criminal. But I won't stand around and watch the two of you anymore either." He threw his hands in the air. "Don't know why I'm still in this damn town, torturing myself this way ... I don't have to stay here." It was said under his breath but she heard it. He opened the door and stormed out, forgetting the cups he came in for.

T E N

On Christmas Eve, John gave Daisy an engagement ring and proposed marriage. She accepted both with dignity and reserve. On Christmas Day, John proudly announced it to a room full of guests as sheets of dreary, unseasonable rain pelted the picture window and almost drowned him out. It was official now; they were engaged. While Daisy's mother gushed joy, her father leaned in with a congratulatory hug and whispered, "I just want my Petunia to be happy. Are you sure this is what you want?"

Thoughts of enlistment consumed Corbin again. The only thing stopping him now was parental resistance; he did not look forward to the fight. He considered doing it without telling them but it felt cowardly, and cowardly seemed a bad approach to war.

Gil continued to offer daily broad-view summations of the war at the supper table. He had a lot to say for someone who'd never been, but war seemed to be the subject of every conversation nowadays. U.S. troops – the first to be shipped across the Atlantic – were now fighting Hitler in North Africa. And in the Pacific, though Japan's advance was finally halted, they still controlled the ocean for thousands of miles. The family had grown weary of Gil's war talks but lately Corbin actually welcomed them, on the lookout for a good moment to break his news. The moment soon came with a meal of liver and onions. "We're fighting across both oceans now," Gil said. "Like it or not, we've got a two-front war."

Corbin hesitated just long enough to form the words. "So now more than ever, it's the job of every able-bodied man to step up ..."

Opal knew what was coming. She jerked her head in his direction with eyes conveying concern.

"... which is why I've decided to enlist after the new year."

Opal suddenly hated her husband as though his remark were to blame. But she knew it had more to do with Daisy than with patriotism or anything Gil said. In truth, her son was being pushed into war by a diamond ring in a black velvet box.

Arguments and pleading followed. "You're a farmer, a soldier out of uniform," Gil said with his chin in the air. "You should be proud to serve this way, proud to grow food for the troops. They'd starve without us."

For Corbin, that was the same as comparing a soldier in the trenches to the one peeling potatoes in a mess tent.

Opal begged him to view life with a wider scope. "Your future goes beyond what's happening here," she said, giving him a pointed look.

But nothing they said made any difference. His mind was made up.

Later that evening, John reacted with alarm. "I thought you'd given up on that. Gad, Corbin, my parents will kill me if I quit college to enlist."

"Who said anything about you?"

"Well …"

"You don't need to go just because I'm going."

"But, won't it seem odd for you to go without me?"

"Yeah, but we need to go our own way on something like this."

John didn't try to hide his relief. "All right then, if you're sure."

Corbin broke it to the women the next day as the four sat eating burgers at the diner on Velma's day off. He rapped his knuckles on the table in an attention-grabbing manner and just blurted it out.

Velma's eyebrows came together as the brain behind them panicked. Her time was about to run out and all she wanted to do was go off in a corner to plot her next move. Daisy's reaction proved more complex – a jumbled reaction that traveled quickly from guilt, to respect, to fear.

John began at once to study Daisy's face. For him the guilt was hard to identify, but he recognized the respect and certainly the fear, unable to decide which bothered him more. One thing was sure – Daisy had never shown respect like that for him, or such fear for his safety. John was not aware of it then, but from the time he sat down until the time he stood up, life's path had changed for him. Building inside him, born in the moment, was his own surprising need to enlist.

They went to a movie at the Monarch afterward and sat behind two uniformed youngsters on three-day passes and a long way from home. "That'll be us in a month," one of them said watching newsreel footage of blank-faced GIs filing up the gangplank of a troop carrier. "And I hope we're going over there," he added a moment later seeing Hitler's armies march in goosestep across the screen, thousands in perfect formation as far as the eye could see.

"Don't blame you a bit. It's where I hope to go," Corbin said.

"Those guys aren't so tough. They must be wearing themselves out with that crazy goosestep. Have you tried it? I tried it just for the hell of it and I'm telling you, it'll wear you out. And it's hard on the knees ... "

John made the snap decision on the way home to tell Daisy he was enlisting. Later he would question whether his entire motivation was to see her face, but even so it didn't matter; once the words came out of his mouth he couldn't back down. The next day he told a surprised Corbin and even pressed him to enlist right then rather than wait. So on the second to the last day of 1942, they went together to fill out papers and sign their names, relinquishing the coveted occupational deferments that would have saved them from the war.

John had never done well against his father's persuasive reasoning so he delayed telling his parents until afterward. Predictably, George Ottinger called it impulsive and absurd. "The least you could have done," he said, "was let me try to get you a commission. You're going in as an enlisted man when you might have gone in as an officer."

As an officer! John shrieked to himself. That would have been the absurd part. The very idea of having to lead anybody anywhere, especially in a war zone, sent growth-stunting fear through him.

Over the next few weeks Corbin managed to get a grip on his emotions, resigned himself enough to once again give loyalty its proper place. He had not actually talked to Daisy since that night at the armory in December, and it seemed an inadequate end as his March departure drew near. On a frigid afternoon he walked into Hall's Market for the first time in a month and asked her for a candy bar. She took it from a display rack and set it on the counter with a sad smile. He fished a nickel out of his pocket, handed it to her with a note that read *storeroom tonight at 8*, and left before she could respond.

A few hours later he entered the dark armory through a side entrance nobody ever bothered to lock, felt his way to the kitchen and switched on a light. The heat was off so it was cold in the building, nearly as cold as outside. He found the storeroom key, unlocked the door and wondered whether she'd come.

She did. The side door opened and closed. He heard footfalls on the old wood floor and the swish of skirts, smelled her scent of lavender.

"I wasn't sure you'd come," he said.

She gathered her coat collar around her neck and nodded.

"I know ... it's freezing in here. I won't keep you long."

"That's okay. So you're leaving soon."

"Yeah, and I don't want to go without smoothing things out. What we said in here last time, well ... we shouldn't leave it like that."

"No."

"Not just for us but for John and me, too."

"Yes, you two have to stay close."

"I need you to know I understand about not wanting to hurt him. I feel pretty guilty right now. Not sure who I feel guiltier about though ... John or Pop Ott. He'd expect better things of me." Corbin reached in a pocket for her handkerchief and handed it to her. "Here, this is yours. I stole it."

"You did? Well, you can keep it."

"Better not ... means entirely too much to me. Besides, it isn't olive drab."

Daisy smiled at that.

"The truth is," he said, "neither of us is free to love the other, there's too much in the way."

"You'll find somebody else."

"Maybe, but she'll have to be just like you. You're my standard ... I'm gonna have trouble settling for less."

"I'll be jealous of her. I'm jealous of her now, whoever she is."

"Then you know how I feel." He studied her for a moment, questioning. "You've never seemed jealous of Velma, though. Why is that?"

"The Velmas of the world ... they're never a real threat. Would you marry her?"

"No."

"See what I mean? Girls like her are not wife material to any man I'd want." She cut her eyes at him. "It's none of my business, but why do you mess around with her?"

He shrugged. "Well, I can't have you, so who I *mess around with*, as you put it, doesn't matter. And there's no ties with Velma. She'll be easy to leave and she won't mind letting go."

"Won't mind letting go? Don't be too sure."

"Now you sound like my mother."

"Did she tell you that? Wise woman, you should pay attention to her. You'll probably fall in love with a European girl and bring her back as a bride."

"Between you and me, I don't plan to come back."

"Where will you go, then? After the war I mean."

"New York City, maybe."

"Then, I'll never see you."

An awkward silence filled the tiny storeroom while each tried to think of something to say. "John tells me you're waiting until after the war to get married," Corbin finally said, wondering whose idea it was to wait.

"We both agreed it's best," she said, seeming to read his thoughts. "Well ... please take care of yourself and John. The two of you need to watch out for each other."

"You sound like my mother again."

"Never mind. I already made John promise the same thing, to take care of himself and watch out for you. Now you need to promise me. It's important that you promise me," she said as her eyes filled.

"Okay, okay, I promise. And I promise something else, too. I promise not to pressure you again. If we ever speak of how we feel after tonight, it'll be because you start it." He stepped close enough to touch her face, traced a path from temple to chin with his thumb. Then he took the handkerchief, dabbed at the tears on her cheeks and handed it back. "Just never forget, no matter what happens, it'll always be you." She did not step away. He slid hard arms inside her coat, encircled her waist and pulled her close. It would have been difficult now to get away but she didn't try. Proceeding cautiously he kissed one cheek, and the other, then a light touch on the lips. He wanted to really kiss her. In all this time they had never kissed and he felt justified, just this once, as a reward for good behavior. He supposed he should get permission but was not the type to ask, so he just did it without preamble and she didn't resist. Instead she became a rag doll in his arms, gave in to the kiss completely, allowing one delicious intimacy before he was gone.

The impending departure pushed Velma into a corner. She viewed as a definite handicap this odd need to appear virginal. He was leaving in ten days and had not yet popped the question, which left her no choice but to be bold.

"Corbin, let's get married." Velma said this the moment his truck pulled up at the curb and she opened the door. She plunked down on the seat and turned to him. "We can have sex as much as you want until you go. We could even do it tonight if you want."

He stared at her in disbelief. "I don't want to get married, Velma. We've never mentioned marriage before, neither of us, and now you bring it up just when I'm leaving."

"That's *why* I'm bringing it up, because you're leaving."

"Well, it's a lousy idea."

"Don't you love me?"

"We've never mentioned love before either, so don't ask me that now." He banged on the steering wheel with both hands and peeled away from the curb, beginning to feel betrayed. They went to a movie, watched it in silence, and he took her home without their usual stop at Linden Lake.

Back in her bedroom Velma stood in front of the mirror and spoke aloud to her reflection. "Hmm, that didn't work." But she was far from deterred. She would write him sweet letters while he was away and he'd surely miss her. Didn't people always say, *absence makes the heart grow fonder*? An encouraging thought. But they also say, *out of sight out of mind*. Well, which one was it?

They left on March 12 with two boys joining the Navy. To Opal they all looked like babies. Conducting herself to please her son she clutched him in a single embrace and reminded him to eat, then let go and told him to write. She'd never been one to gush over her boys anyhow.

On every train station platform in every city these days, goodbyes were often said with muffled emotions; it was easier that way. A cold and steady rain had reduced the crowd of well-wishers, yet the sendoff wasn't short of brave farewells. Opal saw one mother wield a convincing false gaiety only to betray it with a reluctance to let go. And a father sent his surprised son off with a formal handshake, perhaps to support the notion that he was a man.

When Corbin gave Daisy a brotherly hug, Opal suspected a case of emotions denied. And she suspected emotions embellished in the last seconds before the *All Aboard*, as she watched Corbin with Velma and Daisy with John. Despite her hundred fears about this departure, she saw it as a timely defusing of a powder keg – Corbin and John standing at the same window as the train pulled away, escaping with their friendship intact.

"Blood brothers for life," John said as he held out his fists.

Corbin clicked his against them. "Yep, blood brothers for life."

Opal didn't worry overmuch about Corbin eating right. There were shortages of almost everything now because the military got first dibs. The boys needed meat so the government rationed beef and pork. The boys needed combat boots so they rationed leather. The boys needed dairy so they rationed butter and cheese. Tin was needed for armaments and C ration containers so they rationed canned goods.

The new Office of Price Administration issued ration stamps at the beginning of each month – blue ones for canned goods (48 per person), red ones for meat and dairy (64). Every rationed item had two prices now – the cost in money and the cost in stamps. One can of applesauce, for example, cost sixteen cents and ten blue stamps.

Judson, adjacent to farm country, made out better than most, yet women in town could often serve only half a breakfast – eggs and bread plentiful, butter and bacon scarce. Three hungry men hustled into Opal's kitchen three times a day, plus she had a stripling still at home who could eat his weight in rationed goods. She was lucky to have the farm. Hams and sides of bacon hung in the smokehouse from butchering last November. She could churn her own butter, make her own applesauce out of the Winesaps left from the autumn harvest. Even with much of the farm output going to the Ottinger Cannery, the dairy shelves sagged with her own canned fruits and vegetables, and she was often able to augment the meager sugar ration with honey Wilbur occasionally robbed from a neighboring hive. Coffee, though, was another thing; you could not grow coffee or any worthy substitute on a Pennsylvania farm.

Bootleggers in New York and Chicago were back in business again after twenty years, dealing this time in the black-market trade of rationed goods. Many Americans were glad to pay double to sidestep the ration rules, even with the warning, "Violation of these rules will help the enemy!" stamped on every ration book. But the folk in Judson took the warning seriously, viewed as un-American the hoarding or illegal come-by of anything scarce.

Sometimes, it was okay though. One of those things that, like speeding, was permissible for oneself but not for the other guy. Charlie Hall discovered that shady transactions from a neighborhood grocer were even expected at times, when regular customers desired him out of loyalty to produce from the back room a coveted pound of coffee, pack of cigarettes, can of tuna or favorite candy bar the sign said was out of stock.

It was easy for a grocer and his family to function outside the ration limit themselves. Julia Hall lived outside the limits and felt no qualms about it. She had done all her usual baking in December despite the butter and sugar shortage; smoked unlimited cigarettes even when they were scarce; drank two cups of coffee each morning though ships that previously carried coffee beans from South America had been diverted for military use and her own son was probably steaming around on one of them. In her mind she was no different with her little excesses than the gas station owner who put an extra gallon in his tank, or the department store manager who set aside from a long-awaited shipment a coveted pair of nylons for his wife.

Cigarettes were in short supply because so many went overseas. Just when everybody needed a smoke, none were available for weeks. When a shipment finally did arrive and word got around, smokers scurried in from all over town and would have bought up the entire supply in a day if Charlie hadn't limited them to two packs apiece.

He tried to keep a lid on the arrival of any scarce goods – at least until he got it priced and stocked in an orderly fashion. A delivery of bacon or butter invariably meant a long line of eager women with cash in hand, ration books at the ready. A new shipment of bobby pins, which Charlie managed to discreetly stock in the usual place in the hair-grooming section, caused such a scramble among these well-bred women that he decided to keep them, when he had them, behind the front counter next to the cigarettes, when he had them.

The double currency forced him to label every rationed item twice – the cost in money and the cost in ration points as prescribed by the government's latest rationing regulations. It was particularly laborsome with cans. The market owner knew he'd never be able to cope now without Daisy. Ration stamps and the related paperwork had become one of her jobs

– collecting the stamps from customers and sending them to the wholesaler, who passed them to the manufacturer, who in turn accounted for them to the government. No getting around it, they had to comply if they wanted more rationed goods.

This widespread rationing and the fear of telegrams from Washington reminded Daisy and her dad every day of the war. To live within the ration limits and cope without complaint seemed the least they could do, made them feel useful to Wally when they couldn't help him any other way. And maybe with continued daily sacrifice the war would end before John and Corbin even shipped out.

ELEVEN

March, 1943
Fort Jackson, South Carolina

"Left, left, left-right-left. Left, left, left-right-left ...." the drill instructor droned to the fresh column in his charge, rapping it out in the same clipped manner he continued in his dreams. These men and thousands more like them were to be molded into a new fighting force for the Army, the 106th Infantry Division. "You've got to be the sorriest bunch yet ... you're even dumber than I'm used to," he bellowed, using one of his typical lines as he sized them up on a scale of best to worst. He poked a finger at one of the worst. "You. Yeah, you with the big ears. What's your name?"

"Donaldson, sir."

"Well, Donaldson, don't you know your right foot from your left?"

"Sure I do, sir."

"Keep going, keep going, all of you! Then when I say *right* foot, why aren't you using your right foot? Are you deliberately trying to annoy me?"

"No, sir!"

"With those big ears, maybe you fly better than you walk. Is that it, Dumbo?" the drill instructor jeered, saddling the nineteen-year-old with a nickname he'd never shake. "We *walk* in the Army, Dumbo. We do one hell of a lot of walking and your whole line is a disgrace! Keep going, keep going ... left, left, left-right-left." He took a few steps back as the column lumbered by. "Ready ... halt! I said halt! You ... you on the other end of this row. What's your name?"

"O'Connell, sir."

"And that pale drink of water next to you?"

"Ottinger, sir."

"How the hell is it O'Connell and Ottinger, that you know how to march when the rest of these dolts can't walk?"

"High school marching band, sir."

"Well hallelujah, my lucky day. Somehow, I have to teach this sorry bunch to move from one place to another in orderly fashion, and you two are going help me. You're going show the rest of these idiots how to march." He shoved his hat back to scratch his forehead. "O'Connell, take the front half, from this row forward," he said, lining himself up with the middle of the column, "to that grassy area to my left. And Ottinger, you take the other half over there to my right. Okay? Can you handle it?"

"Yes, sir."

"Good. You both just got spot promotions to acting corporal. If you do this right and I'm in a good mood later, maybe I'll recommend they make it permanent. If you don't do it right I'll cut off your thumbs. Now the rest of you guys ... I suggest you learn how to march by 08:00 hours tomorrow. Otherwise you'll look bad, and when *you* look bad you make *me* look bad. And believe me ... I get real cranky when somebody makes me look bad. Swear to God, if I don't see quick improvement I'll suspend every chance at a weekend pass 'til the end of this war. Now get going!" Over the heads of scrambling men he added in a loud voice, "Hey, what instruments do you two play? Please don't tell me the lousy drums."

"Trumpet sir, both of us," Corbin yelled.

"Well hallelujah, do you play Taps?"

"No sir, but we can learn."

"Good. One of you needs to be at HQ by 22:00 hours. We just lost our bugler to the 28th."

It was fine with Corbin to take on the bugle playing and fine with John to let him. Though his hastily prepared first rendition over the loudspeaker did not make him proud, and the unexpected order to play Reveille the next morning resulted in a laughable attempt, Corbin soon conquered both and played for two weeks until they found a permanent replacement.

The spot promotions came with armbands to distinguish them from the others in measureless marches and close-order drills. The distinction did not win them many friends. It excused them from KP and latrine duty, however, which was probably what the others most resented. The acting corporals met with excessive formality during the day and freeze-outs in the barracks at night, but at least they had each other in their unpopularity.

Corbin managed to strike up a friendship with a guy named Dutton who'd been in the Army before and had a reputation for being a crack shot. He was considered an old man compared to the rest, probably all of thirty, so when an Italian named Cartuzzo called him *Pappy* one day, it stuck. Dutton didn't seem to mind the nickname though, or anything else for that matter. He shrugged off every petty taunt and challenge that would have provoked somebody else, displaying a sharpshooter's essential mild manner. Corbin studied the man and decided he was worth imitating. Pappy Dutton seemed to have hit on the best way to survive in this place, perhaps from his previous four-year stint.

And he seemed to be the only one other than Corbin who wanted to be there. The rest appeared homesick or lonely or scared. Few were prepared for basic training – the Army's toughening-up period where drilling was relentless, workouts brutal, lodging dreary, inspections humiliating, food institutional, discipline humbling, persecution encouraged, privacy nonexistent and home seemed a planet away.

The importance of privacy had never occurred to Corbin, yet now he was sleeping in a hall the size of the armory with men that snored louder than he. His personal space had narrowed to a metal locker and bunk, the bunks close enough for him to stand between two and put elbows on both. His room at home was a secluded island by comparison. Privacy had never been an issue on the farm; there'd been a dozen places to escape to within a few feet of the house. But there was no privacy anywhere here, not even in the bathroom – especially not the bathroom. Amid the off-putting sounds and smells of a latrine used by fifty men, he was openly contributing to the sounds and smells himself. And he'd never quite adjusted to the buzz-cut they gave him, reaching in a pocket throughout the day for a comb that wasn't there and he didn't need.

Nevertheless, even taking all this into account, Corbin still preferred the Army over the farm. But that didn't stop him from eagerly awaiting Mail Call – the best part of the day except to the guys who never heard their names. Every evening after dinner the men returned to the barracks hoping for letters, which they oftentimes faithfully answered that same night. John usually got a stack of mail, what with Daisy and each member of his family writing three times a week. Corbin, too, could count on regular mail from home, including frequent letters from Velma that were scented with cologne and written with misspellings in a curlicue hand. There was even an occasional sisterly note from Daisy, her elegant script immediately recognizable on the envelope. He opened hers with a hope of ... something ... then reacted to that hope with a pang of guilt. John had remained so completely trusting. *He thinks I'm as loyal as he is,* Corbin often reflected with shame. Though loyalty had to be easier for the guy with the girl.

After weeks of calisthenics in the South Carolina sun, miles of marching with full field pack in sandy soil, the entire unit appeared tan and reasonably lean, even the ones who'd been flabby on arrival. Corbin didn't look much different but there was a noticeable change in John – hints of definition in his chest muscles, face and arms the color of the sand. "I wish Daisy could see me now. I've never been in this good a shape," John said to his reflection in a mirror. "Don't you think so, Corb?"

Tucking the end of his tie between the second and third shirt button, Corbin studied him and responded favorably. John *did* look good. Yet from a distance he could have doubled for any other man in the room. Same uniform, posture, attitude – everything about them strictly government issue now. They were clothed in government issue from underwear to helmet, toted government issue gear, smoked government issue cigarettes, suffered government issue haircuts, rode in government issue trucks. After marching as one, eating as one, sleeping as one, thinking as one, the entire division to a man had actually become government issue – the American GI.

***

"I need four volunteers," a freckled sergeant announced on a Monday morning. The men stood like statues without so much as a clearing of throat or scratching of head, lest it be mistaken for an offer. Conventional Army wisdom warned against volunteering. If volunteers were asked for, one could assume it involved an unwanted job of some sort, such as sewage disposal or pushing a wheelbarrow full of something up a steep hill. The 106th had already picked up this wisdom from somewhere, as though it had been painted on the barracks walls or scribbled on mattresses by the men who'd slept and prayed and sweated there last. "Come on, you heard me. I need four volunteers."

Pappy Dutton stepped forward first. Corbin took the older man's lead and stepped out next, followed by John and Dumbo Donaldson.

"Okay, I've got four," the sergeant said. "Report to the Motor Pool."

The four hoofed over and found the Motor Pool Sergeant rocking from heel to toe in front of a row of trucks, arms crossed as if he'd been waiting all morning. "I'll get right to it," he said. "There are four vehicles here. Each of you take one, clean it up, familiarize yourself with its operation. And remove every inch of that gunk. I wanna see them shine."

It took days to carry out the order. Each vehicle as it turned out was a new 2½ ton, tenwheel truck with a double-range transmission and front-mounted power winch. The gunk as it turned out was Cosmoline, a gooey substance intended to protect whatever it covered and resist removal. It reminded Corbin of Vaseline, except it was green and stiffer. Hours and hours were spent on the "clean it up" part. They tried hot water first but it didn't work. The only thing that did work was diesel fuel.

The "familiarize" part was completed in a half-day. The trucks had starter-buttons to push instead of ignition keys, which seemed odd to them at first. But it would have been odder still, they decided, to stand in enemy territory yelling, *Hey, who's got the keys?* Corbin particularly enjoyed all this new-truck tinkering – no need to rebuild something or flush something or patch something in order for it to run.

On Thursday an unfamiliar staff sergeant showed up and planted himself in front of them, posture relaxed, manner nonthreatening. "I am Wire Sergeant Martin. You've all been assigned to me. These are wire trucks you've been working on, for laying communication wire. They're your trucks now ... your responsibility," he said, nodding toward the vehicles that sparkled in the sun. "Each of you will be given a crew of three, and with your crews you'll provide a communication network for the four artillery battalions in the division. Specialized training in this area will be your immediate focus.

Gentlemen, we are all part of Division Artillery's HQ Battery, an arm of the division elite. Never forget that, and look sharp. I congratulate each of you ... you've just been promoted to wire corporal."

Their official orders were ultimately to install telephone wire, establish radio communication, encode messages, run surveys for gun emplacements and coordinate artillery operations among the battalions. The gist of it in laymen's terms was to hook nests of howitzers together and feed them information so they could successfully blow things up.

Each crew first had to master the skill of installing wire. With a heavy steel spool loaded onto a frame in the back of the truck, they spent the next few weeks practicing in the low-lying hills and scrub-oak forests of South Carolina. Lines often had to be positioned high in the trees in order to cross a road or body of water. Corbin had the best crew for that, one of them a lineman in civilian life, able to strap on a set of pole climbers and whiz up a tree like a pro. The goal was clear: get those lines where they're going and get them there right now, regardless of obstacles. The trucks could do it – powerful enough to clear a path, move debris out of the way, take out unwanted trees and generally rearrange the landscape. Corbin relished the job and its $66.00 a month paycheck. The money didn't mean much to John, but the way Corbin viewed it, the Army was giving him good money just to play on the range all day with a new truck.

Rumors began of going to the Philippines. Furlough lists were supposedly being drawn up and scuttlebutt had it that this was *the* furlough, the one prior to going overseas. Emotions ran high for a while and then fell flat. Furloughs were issued, but nothing so final – just the ordinary ten-day kind handed out in shifts. The wire crews got theirs over Thanksgiving, a lucky break. John was pleased beyond words to be going home. Even Corbin looked at it with favor and began to make plans: he would hunt, fill up on his mother's cooking, and attempt once again to score with Velma. If her letters were any indication, she was ready.

They stepped off the train to celebrity treatment like others returning home after so many months. Velma waited on the platform like she belonged there as much as Daisy, and attempted to copy the same air of quiet dignity. Impossible. In an overwhelming burst of pride she sucked in her breath at the sight of Corbin looking so manly and grand. It was one thing to have seen him in a band uniform or dungarees, but in an Army uniform? Well, that beat everything. *I've got to get this guy, I've got to get him*, became her silent mantra.

She was encouraged when he hugged her with that dangerous look in his eye and said, "I never thought I'd say it but it's good to be home." He obviously still wanted her. If men weren't so silly about virgin brides it would have been nice to just let it happen. As it was though, men *were* silly, and she wasn't so filled with wisdom herself when they parked at Linden Lake on his second night home.

It was a clear crisp night; they could have gazed at a brilliant moon if they hadn't steamed up the windows. For the first time, she let him reach a hand inside her underpants and explore there until they both were in a state. Then abruptly, she pushed his hand away.

He straightened in the seat and placed both hands on the steering wheel. "You're never going to do more than play around, are you?"

"I would if we were married," she muttered, knowing she'd let things go too far without a willingness to go all the way. "Don't you think I want to do it, too? But we have to get married first. Then we can do it as much as you want. I'd treat you real good if we got married, Corbin."

"Velma–"

"And you said it was good to be home. I could get a cute little apartment right here in town and have it all fixed up when you get back." The words tumbled out as though she'd saved them up.

"I don't want to spend the rest of my life in Judson, Velma, you know that."

"Okay ... okay, I won't get an apartment. I'll stay with Daddy and work real hard and save money. Then when you get back we'll have enough to go to New York City. That's where you want to go, isn't it?" She paused to give an inquiring look, then plunged ahead before he could answer. "Anywhere you want is fine with me. Only let's get married now. I'll treat you real good."

Without another word, Corbin started the truck and left.

She studied his blustery profile. "Are you mad because I stopped you?"

"No, I'm not mad about that, I actually respect your decision. I'm just ... I'm weary of all this marriage talk." He let out a frustrated sigh. "I get the feeling you're trying to maneuver me into it and I don't want to get married. If it means we need to stop all this fooling around, I accept that. But, once and for all I'm not getting married, Velma, so stop nagging me about it!"

She shouldn't have gotten angry then; she nearly blew the whole thing. Corbin took her home and avoided her. She might not have seen him again at all had she not shown up at the train station for his departure the week after Thanksgiving. She kissed him on the cheek, said she was sorry, took her place beside him with an arm linked possessively through his.

He smiled down at her and rubbed her cheek with a knuckle. "Oh, that's okay. I'm sorry, too. And in case I forgot to tell you, I really appreciate the way you wrote to me. It means a lot getting letters from home."

"Then I'll keep writing." Relieved that all was not lost she moved closer, pressing a well-developed breast against the back of his arm. They stood together on the platform just like a couple while people mingled around saying good-bye. It was heaven for Velma until Daisy glided regally toward them in a red coat with a fox collar. At the sight of her Corbin shifted his weight, shifted away from Velma just the tiniest bit – imperceptible to the eye but Velma felt it.

She was awake half the night. Maybe it didn't mean a thing. Maybe his left foot got tired so he transferred his weight to the right. Or maybe it did mean something. Maybe it meant he was in love with Daisy like every other man between sixteen and sixty. But even if he were, what did it matter? Daisy was John's girl; she'd been wearing that rock of an engagement ring for nearly a year.

Well, one thing was certain: the last two years had been a failure for Velma. This business of protecting her virtue (already somewhat soiled) had been a plain and simple failure, putting her no closer now to her goal than she was back then. She wondered about all the recently-married women. Had they withheld their favors to the end? Truthfully, who would know? Maybe even John and Daisy were doing it. Maybe she and Corbin were the only couple in town who hadn't. She might be married by now if she'd pleased him, the poor frustrated guy.

She decided to proceed with her plan. It was this town he wanted to escape from, this place that bothered him, not her. Until the war was over she'd work hard and save her paychecks as seed money for their fresh start in New York. There wasn't much to buy these days anyway. And she wouldn't just write letters; she'd visit. And during that visit she'd give him what he wanted, and things would be different from then on.

TWELVE

On one hand it had been a lucky break to be furloughed over Thanksgiving, but it meant being stuck at Fort Jackson for the Christmas of 1943. Cards and packages arrived from home as the holiday approached. It was especially tough on the guys who rarely got mail, each tending to loiter in the shadows at Mail Call to step forward if he heard his name or steal away unnoticed if he didn't.

The men leaned on each other more now, Corbin noticed, as a sort of surrogate family during this first Christmas away from home. Surrogate names, too, played a big part. Even Larry Donaldson had grown proud of his "Dumbo" label. Pfc Vinnie Cartuzzo seemed especially gifted at labeling guys, usually with something that involved one's heritage. It might have been unintentional, but Cartuzzo had a knack for binding men together just by slinging harmless insults everyone else then picked up on. To be the brunt of Cartuzzo's ribbing had become a symbol of belonging and marked a man for life. Neither Corbin nor John had been graced yet with a Cartuzzo insult, evidently still paying for the acting-corporal armbands they'd worn in the beginning. Corbin pretended not to care.

Pappy Dutton suggested the wire corporals take over KP for the battery's Christmas dinner. It would give a break, he said, to those who got stuck with it every day. And if men still resented those who'd skipped out on the grunt work all this time, it might smooth things over to work Kitchen Police on the biggest day. Especially since Christmas was on a Saturday and those with families within a hundred miles might be dreaming of a weekend pass.

Pappy seemed to know his way around the mess kitchen. He made fast friends with the battery's mess sergeant to avoid tromping on any toes, and he signed up the volunteer crew for *all* the KP duty, from food prep to clean up, so everyone else could be off.

The cooks and bakers cut few corners for Christmas dinner that year. The menu started with oyster stew, continued with turkey and ham and every side dish the average GI craved, and ended with mincemeat pie, fruit cake and ice cream. With so many different foods available, the men filed through multiple times so as not to overload their partitioned metal trays.

After standing in a chow line three times a day for the past nine months, it was eye-opening for Corbin and John to observe one from the other side, and it must have been fun for the rest of the men to be served by mess attendants with two chevrons on their sleeves. Some were finicky about where food was placed on the tray. "Put the turkey and dressing here," one soldier pointed, utensils held precariously in the crook of a little finger. "Whatever you do, don't put gravy on the cranberry sauce," another said, his tray held solidly between both hands. A few attempted to control the food placement without a word just by rotating the tray and gesturing with it. Others didn't seem to care at all where the food landed.

The sun had gone by the time the last large pot was scrubbed and stored, last table wiped and section of floor mopped in the mess hall. Corbin felt lonely for home most of the day so it had been just as well to stay busy. When he dragged a garbage barrel full of turkey carcasses out the kitchen door, a light snow was falling.

"Hey Spuds," a familiar voice called from the dark.

Corbin peered at the shapes of two GIs.

"I'm talking to you, O'Connell."

He picked up on the voice then; it was Cartuzzo.

"You must love spuds ... being Irish, I mean."

"Yeah, Cartuzzo, I love spuds."

"Thought so. That's why there weren't any lumps in the mashed potatoes. See I told you," Cartuzzo said, nudging a private named Dorkman. "And being Irish you must be a Catholic, right?"

"Yeah, I'm Catholic. I'm guessing you're one too."

"Hey, I'm Italian," Cartuzzo said, raising both hands, "of course I'm Catholic. So's Dork here."

"We have that in common, then."

"Hell, we're practically brothers. Like I said, you guys mashed up the potatoes real good."

"And the gravy was good, too. No lumps there either," Dorkman said.

John pushed the last garbage barrel out the door and dragged it to the corner of the building where trash detail would pick it up in the morning. "Hey Ottinger," Cartuzzo said, "You guys did real good today."

"Thanks, glad you enjoyed it."

"Ottinger ... what kind of name is that? Jewish?"

"No, it's German, actually, German Catholic."

"German?" Cartuzzo shrieked. "What do ya think of that, Dorko? Ottinger's a damn Kraut!"

"Yes, but I'm fifth-generation American so don't hold it against me."

"I heard your family's loaded. Is that true?"

John just shrugged and smiled.

"Ottinger's a gatsby, he's a gatsby boy! Well, Spuds and Gatsby, you did real good today," Cartuzzo said as he and Dorkman melted into the shadows. "Hey Spuds, one more thing. Somebody said all Irishmen are boozers and barroom brawlers. Is that true?"

"Hell, no. I haven't fallen off a barstool yet. But just hearing that makes me want to get drunk and punch somebody in the face."

This struck Cartuzzo and Dorkman as hilarious. They roared with laughter clinging to each other for support. Their laughing went on for what seemed a long time, fading rather than ending as the pair got further away in the dark.

Spuds and Gatsby, Corbin smiled to himself. Well, at least now they were in. Being accepted was a nice Christmas gift, and he'd certainly grown enough potatoes to earn the name.

The 106th left South Carolina after the new year and convoyed three days to Tennessee for field maneuvers with the Second Army. Though calendars said January, the sun radiated warmth more like springtime in the long thin state.

While the infantry and the field artillery advanced across rivers, seized bridges, broke through lines, encircled and captured a mock enemy, the wire crews ran miles of field wire in the mud. Corbin asked Pappy if he felt misplaced in communications since running wire seemed like such a waste of sharpshooter talent. But the man just said, "They'll figure it out eventually I guess, and if they don't ... I'm not going to miss the front lines."

After ten long months, Corbin felt as far from combat readiness as if he'd stayed on the farm, and though he celebrated his freedom from home, it was the Army calling all the shots. He found himself booted into communications training at Fort Sill, Oklahoma whether he wanted to or not, in a classroom to learn Morse code.

According to the staff sergeant instructor, the code for "V" had become the sound for Victory, not only to the Allies but to those waiting to be freed. And on that day of victory, he predicted, people everywhere would bang out the dot-dot-dot-dash, not just through the expected means of telegraph and radio, but by gun blast, light flashes, smoke signals – any method available.

The ease in which the class of twenty-five memorized the dot-dash combinations for each letter, and interpreted code sent at six words-per-minute, deceived them into thinking the whole thing would be a breeze. But the instructor declared it impossible to hear the actual dots and dashes sent at faster speeds, so they should not even try. "Treat Morse as a form of music if you want to succeed," he warned. Corbin smiled at this, having already noticed the "V" sounded just like the first four notes of Beethoven's Fifth Symphony.

Six hours a day they listened, attempting to decipher a faster and faster stream until their minds were mush and each felt like bawling. Some dropped out. Corbin might have been one had he not related the whole thing to music – listening from a distance to pick up the rhythm like a Gene Krupa drum solo.

The division had moved to Indiana's Camp Atterbury when Corbin caught up with them in late spring, 1944. The war news sounded brighter by then. In the Pacific the Allies were making a costly but steady island-to-island hop toward Japan. And in Europe they were advancing toward Rome and relentlessly bombing Germany day and night. For the first time in two years people dared to imagine a victory in Europe, yet everyone knew they must shake Hitler loose from the occupied continent before they could march on Berlin.

While the 106th settled in Indiana, other divisions were gathering all over England. Airmen, ground troops and paratroops lived in tents and practiced maneuvers while officers wearing fancy insignia made plans. Immense quantities of airplanes and landing craft, a replacement rail network, prefabricated harbors, cigarettes, toothbrushes, maps by the millions, pints of blood plasma by the tens of thousands rolled in like a tidal wave from the United States – all in preparation for the sweeping invasion that would begin with an arduous crossing of the English Channel.

Big changes were in the works for the 106th but not the kind anybody wanted. Even while the division had its collective foot on the gangplank, it was robbed of half its strength – soldiers unceremoniously snatched away and transferred overseas as replacements. New men were brought in to fill the vacancies but most were rejects or just plain green. So the division reverted to training instead of shipping out. Somebody else got Corbin's wire crew and beloved truck when he was promoted to staff sergeant and assigned as Message Center Chief. But promotion or not, he wanted out. He wanted it enough to stand in front of the company commander and beg to be transferred overseas.

"It's too late, we can't spare you," the captain said. "They've already taken too much of the cream."

"What were they thinking, Captain, pulling us apart like that?"

The mild-mannered officer frowned at the tone but decided to let it go. He'd grown to like the twenty-year-old standing in front of him. "The Army knows what it's doing," was all he said.

"I'm not so sure about that," Corbin went on. "Look at Dutton ... best shot in the division and they've got him stuck in a communications."

He was pushing it, judging from the captain's narrowed eyes. "You're out of line, O'Connell. I suggest you stop talking and get out of here."

But a few days later Pappy was transferred to an infantry unit in a shift of personnel.

～～～

June, 1944

The invasion of Europe was a secret everybody knew. Even the enemy expected it – they just didn't know where or when. As the build-up of men and materiel continued in England, the home front held its breath for invasion news. Gil, when he could get away, spent afternoons at Western Union with Ezra. Nights, he spent on the living room sofa hugging his Philco radio, as much a permanent fixture in the house as Opal's cast-iron skillet.

Finally, before daybreak on June 6, news of the invasion of France filled the airwaves. While America slept, Allied troops by the hundreds of thousands had stormed the beaches and dropped from the sky. Victory was not yet certain but at least the boys were now in France. In a letter to Corbin, Opal described the mood at home as a mixture of jubilation and fear. She was just thankful, she said, that his division had not left the States.

Leave it to mothers to be grateful about sons sitting out a war. Corbin envied the ones over there, seeing only the glory without much thought for the ocean of anguish riding in on telegrams, or what it would mean for his mother to live in constant fear. Well, she could relax for now. The only enemy to fight in Indiana were the flies, and it was riskier to drive the tractor on a hilly field at home than to encode and decode messages there.

The Message Center had become a twenty-four-hour operation, Corbin taking the day shift and his likeable owl-eyed clerk, Pvt. Charles Ragsdale, the nights. They had to set up in the field sometimes with no tent, no table, no light. Just a field desk – a legless three-foot cube with one side that folded down to form a writing surface. Everybody groused about field operations except Corbin; at least in the field he could *pretend* to be in combat.

It seemed odd that the military had not seen fit to provide him a rifle. Shouldn't every war-bound soldier, regardless of position, be armed with a decent weapon? Corbin had been issued a combat knife and 45 caliber pistol, but what good would they be unless you got up close? He fiddled with somebody's M1 Garand enough to know how to load it and appreciate its marvel. A man could fire eight rounds before reloading, and even the reloading seemed almost automatic – the rifle of its own accord ejecting the empty clip. The M1 was heavy at nearly ten pounds, twice the weight of his shotgun at home. But then Corbin couldn't find a single thing the M1 had in common with a shotgun, except they were both firearms.

In late summer, sharpshooters in the 106th received the long-awaited M1C sniper rifle – basically an M1 Garand with a built-in scope. Somebody on the Division staff decided others should be familiar with the new weapon, and Corbin managed to worm his way onto HQ Battery's short list to be trained.

On the day of training, just by happenstance, Pappy Dutton showed up as instructor. He demonstrated the M1C for the group, mesmerizing them with the obvious power to annihilate that came from handing a skillful sniper such a gun. "I'm feeling a twinge of pity for the Germans," Corbin said with awe to the guy next to him. "Damned if I'd wanna fight us in this war."

When it was Corbin's turn he cracked off a casual shot and missed the entire target positioned some 400 yards distant.

Pappy was a frowning witness. "Hey ... slow down. Take more time to aim."

"Yeah, you'd think I'd know that by now. My dad must have said it a hundred times teaching me to hunt with a shotgun."

"Well, this is not a shotgun. Bad aim is magnified with this weapon, so taking your time is even more important here. Learn to use the power of the scope for heaven's sake. When we fire at somebody he'll be firing back, so we might only get one chance to kill or be killed. Now try it again ... and take your time."

Corbin took another shot.

"Okay, better."

With the next one he hit the target's center.

"Better, much better." Pappy slapped him on the back. "With a little practice you could be deadly."

On an impulse Corbin showed up at the company commander's office and asked for an M1C of his own. The captain, a flyswatter in his hand, gave him a deadpan look and said, "You can't be serious."

"But I am, sir."

"You're never happy doing what you're doing. Is that right, O'Connell?"

"It's just that ... I hunted at home a lot and I think I could be an expert shot with that gun, given a little practice."

The officer took aim at a trio of flies on a corner of his desk, delivered a blow and wiped the dead three to the floor.

"Anybody could be an expert shot with that gun. My mother-in-law could be expert, God forbid."

"Yes sir," Corbin said. He wanted to laugh out loud but offered a safer smile.

"If they were as abundant as these damned flies, you might have a chance. But as it is, most of the first issue went overseas. The few available to us were doled out with common sense, O'Connell, to infantrymen according to their riflery scores. Now get out of here before I revoke your weekend pass."

The next day, Corbin left the base with five other GIs and took the bus to Indianapolis intending to find a girl. On weekends, Atterbury men with passes overwhelmed the local town or traveled forty miles to the larger city. Corbin was looking for a simple night of fun – nothing serious, nothing permanent.

Pappy Dutton had advised against anything serious or permanent. No good ever came, he said, of soldiers cementing relationships that ought to remain temporary. He did not look fondly on nights of fun, either. "You'll be caught if you're not careful," he'd warned.

Corbin wondered about Pappy. He talked like he had gotten a girl pregnant, though he'd never mentioned a wife. Corbin promised himself no girl would ever catch him that way, thinking of Velma. He seemed to forget it was her relentless refusals that had protected him thus far.

John spent time in Indianapolis the same way he did on the base: putting coins in a jukebox to hear *Among My Souvenirs* and a string of other tunes with equally mournful lyrics. He'd become downright gloomy in recent weeks over his decision not to marry until after the war. "Do you think it was right to wait?" he'd been asking at least once a day until Corbin had tired of it.

Dumbo Donaldson was another with a fiancée at home, and together they analyzed the dangers of waiting as they fed the jukebox and each other's doubts. John now questioned whether it *had* been his decision or whether Daisy had actually been the one to put things off. And if she had been the one, why?

Corbin left them in their gloom to escape elsewhere, relieved not to be tied down to anyone by need or duty. Watching them had dampened his plans of conquest for the moment. He was content to simply stroll through the streets of Indianapolis, free as the plump pigeons that bobbed on the sidewalk and perched atop buildings with equal ease. He sat on a park bench to make a study of them. With all their freedom the birds could fly anywhere, yet they chose to be here in the city. Corbin understood. If he were a pigeon that's where he'd be.

THIRTEEN

Judson fit the image of a boomtown in early July, 1944. The war industry had attracted workers, most of them women, from all over the countryside. It was hard to find a place to live, hard to find a restaurant table to get a meal, hard to find a spot to park – even with gas rationing. The town had mushroomed enough to even impress the likes of Corbin O'Connell, if only the sidewalks weren't so devoid of under-forty males.

George Ottinger had to hire two new foremen for his burgeoning factories. The younger one, Mitch Kenny from Philadelphia, looked young enough to be drafted and certainly appeared fit for duty – handsome and healthy, able to walk a female assembly line sixteen hours out of every twenty-four. Yet he was here.

All the cars for sale in front of Ottinger Motors these days were used cars with heavy price tags. John's Desoto had cost $900 in 1941, with tax and white-wall tires. Seemed like a lot of money then, but a new car could not be had now at any price.

The O'Connell farm hadn't changed much. Even with Corbin gone, the daisies were blooming, the apples growing, the hogs reproducing, and the corn stood tall despite a recent drought.

Yet with all the vitality of production there was a pallor about Judson, born from the growing list of names in Memorial Park, and the fear of more. Most families in town had sent away a husband or son – each represented by a blue star on the front window.

Telegrams with news from D-Day changed blue stars to gold and made Ezra Knox an even more dreaded sight. It didn't help that he was tall and cadaverous. The only thing saving him from an altogether macabre likeness to Ichabod Crane was a laugh you could hear next door. Yet reasons to laugh had become scarce as silk. He sensed people watching from windows wherever he went, which made him feel a bit like a dangerous animal in a zoo. He had stopped dropping in unannounced for a visit, couldn't remember the last time somebody invited him to Sunday dinner. The poor man even tried to dress more cheerfully to help dispel the gloom. But there was no getting around it; they would dread the very sight of him, no matter what, until the end of the war.

Then, in an old trunk in the attic, Ezra found a dusty black fedora that once belonged to his father. He gave it a good brush and decided to wear it to deliver the next sad telegram, and the one after that. It didn't take long for the town to catch on: Ezra in a black hat meant trouble, while Ezra in a tan hat or a blue hat or no hat meant a harmless telegram or simple walk down the street. The distinction saved him. He found he could endure being treated like a leper for the dark trips if treated like a friend for the rest.

People learned to interpret another of Ezra's signs: walking meant going no more than three blocks; bicycling meant further but within the town limits; driving meant somewhere beyond.

His comings and goings soon became a point of daily discussion at the Star Diner. About midday on a recent Thursday when he passed on the street, a woman near the window said, "There he goes," without a mention of his name.

Everybody stopped eating. "Black hat?" somebody asked.

"Afraid so."

No black hat and the rest wouldn't have mattered, but in this case the diner went on alert. "East or west?"

"West."

"Walking?"

"Yep."

"Turning the corner or going straight?"

"Looks like he's ... going straight."

"Could be one of the Patterson boys, then."

"Could be."

Velma observed these dramas pretending a concern she didn't feel. Her only true emotion about the war was annoyance. Anything worth having was either scarce, or on the ration list, or both. Searching out necessities like bobby pins and stockings, which she'd formerly taken for granted, had become a second job. It was all in the timing as everybody knew – to hear of a shipment and get there before it was gone. A particular problem working at the diner since she couldn't just leave on a whim. Especially now, with every restaurant in town busy day and night.

Bobby pins weren't rationed but they had become scarce because of the metal shortage. Women searched for strays in old purses and coat pockets. And in the same way people had scrounged for coins during the Depression, they were using flashlights and magnets to rescue bobby pins from behind dressers and inside couches, even from dark cellars and crawl spaces under porches where they might have fallen between cracks in the floor. A challenge even existed to this kind of scavenging in a shortage of flashlight batteries.

The scarcity of nylon proved particularly annoying to Velma who had dutifully switched to nylon stockings when silk went extinct in 1941. Now the same thing had happened with nylon, the military grabbing it for parachutes after exhausting all available silk. In self-preservation, she had learned to apply leg makeup in a nice even coat and could deftly draw a believable seam down the back with an eyebrow pencil.

Velma thought about Corbin every day and faithfully wrote as promised, yet for the second time in her life she surrendered to another guy. There were so many to choose from at USO dances, men who watched with longing and vied for her attention. That heady feeling of being desired – there was nothing else like it in this world. She'd put on the brakes with a whole line of them first, so she deserved some credit, but then she met *the one* at the armory in June and had to sneak in the house late at night. No plausible excuse, except that he was handsome and a delightful kisser, and it just felt good to let it happen instead of posting the usual barriers. Besides, she didn't really care what *he* thought of her.

The surprise came when he begged her to marry him. Now, *that* was fun. So much for men wanting virgin brides. He'd even gotten down on a knee and seemed heartbroken when she refused, which only served to strengthen Velma's belief that she'd been handling Corbin all wrong.

There was a girl in town who'd recently rushed to the altar after getting pregnant by a young GI. Velma heard tongues wag at the diner because she was showing already and trying to hide it. It was almost as bad as it had been with Francine Pine who'd been "easy" in high school and the gossips' favorite target. Going to school with Francine had been fortuitous for Velma, else the favored-target status might have fallen to her. Nobody said much about Francine anymore though – not since she sank below the range of judgment by offering her services for money.

Velma pitied the pregnant bride in a way. On the other hand, maybe she got what she hoped for; at least she was married now. Velma had so-far escaped getting pregnant. If it ever *did* happen she wanted it to be with Corbin. She had not seen him in a long eight months (another irksome drawback to the war), but she planned a trip to visit him in a week, determined now to give him what he wanted.

FOURTEEN

I n August 1944, Paris was added to the chunks of Mother Earth the Allies won back from Hitler. GIs by the thousands swept into the city and paraded through the streets, hugged and kissed and handed gifts by grateful Parisians who were overjoyed to see the giant Swastikas torn from their buildings after four long years.

People were saying the war was almost over as Hitler's armies retreated to Germany at last. The optimism carried some weight this time, originating at the top when General Eisenhower, Supreme Commander, allegedly made a bet with Britain's General Montgomery that the war in Europe would end by Christmas.

At the PX, Corbin found Pappy buying socks and a pair of gloves without a trigger finger. "Neat little invention," Pappy said, trying on a glove for fit. "Have you gotten yourself any extra socks yet?"

"No."

"Well, you should. If we go to Europe it'll be cold and you'll want to double up. You can even wear socks on your hands instead of gloves. Can't fire a rifle as easily, though." Pappy wiggled his free index finger.

"Since I don't have a rifle, that's no concern for me," Corbin grumbled. "If the war's nearly over in Europe, do you think they'll still send us over there?"

"Maybe not, they'll just ship us to the Pacific instead. Still plenty of fighting in that war and you'll need extra socks to keep your feet dry. I hear it rains all the time in that part of the world. Frostbite and trench foot, a soldier's two worst enemies."

"I thought dehydration was a soldier's worst enemy."

"We'll have a lot of enemies besides the ones shooting at us."

"Shooting at you, you mean. The way I see it, nobody will be shooting at me."

"That sounds like a complaint. I don't know anybody as eager to get shot at as you."

"No, I just think when we go out to fight, we *all* need to fight so we can really outnumber the bastards."

"Not everybody can be freed up to fight. We need support people.

"Yeah, but we got too many support people."

"Don't you want to make it back safe and sound for that girlfriend of yours?"

"Girlfriend?"

"The one that's visiting from home."

"She's not my girlfriend. She's just ...." Corbin's voice trailed off.

"You don't love her, then? If you don't mind my asking."

"No."

"She's the fun type?"

"If you mean ... have we screwed around, the answer's no."

"Good, you ought to keep it that way ... unless you want to get married."

"Can't think of anything worse."

"Then be careful, is all I can say. If you decide to screw around, don't forget it only takes once. You could be caught like a rabbit in a snare.

"Why do I get the feeling that you speak from experience?"

"Because I do."

"You got a girl pregnant?"

"Afraid so.

"But you're not married."

"Not anymore. She got pregnant, we got married, she had the baby. Then about a year later, right before my stint was up, she asked for a divorce."

"What?" Corbin gaped at him.

"Yep, just as I started to like the idea of being a husband and father. Then she went and married one of her old boy-friends. Turns out the kid wasn't even mine, it was his."

"What?"

"Yep, she'd gotten herself in a mess with the other guy and came looking for me in a panic. I should have known something was up. She practically threw herself at me one night after refusing for months to go beyond first base. After the kid was born they patched things up, so she wanted to be with him. Can't blame her for that, I guess."

"What did you do? I mean ... you must have been really pissed."

"Sure I was."

"But weren't you relieved, too? I would've been relieved more than anything."

"Yeah, later on, but not then. I felt like her puppet. 'I'm pregnant, we have to get married, you have to be a father, I want a divorce, the kid isn't yours.' That was the worst part ... her calling all the shots. Know what I mean?"

"Hell yes, I know exactly what you mean."

On the bus to Indianapolis Corbin decided to surprise Velma with an expensive dinner. He'd never done that before. And he'd surprise her as well by not laying a hand on her, another thing he hadn't done before.

Velma came in on the train and met him in the center of the city with suitcase in hand and a surprise of her own: rather than stay with her aunt in Greenwood she had reserved a hotel room right down the street, and could they go there first so she could check in?

He waited in the lobby like a gentleman while she went to her room alone like a lady, which set the tone for the entire afternoon. Holding hands, they strolled through the streets, studied the architecture of buildings, peered into the sun at the Obelisk. Corbin shared what he knew of the city's history and Velma listened in rapt attention, enraptured or not.

Men in uniform were thicker than the pigeons on the square, thick enough for Velma to question who was fighting the enemy overseas. "There are twelve thousand men in the 106th," Corbin said, "and half are probably here." It appeared to be true; many wore the division's Golden Lion insignia – a lion's face on a round blue background. A few gave Velma the once-over from a distance, yet she seemed wholly content with the Golden Lion at her side.

Dinner went beyond expectations. Each gazed across their candlelit corner table marveling how much the other had improved. On the romance scale the whole thing measured pretty high. Velma did not say a single word about marriage. Corbin sweetly held her hand after the meal. Had she not slipped off a shoe to run a bare foot up his leg, had she not sent amorous signals with her eyes, he would have stuck to his earlier plan not to touch her. As it was though, he paid the bill and they left the restaurant rather abruptly, the hotel room the unspoken mutual goal. His thoughts were such a tangle – hoping she'd finally give in, determined to play it safe, relying completely on the safety of her refusal.

They left a trail of discarded clothing from the hotel room door to the bed. As they fell half-naked across the quilt, Corbin shoved her suitcase to the floor wondering when she was going to stop him.

She covered his face with little kisses and whispered, "I want ... to show you ... how happy ... we ... can be."

A tiny alarm went off in his head. He hesitated a moment but that was all, swept away as he was with a tide of desire strong enough to trounce caution. Not wanting to hurt her, he tried to be gentle – it being her first time and all. He'd often pondered what it would be like with a virgin. The only other girl he'd had sex with was Francine Pine and every guy in Judson had done it with her. Now that he had, well ... it wasn't that much different, but it was nice, very nice.

Afterward he held her close, moved by tender feelings that she had chosen him to be the first. Even knowing his hard line against marriage, she had come all this distance and given herself freely without the slightest nag. He found himself developing a soft spot for this sweet and loving Velma.

But the nagging came at breakfast with the eggs. It began with a question. "When's your next furlough?" she asked. "Seems like you should be due for another one soon."

Corbin answered naively as he buttered a piece of toast. "If we get one it'll have to be soon. We'll be shipping out before long."

"Shipping out? Gee, I was hoping you wouldn't have to go at all. The war's almost over isn't it?"

"Maybe in Europe, but not in the Pacific."

"Let's get married then Corbin, during that furlough. We could have the wedding right in Judson ..." Velma saw quick anger surface on his face. "Or ... or we could just elope," she rushed on. "That would be romantic, wouldn't it? Or I could come back here. We could get married right here in Indianapolis and have the whole furlough for a honeymoon."

"Please, Velma," He set his toast down and held up a hand. "We've had such a nice time, please don't spoil it."

"Spoil it? What do you mean, spoil it? I'm not trying to spoil anything. I'm trying to make it go on."

And so it went on. The nagging continued in her letters, which took all the fun out of Mail Call. Velma seemed to think she had a greater claim on him now. He'd liked her a lot better as a tease.

The 106th underwent intense accelerated training to prepare for deployment overseas. Manpower and equipment were rounded out, procedures reviewed and tightened. The Message Center got a 2½ ton truck like Corbin's first one, minus the wire drum. This truck was canvas-backed, to haul the Message Center and HQ Command Post tents and equipment. Nobody knew for sure where they were going or when, but everyone knew it would be soon. Men were taking bets on which ocean they'd cross. Few expected to go west.

By the time word came in September of a furlough, Corbin had reached his limit with Velma. To subject himself to more by going home seemed masochistic and incendiary. On a whim he took a train to New York City and sent John to Judson without him.

Corbin had never been to New York City, not even with the Ottingers. As the train sped east he found it hard to sit still. Out the window, mountains veneered in evergreens gave way to orchards and fields. To his trained eye the apples looked ready to pick, the field corn dry enough to store. But it was somebody else's job to bring those crops in, and he was on his way to the city of his dreams. The only sad thought was of his mother – how she expected him home and he ought to be the one to tell her. His ears perked up at a sailor across the aisle describing a telephone center in the city, exclusively for servicemen. "It's right on Times Square, you can't miss it," the guy said.

Corbin's first glimpse of Grand Central Station was something to remember. He gazed up and around in the nation's largest terminal, gawking like a small-town tourist at the grandeur and immensity. On the street he got his first, long-anticipated look at the nation's largest city. Everywhere, buildings towered into the blue. He'd never seen skyscrapers before. Their height seemed exaggerated, almost cartoon-like as they soared into the late-afternoon sky until their tops nearly touched, narrowing the wide street he stood on. He planted himself there to take it all in, an obstruction to those who'd already seen it.

The GI Phone Center seemed like chaos to Corbin at first but he soon saw the underlying order of the dozen or so operators, all of them women. He registered his call to Judson with a red-haired beauty, paid his money and waited for his name to be called. He counted a row of twenty-two telephone booths, uniforms entering and exiting from each every few minutes. A wall of glass looked out on a pulsating Broadway. Vehicles swarmed in both directions despite the gas rationing. The sun had set but the window blazed with headlights and blinking neon, and the Rialto Theatre's marquee across the street.

He joked with men from every service branch and rank – some going, some coming, some injured. Most were happy, if only about their phone calls home. A chain-smoking marine reported missing-in-action could scarcely contain his joy waiting to tell his wife he was not only alive but back on U.S. soil. A young sailor with disfiguring scars stayed in the shadows and wavered when they called him, dreading the moment he'd have to tell his mom. Corbin waited an hour to hear his name and decided in the interval not to tell his mother the real reason for not coming home. He just let her think he was lured to the city, a conclusion she naturally jumped to listening to his excited voice describe the view out the picture window.

John had dreamt for weeks of a happy homecoming but the whole thing turned sour when he met Mitch Kenny. What an unpleasant, unexpected jolt. The factory foreman showed up for dinner the very night John arrived, by invitation no less, sweeping into the house with flowers and a hard-to-find bottle of Brandy. He offered John a firm hand to shake as if he were the heir apparent – not a hint of awe or intimidation about meeting the boss's son. John disliked him immediately.

The man was brazen with Daisy the whole evening, openly flirtatious at the table despite the fact that John sat right there. And saying goodnight, Kenny kissed her hand and held it too long, oozing charm. John complained to his father later. "I don't like him, Dad. I found him bold and pushy, entirely too sure of himself."

"Mitch *is* bold and pushy. That's why we need him."

"But he was persistently flirty with Daisy tonight. Didn't you notice?"

"Mitch is persistent about everything, which makes him an asset. He fits right into our plans for expansion ... I'm hoping the two of you can work together after the war. Don't worry about Daisy, she can take care of herself. And Mitch knows his place."

A shocking response! Just where *was* Mitch Kenny's place? What must the guy be like when John wasn't around if he acted that way in front of him? Thank goodness his mother was her same devoted self, planning the dinner menu around his favorite foods, caressing his face at every chance. And Anna, too, his eleven-year-old sister, who spent the evening in her usual way as she leaned against him or clung to Daisy, clearly idolizing her brother and her future sister-in-law.

John had been eager to sleep in his own bed that night, then ruined it by worrying about the foreman. How could anyone trust a man with two first names who sported a clipped black mustache like Clark Gable? There was also Daisy to consider. John had sensed a change in her, sensed it as early as the train station. Nothing he could really point to, but something had happened to drain all her sparkle. And when he drove her home later in the evening her goodnight kiss seemed limp. Just thinking about all of it made John's palms sweaty but he had to face facts: the possibility existed that Mitch Kenny had turned Daisy's head.

When Velma heard about Corbin she lost her composure. The worst part was, there was nothing to be done. She couldn't very well go traipsing to New York City to hunt him down, but, oh ... she needed so much to lash out. She'd spent her entire savings on that trip to Indiana, what with the train fare and hotel room and that negligee she'd bought for ten dollars and never put on. With the devotion of a wife she had endeavored to satisfy his every wish, carnal and otherwise. She'd given him her best and it still wasn't good enough. What did the guy want?

She finally shook off enough of her flabbergastation to get through a double shift at the diner. It didn't help that her impending period was making itself felt. She snapped at customers and mixed up orders, all the while thinking, *it would serve him right if I were pregnant; he deserves to get a jolt like that.*

At home that night when her period started, she was crampy and irrationally tearful about it. All of a sudden an out-of-wedlock pregnancy and forced marriage didn't seem that bad. In frustration and wishing it were true, she wrote Corbin a letter saying she was pregnant, then crumpled it up and tossed it in the trash. An hour later she retrieved it, smoothed it out and hid it in a drawer.

The letter beckoned for weeks until she sent it. No harm would really be done, she told herself, as long as she followed it up with another declaring a false alarm. How would he react to the first letter? Would he call her on the telephone and promise to make everything right? Or send a cable? She'd tell him the truth, of course, no doubt about that. The only real question was how long to make him squirm.

Corbin got a bed at the YMCA for three dollars a day. New York City was still in the grips of summer in September, with no escape from the heat or crowds. Once or twice he even found himself longing for a few minutes in the dairy. It wasn't so bad at night and he soon settled in with the rhythm of the natives – in bed at three in the morning and out long after the sun came up when barracks-style clatter made it impossible to sleep.

The magic of 52nd Street beckoned after dark. The greatest live jazz on earth was commonplace there, some of it conceived on the spot, flowing out of one club after another late into the night. Corbin loved every minute of it. His one regret was not seeing the family when he had the chance, since another might not come again until after the war.

When he returned to Camp Atterbury most of the flies had gone. The ones that remained were large and lazy, easy to swat. The heat and humidity had eased, replaced by raw anticipation that seemed electrically charged. A quiet undercurrent for the most part, surfacing in occasional bursts of quick anger from men advised to sign their Army-provided life insurance policies while waiting for departure news. Some even wrote up wills and mailed them home.

In early October word finally came down to "pack your gear, we're moving out in two days." Corbin went to the PX and bought three extra pairs of wool socks and a GI wristwatch. The men had an emotional Mail Call that night, each silently fearing what he received might be the last he'd ever get from home. Corbin opened a lumpy envelope from his mother containing his rosary wrapped in a note. No doubt she'd found it where he'd left it, coiled in a little pile in a top dresser drawer. The note simply said, "Thought you might need this." He'd never had more than an obligatory relationship with his rosary, yet he clutched it in his fist and took a sharp involuntary breath. Others had come away with their rosaries – John for one, Vinnie Cartuzzo for another. Numerous times in the barracks at night, Corbin had watched the seemingly irreverent Vinnie caress his rosary while mumbling familiar words. He glanced across now at Vinnie sprawled on his bunk reading something on pink paper with the shine of tears in his eyes.

Dumbo Donaldson opened and read a short note, then thrust it at John and left the barracks. John set aside a letter from Daisy to read Donaldson's – a terse confession from his fiancée that she'd fallen for another guy.

Corbin thought it was ill-timed and mean. In his opinion the woman should have kept it to herself and lived with the guilt of deceit. The whole thing served to further solidify his *no strings* philosophy. He tended to be smug about his own free situation, perhaps because it eased the pain of not having the girl he loved. And it seemed fate was going to permit that smugness a few more weeks: though Velma had already mailed the *I'm pregnant* letter, Corbin would travel across an ocean before it caught up with him.

FIFTEEN

Without fanfare, the 106th boarded troop trains on a sunny day the second week of October. Though they still hadn't been told where they were going, the position of the sun said they were headed for the eastern seaboard. So it was Europe. As the train carrying HQ Battery snaked its way across Pennsylvania it passed the same orchards and fields Corbin had seen a month before. Donaldson sulked in his seat and stared out the window, inconsolable, certain his decision not to marry had been a mistake. He seemed to have deflated overnight, like a balloon with a pinhole leak.

Vinnie Cartuzzo offered a well-meaning, "Don't take it so hard, Dumbo. Hell, she ain't worth it, doing what she did." He slapped Donaldson on the arm. "You're free as a bird now, like me and Spuds here. We've got the right idea ... shipping out free as birds."

John tried to be a source of consolation but was the last person who could have succeeded. He'd reacted to Donaldson's letter with quiet alarm fearing the same might happen to him. "I just don't know if waiting to marry was the right decision," he said. "It's one thing to be here in the states, but – "

"If Pappy was here, he'd say it was right," Vinnie said.

"But what if she finds somebody else while I'm gone?"

"You're just worried now because you're going overseas."

"It isn't just that," Corbin said. "Ever since he got back he's been worrying about that new foreman his father hired."

"Afraid she'll jilt you for him?" Vinnie asked. "She ain't gonna do that ... not if she's worth marrying."

"Well, my girl is certainly worth marrying ... that's the problem. Tell him, Corbin."

"John, you need to stop this. She wouldn't jilt you for somebody else, you should know that by now." *I certainly know it well enough.*

They slept sitting up on the train and arrived at Camp Miles Standish near Boston the next day, happy to stretch out on bunks that night in barracks just like the ones at Atterbury. Plenty of difference otherwise, though. They were all confined to the base, and censorship of mail began there. Though everyone felt sure they were headed for Europe, they couldn't tell the folks at home. Once they went into battle the entire country would hear about it on national radio, but for now the division's whereabouts had to be veiled in secrecy.

A few had worked out ahead of time some clever little clue of their direction. Corbin was to mention apples in a letter if headed across the Atlantic, or peaches if the Pacific, to help Jimmy track the 106th on a map of the world he'd mounted on his bedroom wall. So at the end of a letter to his mother he wrote, "To Jimmy: Hello little brother, sorry I'm not there to help pick the apples."

The division left Camp Miles Standish in three groups at three different times to cross the Atlantic on three ships: the Queen Elizabeth, Aquitania, and Wakefield – former luxury liners retrofitted into troop ships. On November 10,

HQ Battery (among the last to leave) climbed on a train in a downpour and then stood in line at the Port of Boston in a cold drizzle to board the USS Wakefield, each man with a heavy duffle bag either flung over a shoulder or shoved inch by inch up the gangplank with a booted foot.

Inside the hull of what was once the SS Manhattan, all the luxurious suites, fixtures and furnishings of a cruise liner had vanished. For the six-day voyage, home was to be one of several open caverns jammed with rows of steel bunks stacked in five-high tiers.

When the Wakefield left port it headed straight into a North Atlantic storm. The ship rolled, pitched and yawed for hours on battering waves, vibrating violently as the stern lifted out of the angry ocean until it fell back again. Walls of gray water crashed over the bow onto the low-lying foredeck – a foredeck that ran a good fifty feet above the water line in quieter conditions. The first night was not pleasant; nearly everyone got sick. Some in their misery viewed this harsh beginning as an ill omen of what lay ahead. Corbin decided it might actually be better to eat, but the chow line extended half the length of the ship and took two hours to reach. When he arrived there he had to grip the sloshing mess kit and cup in his hands to keep them from sliding away. He managed to consume a little of what he'd waited so long to get, though most of it sloshed out with the lurch of the ship.

The sun came up the following morning on a calmer sea. To escape the smell of stale tobacco and seasickness, anyone steady enough to walk made his way up on deck. Schools of porpoise cavorting alongside raised spirits, and men began to move their watches up an hour a day toward Europe time.

It was pleasant on deck, and therapeutic. Especially at night, Corbin discovered. Suspended in a world with no horizon where the black ocean blended with a sky full of stars, he felt free, almost weightless, as though he could soar off the deck, away from the inky ocean into the inky sky. He feared the future. Everybody did. Yet his fear at least was tempered by zeal for the new. It was all a big adventure to him, this traversing of the Atlantic Ocean on a cruise ship to another part of the world. Such a thing would never have happened without this war that was nearly won. After the war he could plan and build his future – a future all his own. Until then he had only to help finish the job and get through it alive. It seemed so clear and simple in the dark as he leaned on the rail listening to the waves break below. Such clarity tended to be short-lived, often fading the moment he left the deck, but he was able to carry away the core of it: the war's nearly over so just finish the job and get through it alive.

This view of imminent victory continued to be shared by those at the top. The Allies had failed in their September push to break into Germany through Holland so all bets were off for peace by Christmas, but they knew it was no more than a matter of time. Hitler's war machine was close to ruins – armies devastated, materiel destroyed. And whatever remained was stretched to the breaking point between the Soviets in the east, America and Britain in the west. How could he amass the power to launch another offensive? Even Hitler couldn't grow more armies overnight and he had run out of resources to produce more war materiel.

Or so they thought. While the Golden Lions crossed the Atlantic, Hitler was doing just that. From the weakest of Germany – children, grandfathers, convicts – he was building the Volksgrenadier (the "people's infantry"), which he would then combine with the strongest of Germany – the Waffen SS, his carefully-selected heavily-armed units of the SS. And somehow he *was* producing more war materiel, cranking out tanks, artillery and ammunition in underground factories that evaded detection from the air.

<center>~~~</center>

Mid-November, 1944
Europe

The Wakefield sighted land through the mist on November 17. Every off-duty soldier aboard came up on deck to watch a British destroyer escort the troop ship into Saint George's Channel where she was to drop anchor for the night. As the day faded they saw their first real evidence of war in the anti-aircraft batteries mounted everywhere, the obvious destruction by the German Luftwaffe to England's shoreline and the city of Liverpool. The entire area, under blackout restrictions, fell silent and motionless as the sun went down on the Channel's opposite shore.

The next morning the ship docked at Liverpool. A cheery brass band played the *Star-Spangled Banner* to welcome the long line of men waiting to disembark. "This is nice but why are they playing for us?" Corbin wondered aloud. "We haven't done anything."

"Playing for what they think we're going to do, I guess," John said.

They journeyed by train to the midlands of England and moved into the quaint stone buildings of a British military installation. In a matter of hours Corbin and Charlie Ragsdale had the Message Center set up and operational in one of them, not far from the HQ Battery Command Post. It was to be a twenty-four-hour operation here as in the states – Corbin taking the days and Ragsdale the nights.

England in November was about the same temperature-wise as home, but the cold seemed damper, more penetrating. And it was chilly in those old stone buildings, chillier at times than outside. Other than that they were comfortable and, for the moment, safe. Corbin traveled a good bit the first few days between the Message Center and HQ, imagining what it might be like to duck bombardments in field tents near the front.

They obtained evening passes for walks to the nearest town. There were places to eat and drink but the food was sparse, the beer warm and bitter. The civilians, though, were a picture of friendliness – curious children, perky women, merchants lending a patient hand with British currency despite the constant flow of troops day and night.

The Army chow was good; the GIs even had a fine turkey dinner on Thanksgiving. Some didn't feel right about eating so grandly while others in combat zones had to live on C rations. Then word got out that Eisenhower had ordered every soldier in the European Theatre of Operations to get a turkey dinner, no matter where he was.

Armed Forces Radio broadcast music at night. Though they'd been in England only two short weeks, the sounds of Bing Crosby and Glen Miller, taken for granted at home, already meant more to them here. And with the holidays only a month away, *White Christmas* was bringing tears to tough and hardy eyes.

Corbin had picked up a cold the day before Thanksgiving, still nursing it the day after. He managed to spend a quiet morning slumped in a desk chair, topcoat over his uniform, wool helmet liner pulled low on his head. The entire day was blessedly uneventful for the most part, until late afternoon when an unfamiliar officer entered the Message Center from a rainstorm. Corbin jumped to attention and saluted.

The ruddy-faced man gestured sharply in return. "I am Major Stewart Shiller." His clipped accent sounded like New England. "I'm expecting a critical dispatch from SHAEF G4. It should have come by now."

"We have received nothing for you yet, Major."

"Are you sure?" The officer's eyes traveled the surface of the desk.

"Yes," Corbin said, fighting to hold back a sneeze.

"The dispatch must be delivered to me the moment it arrives."

"Of course, sir. Delivered where?"

"To my quarters."

"And where are your quarters, sir?"

"This is a communications center, is it not?"

Corbin lost the battle and sneezed into a handkerchief. "Yes, sir."

"And you are in charge of it?"

Another sneeze. "Yes, sir."

"Then you ought to know. And one other thing ... you are wearing a helmet liner without a helmet. It looks ridiculous. You need to either remove the liner or put on a helmet."

Corbin stood there with a blank face, still at attention, as the man turned on his heel and left.

Charlie Ragsdale came in soon after to begin his shift, dinner tray hidden under a dripping raincoat. He pulled off the raincoat and tossed it aside.

"Smells pretty good, Rags. What is it?"

"Spaghetti. I think I actually like this routine of getting up for dinner and going to bed after breakfast."

Corbin blew his nose into his last clean handkerchief. "Who's Major Shiller?"

"Beats me. Why?"

"He came in a few minutes ago looking for a dispatch from SHAEF G4. Demanded we deliver it the minute it comes."

"What else would we do with it?"

"I asked him where to deliver it but he wouldn't say. Just chewed me out for wearing my liner without a helmet."

"Oh Jesus, one of those. Well, we can't deliver it if we don't know where he is."

"I'll run over to the Mess Hall and ask around."

"Got a raincoat?"

"Not with me."

"Take mine, it's miserable out there."

Corbin pulled Ragsdale's wet raincoat over his head, adjusted the hood snugly over the helmet liner and went out the door. In the Mess Hall he found out what he needed to know: Major Stewart Shiller from SHAEF G3, billeted in the Officer's Quarters in Building Six, third floor. He scurried back toward the Message Center in a curtain of rain, coffee cup in his right hand and a full mess tray in the other, all of it under Ragsdale's raincoat. When he passed Shiller on the sidewalk he chalked it up to bad timing and politely stepped out of the way. He raised the hidden cup in an attempted salute and offered a respectful, "Good evening, Major." There was no reply.

The rain had slacked off an hour later when Corbin left the Message Center for the night. He returned to his billet in time for Mail Call, the first since Boston. Dumbo Donaldson stayed away but had given John instructions to listen for his name in case another letter arrived – one filled with flowery remorse and a declaration that she'd changed her mind.

Corbin collected his and Ragsdale's mail and carried it all to his bunk. He stuffed Ragsdale's in the pocket of his coat and thumbed through his own. The letter from Velma was in a flat featherweight envelope, clearly just a single folded sheet rather than her usual multi-page harangue. He tore into it with mild curiosity and cool detachment. No way to know it then, but this letter was to be the last he'd ever open in such an offhand way. In fact he'd never be so coolly detached again about anything.

Dear Corbin,

I'm very, very disappointed you didn't come home during your furlough. It was really mean after the way I gave myself to you in Indianaplus. Were you avoiding me? I sure hope not since I thought I meant more to you than that. And it's going to be hard to avoid me in the future, because I think I'm pregnant. That's right, it looks like I'm pregnant.

People are saying the war is almost over and I hope there right so you can come home and we can get married. We can live here or someplace else, whatever you want. But we <u>are</u> getting married. I haven't told anybody yet but when word gets around, I won't be the only one to think we should get married. Everybody in town will be expecting you to do the right thing.

Yours truly,
Velma

It was hard to breathe at first. He escaped to a porch and inhaled large amounts of cold night air, which made his chest hurt. Though he wanted to rip the letter to shreds he found himself reading it again and again, almost involuntarily, as though he might have read it wrong. He stayed out in the cold for the longest time, nailed in place under the dim porch light.

John finally came looking for him, saw his face and the letter. "Good God, Corbin, what is it? Did somebody die?" he asked in a panic, fearing for Daisy.

Though Corbin had decided not to share the letter with anyone, he shoved it into John's hands.

"Uh-oh, I see. Gad, I'm really sorry, Corb. Is there anything I can do?"

"What could you possibly do, John?"

"I don't know ... I just hate to see you–"

"Wait, there is one thing. You can promise not to write about this to anybody at home."

"Of course I won't."

"I mean, not *anybody*." What Corbin really meant was, *don't tell Daisy*. Somehow at that moment, levelheadedness being scarce, the idea that Daisy would find out seemed the worst thing.

He went to bed and tried to sleep but, on top of everything else, his left ear hurt. He spent a portion of the tormented night wondering who Velma would tell. *She* might tell Daisy. She might tell his mother. Then his mother would have to tell his father. What would he say? And what about John's father? The thought of Pop Ott produced an audible groan. And Daisy's father – what about him? On and on he went, worrying about what people would think until he decided there wasn't a scrap of difference between himself and the women in his mother's sewing circle. There was nothing to be done anyway; the whole town would know soon enough.

He escaped into a restless sleep until an hour before dawn. By then all the petty concerns had been cast aside for the real problem: he'd be stuck in Judson forever, stuck on the farm forever, married to a woman he did not love, raising a passel of kids who'd grow up just as discontent. It was the gloomiest possible outlook, magnified by the darkness of night like the pain in his ear.

At breakfast, Corbin moved the eggs around on his plate thinking he'd rather do anything than face such a future at home. He felt like hell – his ear hurt again and he had the chills. Why now? Weren't earaches for kids? If this kept up he'd have to visit the infirmary. In the foulest of moods he trekked to the Message Center, helmet on over the wool liner. He tossed Ragsdale's letters on the desk beside an empty breakfast tray.

"Hey, terrific! Mail from home!" Ragsdale said. "Uh, what's eating you?"

Corbin waved the question away as he removed his coat and helmet.

"Would you believe the visiting Major stomped in here again last night looking for that damned dispatch from SHAEF? Caught me with my feet on the desk and gave me the business for it."

"Dispatch ever come?"

"Nope, and he acted like it was my fault. The guy's a jerk from what I hear. A spit-and-polish type ... showed up with three footlockers and his own special mattress some poor sap had to lug up to the third floor."

When Ragsdale left, Corbin took over the desk pondering what to do about the wool liner. Better judgment said to remove it, but he was feeling especially lousy just then and Velma's letter had incited rebellion. He pulled the liner down over his throbbing ear and barked to the empty room, "It's almost December and damp as hell." Why should he remove it? Only to please a pompous ass not in the chain of command? Even unannounced drop-ins from Brigadier-General McMahon, Commander of Division Artillery, caused less angst.

About mid-morning when he heard the door open, Corbin ought to have hidden under his desk. But he jumped to attention and chirped, "Good morning, Major Shiller. We still haven't received your dispatch from SHAEF ... if it's what you came for."

"It is."

"Sir, you don't need to trouble yourself. I promise you it will be delivered the moment we get it."

"I don't have such confidence ... maybe it will and maybe it won't." The major gave him an arrogant once-over. "I see you did not take my advice about your appearance."

"Sir ... it's just that I'm here by myself much of the time, it's so chilly in this building and I caught a blasted cold –"

"You are a non-commissioned officer in the United States Army. You should look the part at all times. This dispatch is an important communication from the highest levels of SHAEF G4. I will keep coming in here at regular intervals because, frankly, you have not earned my trust."

"You think because I'm wearing this cap to stay warm, I can't be trusted to do my job?" Corbin tried to steady his voice.

"A shoddy appearance reflects a shoddy operation." With overblown dignity Shiller paced in front of the desk. "I was sent here on a simple assignment to review your unit's combat readiness regarding equipment and vehicles. But this incident has raised the more basic question of your overall combat readiness."

Corbin couldn't believe what he was hearing. *This incident? Questioning our combat readiness because of my cap?* It was too rich – a rear-echelon officer who'd never be near the front, picking on a point that had nothing to do with the war.

"I am not your commanding officer," Shiller went on. "If I were, you would stand for inspection every day, required to dress in regulation uniform at all times."

"No, you're not my commanding officer … that's *one* thing to be thankful for." He shouldn't have said it, but the words had rushed out on their own.

"I do not like your attitude Sergeant," Shiller bellowed. "It's an insubordinate attitude and there is no room in the Army for insubordination. I may not be your commanding officer but … if I have my way, this will cost you your stripes!"

Corbin fell into his chair afterward, stupefied. How had he so quickly fallen foul of this man? When the dispatch from SHAEF came in an hour later, he immediately sent a runner over to Building Six with it. "If Major Shiller is not in his quarters," he said, "find him and put it in his hands." The runner returned ten minutes later and gave him a thumbs-up. Corbin hoped it would end there, but the following morning he was summoned to the company commander's office.

The captain waved him in and said, "Have a seat, O'Connell."

Corbin took a chair and sat stiffly.

"Major Shiller just filed this report charging you with insubordination." The captain scanned the official-looking document he had already read once, then looked across the desk with incredulity. "He says you passed him on the sidewalk without saluting and later spoke to him with flagrant disrespect. What the hell happened?"

Corbin explained about not saluting, explained about the cap, repeated exactly what he said and called it wrong. Not so much to defend himself as to make certain the captain knew the whole story because he respected the man. He left out the extenuating circumstances – that his ear hurt, his former girlfriend was pregnant and he wanted to run from both.

"I get the picture, but the fact remains that an officer from SHAEF came down to review our combat readiness and you insulted him."

"Sorry, sir ... I'm really sorry."

"Well, you've presented me with a real problem here. His report is on the record now. I have to act on it."

Act on it? Corbin squirmed in his chair.

"Shiller wants me to take all your stripes, bump you down to buck private. Hell, you'd be cleaning latrines if he had his way. You really pissed him off." A flicker of amusement came and went in his eyes. "But lucky for you I can't afford to lose you at this late date. We're crossing the English Channel in a matter of days, I'll never train a replacement in time. So I'm taking all your stripes but one ... you can thank the war for that." The captain wagged a finger at him. "You're PFC O'Connell now. You'll remain in your position as Message Center Chief and you'll do the job right. Is that clear?"

"Yes sir, of course."

The officer's eyes softened and he leaned forward in his chair. "Maybe later ... I'm making no promises now ... but maybe later when this business settles down, you'll get the stripes back."

"Yes sir, thank you, sir."

"Now get outta here. And O'Connell ...."

"Yes, sir?"

"Stay away from Major Shiller."

Corbin returned to the Message Center in a kind of daze. He had *never* been Private First Class O'Connell, bumped as he had been to acting corporal in the early days of basic training. So this was a blow, a real blow. Added in with Velma's letter, it seemed like his whole future had just plunged into a canyon.

SIXTEEN

December, 1944

The Army issued them new field jackets – the longer kind with tight cuffs and a drawstring around the waist – a precursor to moving out. A day later they crossed the turbulent English Channel aboard a fleet of Landing Ship Tanks and found themselves anchored in the Seine Estuary of Le Havre, France that night, December 1. The Allies had invaded Le Havre back in September and leveled it while they took it from the Germans. Scores of Americans had died in the process of liberating this land, but there was no danger now.

They sailed up the Seine River to Rouen, the waterway lined with French citizens cheering in gratitude for what others had done – men they could not thank. The Golden Lions took it that way, humbled by it.

They stayed near Rouen almost a week, sleeping in pup tents in the rain. The conditions encouraged niggling. It was hard to remain completely dry, and once uniforms got damp and uncomfortable they stayed that way. Warnings of trench foot conditions filtered from the top with reminders to keep feet dry, but feet were already the driest of their parts because socks were about the only things getting changed daily.

Corbin joined John and Dumbo Donaldson as one of the gloomy ones, fretting over his predicament with Velma. Her letter required an answer so he scribbled a thoughtless reply. Then, reading how angry it sounded, he threw it away. Even more now, he felt no sympathy for John. And as for Donaldson, Corbin envied him. What was so bad about a Dear John letter? He would much rather have received one of those than the one he got.

It was still raining the day they moved out. Charlie Ragsdale maneuvered the Message Center truck into its assigned fourth position for their trek east to the front. The order of the sixteen-vehicle HQ Battery convoy was always the same – starting with the command car and ending with CJ Murphy's maintenance truck.

Across France they passed hundreds of German vehicles strafed, burned and abandoned in ditches on the side of the road – encouraging signs of a weakened foe. Crossing into Belgium, Corbin saw a farm that reminded him of home. The same front porch, same giant oak tree in the yard, tree branches bare as they would be now at home. The same meadow stretched northeast bordered by the same line of tall trees. This meadow, though, was littered with burned-out artillery, the farmer's few remaining cows grazing around it like nothing was amiss.

The convoy reached St. Vith, Belgium after a two-day motor march in freezing rain. St. Vith had been liberated by the Allies just three months earlier after four long years of German occupation. It was prime real estate: significant roads and a railway junction, strategic location in the dense Ardennes Forest near the front on Germany's western border.

They set up bivouac on the edge of town amid giant evergreens. After the rough and rattling ride it was silent and peaceful there. Corbin had never heard of the Ardennes Forest. Certainly not something he'd studied in school, and no forests at home were as dense and untouched. He tried again to answer Velma, this time managing to compose a more civil reply from a string of carefully-chosen words. He put it in his duffle bag to mull over.

The plan was for the 106th to relieve the 2nd Infantry Division, sent to this quiet sector to rest after engaging in heavy combat since D-Day. For these battle-worn veterans the stay had proved quite a contrast. Stretched sparsely along a section of the eighty-mile front, they'd been lulled into complacency by the placid fir-tree forest that required no watching, offered no threat.

The *Stars and Stripes* peddled the notion that Germany was finished. The magazine even went so far as to outline the American discharge plan for the European Theatre: eighty-five points or more bought an honorable discharge from the Army; less than that meant redeployment to the Pacific. (One point earned for each month in service; five points for every combat award). Some in the 2nd Infantry Division actually had a shot at going home. But the men of the 106th, most with a measly 27 points, would be sent to the other war when this one was over.

The entire Allied chain of command all the way to Eisenhower rested in the illusion of a broken foe. Some even thought Hitler was dead. But he wasn't dead – underground to be sure, but not dead. To keep the Allies from intercepting radio communications he had ordered radio silence. To keep spies from leaking information he had abandoned his highest commanders, retreated to a subterranean bunker to direct his last and greatest attack: a massive counter-offensive designed to seize the crucial port of Antwerp in northern Belgium, and to split British and American forces to try for a separate peace. Hitler crawled over maps for days without sleep and decided the initial attack should be launched through the Ardennes Forest – in the center of the thinly-fortified western front.

It was December 10 when the 106th relieved the 2nd Infantry Division, moving north along the front. As far as setup, there wasn't much for the new men to do. The rookie artillery battalions moved their guns into pre-established positions. The rookie infantry regiments took over existing bunkers and foxholes on Schnee Eifel – the wooded ridge a few miles northeast of St. Vith. Corbin and his unit inherited the existing Message Center with communications network already in place, needed only to occupy warm seats and take over operations.

"How long you been here?" Corbin asked his 2nd Division counterpart.

"Couple a months."

"How's it been?"

"Hell, this is nothing. It's a ghost front, there's nothing out there." He waved an arm in the general direction of Germany.

"Have you been able to intercept their radio communications?"

"Nothing to intercept. Seems like Hitler's boys have nowhere to go and nothing to say."

"This division's never seen combat. We're here to ... get acclimated, I think was the phrase. Not that I'll ever see combat anyhow."

"Count yourself lucky."

"Doesn't it irk you to be stuck back away from the action?"

"No, and you can get killed doing this job, too, if it makes you feel any better. I'm a replacement, in fact. Took over for some poor guy who got it at Normandy. Only been with the unit since July."

"Think the Krauts are really done for?"

"Looks that way. Count yourself lucky again for showing up late."

For the likes of Pappy Dutton, a bunker at the top of Schnee Eifel was a potential perfect vantage point, if there were such a thing looking out on dense evergreens floating in fog. The apparent peacefulness suited the nervous new arrivals just fine, all of them buoyed somewhat by the obvious nonchalance of the departing. But after a day or two, nothing about the trees and fog seemed peaceful. They were told the Germans were finished, that nobody was out there, that the most dangerous enemy here was Mother Nature. But it was hard to accept. It sure felt like somebody was out there, especially at night. They imagined an encroaching enemy in every shift of fog and sway of trees, which shrouded them in a cloud of uncertainty and robbed them of decent sleep. Maybe all this waiting in the cold just made the rookies nervous, or perhaps they truly sensed the impending strike of an army with a three-to-one advantage in infantry.

While the Americans shivered in their foxholes, columns of German soldiers were stealthily closing in. On December 14, a flustered St. Vith woman rushed into the Message Center after managing to make her way back from Germany on a stolen horse. "Die Boche! Die Boche sind zurück!" With wild hand gestures she jabbered away in rapid German.

They called for a radioman from HQ to come and translate: The Nazis! The Nazis are back! Thousands building up across the border! Trucks and tanks, many tanks. But not on the main roads. They are hiding.

Other frightened Belgians brought similar warnings, desperate to be finished with German occupation. Intelligence officers passed the warnings up the line only to have those at the top take them as loony exaggerations. On December 15, when men at the front reported tank movements in the distance, the brass actually accepted as fact the increase in military activity, then shrugged it off as insignificant. It simply wasn't possible for Germany to wage a counter-offensive after spending the last year in retreat.

Then, in the pre-dawn hours of December 16, while the U.S. infantry was adrift in an uneasy doze, a quarter of a million Germans and two thousand tanks gathered and waited for the light. At daybreak on that calamitous Saturday, dense fog still hovered over the Ardennes Forest – perfect conditions to nullify the Allied bombers Hitler feared.

At 5:46 a.m. they opened up. The far-off boom of artillery barrages that shattered tree trunks and human bones sounded like simple thunder twelve miles away in St. Vith. Word of the stupefying assault came by frantic radio outbursts from the entrenched 106th stretched thin over twenty-one miles of the front.

But those in charge still didn't react, not until news of an actual breakthrough. Suddenly then, came an order to pack. No detail, just the command to be ready – HQ Battery was getting out of the way. A chaotic sort of hugger-bugger scramble erupted across the compound, the calm efficiency of previous moves abandoned. Hurry, hurry, hurry seemed the urgent message conveyed in every step, every impatient gesture as Ragsdale pulled the truck and trailer to the front of the Message Center and they proceeded to load.

Then they waited. It was typical to be ordered to hurry, stand by, and proceed without ever knowing the reason for delay. This hurry-and-wait approach had been typical during nineteen months of Army training, and still now apparently, even in a combat zone. Ragsdale paced beside the truck watching the fogged-over sun sink lower in the sky. "We're burning up daylight sitting here," he said repeatedly. "Don't they know it's gonna be hell driving in the dark with no lights?" Vielsalm, Belgium was their destination, some twelve miles or so to the west. Not very far, but it would seem like an odyssey on a foggy night, on unfamiliar roads, dealing with blackout lights that rendered the human eye almost obsolete. Each vehicle came fitted front and rear with these special lights, which emitted a diffused beam invisible to aircraft. "I know blackout conditions are important at a time like this, but doesn't anybody besides us drivers realize that convoying that way is shaky business?"

It was well after dark when they finally moved out. Ragsdale maneuvered the truck into its usual fourth position, sliding a bit in the mud. As they bumped along he gripped the wheel and squinted at the windshield in an attempt to balance the two opposing rules of blackout convoying: stay close enough to the vehicle in front to see its slivers of taillight; avoid bunching together too much lest the Germans destroy multiple vehicles in a single strike.

Corbin lit a cigarette and left Ragsdale alone. With nothing to do, nothing to see out the window, he closed his eyes and got lost in his thoughts, which were peevish these days. His immediate peeve was this trip – this getting out of the way of the war. For him, armed conflict seemed a lesser threat than what awaited him back home. He even considered the idea of not going home at all, and a short battle raged between guilt and a desire to escape. Guilt soon won, aided by thoughts of what his mother would say. Life ahead was a crumbling ruin. What had gone wrong? A month ago he'd been a well-settled staff sergeant free as air, enjoying the last full day of an ocean voyage on the upper deck of the Wakefield. What *had* gone wrong? He pondered the question warily and not for long, suspecting he'd caused the whole downward spiral himself.

Ragsdale lost sight of the truck in front of him on an elbow in the road. He leaned closer to the windshield and rubbed it with a hand, trying to see. Nothing but blackness ahead. "Shit, I hate this," he murmured, forced to guess at the lay of the curve. He swung too wide as he rounded it, felt the soft shoulder give way. "Shit! Shit! Ah, shit!" he bawled, jerking the steering wheel to the left a little too late.

Paying attention now, Corbin held on. The right front wheel careened off the macadam, took the rest of the truck and the trailer with it and stopped with a jolt in what felt like a ditch. By the feel of the fall the ditch wasn't deep, but they couldn't see anything.

"Now what do we do?" Ragsdale said. "If they hadn't delayed leaving for so damned long ..."

"Could be worse, Rags. At least we're upright." Corbin opened the door and stepped out. "Let's check the damage."

"Check the damage? It's black as Hitler's heart out here."

"Get the flashlight."

They worked their way around the vehicle, the light held near the ground and shielded with their bodies to violate the blackout as little as possible. Everything appeared okay except the front tires – sunk several inches in half-frozen mud. Trucks rumbled by up on the road, drivers unaware. Even if they had been aware they couldn't have stopped; it was against regulations for any convoy vehicle to halt for another, excepting CJ Murphy's maintenance truck. "Let's get these front tires free," Corbin said, "so it'll be easier for Murph to pull us out."

With shovels from the back they began to dig, ears tuned for the deeper growl of the maintenance truck. They yelled when they heard it. Corbin even took a chance and snaked the flashlight around. But with the noise of his own engine, windows rolled up, Murphy didn't see or hear a thing.

Silence closed in when the last rattle of the convoy faded. "Spooky," Ragsdale said. "For all we know we could be in enemy territory."

"Last we heard, the Germans were east of St. Vith. We're west."

"Could've changed."

"All the more reason to get out of here." With eyes somewhat adjusted to the darkness Corbin studied the ground from the truck to the road. "Once we get these tires free, don't you think you can just drive back up there? It doesn't look that steep and these trucks pull through anything."

"I can sure as hell try."

It took them twenty minutes to get back on the road. "I can't see a damn thing," Ragsdale said, craning at the windshield.

"You're doing fine. Just keep moving like you are ... nice and slow." Corbin managed the calming voice of a leader, even without the extra chevrons.

"What if they turned off somewhere up ahead? We may never find them."

"Rags, would you stop worrying about stuff before it happens? You worry twice as much that way."

No need to worry as it turned out. Within a few minutes they caught up with the convoy, stopped on the road for the night. Murphy's truck appeared so suddenly in the fog that Ragsdale had to stomp on the brakes to keep from plowing into it. They had lost their fourth position, trailing at the end, with nothing to do now but settle back and rest.

The attack began shortly after dawn. Artillery shells exploded on both sides of the road with a jarring BOOM! BOOM! Startled men were bolted out of sleep. Hard to tell where it came from. Did the Germans see them? Just an arbitrary hit? Another barrage screamed in with pulverizing precision! Black smoke and fire ahead!

"Jesus, somebody up there just got it!" Ragsdale hollered. Men scrambled from vehicles not knowing quite what to do. Ragsdale and Corbin ducked under the truck, watched others take cover in a ditch.

"Captain says get these trucks moving! They've zeroed us! GET MOVING!" This from a frantic voice attached to muddy boots. A moment later they were back in the truck with the motor running. They swung around Murphy's maintenance truck, rattled along the edge of the road past vehicles with missing drivers, the order of march forgotten.

"Who got it? Who the hell got it?" Corbin craned his neck in search of John's wire truck, sixth in the line of march. There it was, so it wasn't John. It was the one in front of him, Donaldson's. As Ragsdale bumped alongside John's truck, Corbin yelled out the window, "Did they make it out?" John shook his head and looked away while his driver swung wide around the wreck.

With the advantage of daylight it was a quick ride to Vielsalm. They gathered in clumps when they got there but nobody said much. No point in talking about what happened; they were all there, they all saw. And it felt wrong to talk of anything else. For many it was the start of true, personal hatred for the Germans. So ugly and intimate it had been – the suddenness of it, the randomness of it – a U.S. Army truck with three of their own exploded into a twisted flaming pile.

They were served a pancake and sausage breakfast that most of them consumed standing and in silence, just an orchestra of forks and knives clicking metal trays. After that they seemed to loosen up, already learning to shake off death and leave it behind.

Corbin found John off to himself. "That letter Dumbo got from his girlfriend ..."

"What about it?"

"A rotten thing to do, telling him it was over. She's free of him now, anyway. Should have kept her big mouth shut."

"Yeah, well ... I'm thinking about something else. Do you realize it would have been you?"

"What do you mean?"

"If Rags hadn't run off the road last night, you'd have been in that position and it would have been you."

SEVENTEEN

lthough news of the 106th had not yet surfaced on
national radio, everyone in Judson knew they were in
Europe because Jimmy had spread the word. While
the boys were filing off the ship in Liverpool, Jimmy had read
the *apples* clue in his brother's letter and, feeling important,
bicycled into town to show everyone.

The letter annoyed Velma. Corbin had not seen fit to com-
municate at all since her trip to Indianapolis. She'd expected
a frantic response to the *I'm pregnant* letter – maybe even a
long-distance telephone call or cable. Instead she got nothing.
Nothing. Dutifully, she had sent the *false alarm* letter but now
regretted it. It would've been better to make him sweat.

Corbin was still her favorite, even after this. But she'd tried
everything during the last three years, perhaps her best years,
and she was ready to give up. For months now she had safe-
guarded her only wool sweater for when he came home, kept
it wrapped in layers of tissue paper in her mother's old cedar
chest. But not anymore. With all the wool going for military
uniforms, wool sweaters in general were impossible to find,
and this one was a delicious peacock blue that brought out
the color of her eyes. She liked to wear it reversed with all the
little pearl buttons down the back. It clung to her chest most
becomingly that way, and was the latest look.

Her attention had switched to Mitch Kenny for all the good it did her; he seemed interested in no one but Daisy. Velma turned on the charm during his frequent meals at the diner, but he invariably sat there with his nose in a newspaper and responded with indifferent nods. Although, he did not have his nose in the news the other evening when he apparently ran into Daisy on the sidewalk and coaxed her in for supper. Velma was surprised Daisy accepted since she rarely graced the place with her presence anymore. Forced to witness their cozy hour together, Velma wanted to dump a bowl of chili in Daisy's lap and tell Mitch he was a fool. Didn't the guy see he was wasting his time? Even with his many advantages he was just wasting his time. And how brazen to pursue with such vigor George Ottinger's future daughter-in-law.

Jimmy's letter prompted Daisy to put on a coat and cross the street to Western Union. She had often visited Ezra as a child, attracted to the teleprinter's rhythmic and official rapping. Nowadays she popped in whenever she had an excuse, which was often, taking it upon herself to personally deliver his allotment of a rationed item before it was gone. Last week it was butter; today, a can of peaches and a few slices of bacon wrapped in butcher paper.

Ezra was processing a cable when she came in on a gust of wind and plunked the offerings down on the counter. "Peaches!" he crowed.

"Are you sure you want them?" she asked, laughing. "They'll cost you twenty cents and sixteen ration stamps."

"Worth every stamp." Ezra placed the cable in the cigar box with others. "And what have we here?" he asked, fingering the parcel.

"Bacon ... twenty-five cents and three stamps."

"Even better. Here, let me pay you while I'm thinking of it." He fished in his pocket for coins, produced two ration books from under the counter, and left it to her to take what he owed.

"Nothing bad in there, I hope." She pointed to the cigar box.

"No, thank goodness."

"Did you hear the boys are in Europe?"

"Yes, Jimmy stopped in. Apples for the Atlantic, clever tip-off."

"Clever, but .... they're in Europe now."

"They're probably still safe and sound in England," Ezra said in his most soothing voice. A quiet observer, he often witnessed subtleties others missed, and had come to understand how it was with Daisy – engaged to one man and equally concerned for another. He had never mentioned it but consistently acknowledged it, always speaking of *they* instead of *he*. Ezra gave her hand a pat. "I wouldn't worry too much. It really does sound like the fighting's nearly over in Europe." They'd be sent to the Pacific at that point but he chose not to remind her.

A week before Christmas, headlines of fierce combat on the western front screamed at shoppers from newsstands and crushed any dream that Germany was finished. Worrisome details listed the 106th among the embattled forces in Belgium.

Daisy became obsessed over Ezra's travels after that, and the proximity of the market just across the street allowed her to nourish the obsession all day long. On a frigid noonday she even chased him down the street as he hoofed west donned in black. "Who's it for?" she asked, double-timing her steps to keep up with his long legs.

He seemed slightly annoyed, made no attempt to alter his pace for her. "Daisy, you know I can't tell you. Immediate family hears it first."

"Yes, but –"

"A War Department telegram, any telegram for that matter, is intended only for the person to whom it's addressed. They deserve to at least have it delivered without a leak." He halted on the sidewalk and gave her a pointed look. "This one is not a direct concern for you, okay? Now go back inside before you catch your death. And for God's sake try to get your mind on something else. I hear there's a Christmas dance at the USO tonight. You should go."

Left to shiver alone on the sidewalk, Daisy double-wrapped the front of her sweater and watched him turn the corner onto Irvin. It dawned on her then that she had reacted hastily. Ezra would have driven had he been going as far as the Ottinger estate or the O'Connell farm.

***

The Women's Auxiliary had transformed the armory: pine wreaths at windows and doors, garland festooned on the walls, mistletoe dangling from ropes twined with greenery, punchbowls and platters crowding linen-draped tables – soothingly customary yuletide accoutrements for this, the fourth Christmas of the war. The gathering was mostly females in party clothes and holiday hairdos. Men in uniform made up much of the rest. Those fresh from the war were easy to spot, injury having won them an early ticket home. Some had such dazed looks, as though they did not belong. In a way, they didn't. Too soft here, too comfortable, the contrast too harsh to absorb. The women pampered each one of them, and flirted more recklessly than they ever would have chanced with a healthy man.

An Army corporal in a wheelchair stared out with vacant eyes, head bandage stark white against his weatherworn face. Someone gave him cider in a cut-glass cup, cake on a china plate. He studied them with puzzlement. They looked absurd, so out of place in his hands – swollen right index finger crooked around the dainty cup handle, craggy-nailed left thumb grasping the lip of the plate. The last time he noticed his hands they'd been caked with mud and somebody's blood. Wasn't it just yesterday? It seemed like only yesterday. Now, after the inadequate adjustment of a foggy hospital stay, he was sitting here clutching these fripperies.

A war correspondent for the Philadelphia Inquirer moved deftly on crutches, home from the Pacific with his leg in a cast. He said he was glad to be back where people slept in beds at night, wore clean clothes every day and walked on dry pavement; where chances were good the guy he spoke with tonight would not be blown to atoms tomorrow. As his eyes traveled the room he found it hard to believe that this world occupied the same planet as the one in the Pacific. But they did, and the guys he knew on the front lines were still over there.

Wilbur Dowd showed up with his hair slicked back and shoes shined wearing his Sunday shirt and a new tie, lured by the certainty of a good time with women outnumbering men five-to-one. Mitch Kenny was another out of uniform and under forty. He could have anyone he wanted, just about. He could certainly have Velma; she'd made that plain enough. But Mitch was out for bigger game in Daisy Hall. As clouds of cigarette smoke gathered near the ceiling, its acrid odor spoiling the scent of pine, he managed repeatedly to coax her to the floor. He danced with her a large part of the night, and when he wasn't dancing with her he was staring at her with fervor he made no attempt to conceal.

Daisy nearly forgot the war for a few hours as Ezra suggested, though the pleasant evening brought misgivings later at home. Here she was, engaged to a man overseas, wearing his ring amid talk of a post-war wedding. Shouldn't she want to lean on the jukebox and think of him? Instead, she had monopolized the most eligible bachelor in town, which was hardly fair to the other women. Mitch was difficult to resist as a dance partner. He was light on his feet and owned the floor when he was on it, just as he owned any situation susceptible to an aggressive nature. So much like Corbin in that respect.

Corbin. Life had become such an emotional mess. In the armory storeroom (nearly two years ago now) she had professed loyalty for one and kissed the other. It was that kiss, that single kiss, that had occupied her mind these many months. The very thought of it made her weak and she mourned the loss of ever being kissed like that again. Tonight she might have wanted to lean on the jukebox and relive it over and over if not for Mitch.

Corbin was her first and only real love, and she his. Though she'd never really said she loved him, he knew. That love would transcend all else regardless of the future. In moments of feminine fantasy she placed their ardor on par with the great couples from literature – Romeo and Juliet, Lancelot and Guinevere, Eloise and Abelard – ill-fated lovers filled with unquenched passion destined to burn for all time.

She was not entirely to blame for the predicament – pushed toward John at sixteen, and he toward her, by the combined forces of the mothers. Everybody in town thought it was grand. John had been so charmingly open in his interest, so confident in his claim, Daisy had been coaxed into love – not so much with him as with the grandness of it. And yes, the lavish Ottinger lifestyle had played a part. To stand firm against such forces would have required a stronger will.

But that was then. The truth should have been plain by the Christmas of the ring. Yet, even then the clamor from other people's dreams had muffled her own inner warnings. Everything changed, though, with that storeroom kiss, and life had been a lie ever since.

She slept in short spurts that night – awake to see the clock reach three, four, five – vowing never to let anyone have a say in her future again. By the time a grayish dawn seeped through the curtains at six, she had decided to walk away from both men. It was the fair thing to do, the only thing to do. But, ironically, it would please no one.

She'd keep it to herself – no cruel letters to John, no telling her mother. Nobody would hear about it, except maybe her father. Then after the war when everyone came home, she would simply leave Judson and start over someplace else. Not such a strange thing to do, really. The war had grabbed hold of the country and shaken it hard, picking up people from one place and dropping them in another. Dozens had left Judson while twice as many others had swarmed in.

John would be terribly hurt. He suspected something even now, judging by his letters. She dreaded the day she would have to tell him and there'd always be guilt, but her self-imposed restriction from a life spent with Corbin would be punishment enough.

EIGHTEEN

December 17, 1944
Vielsalm, Belgium

On Sunday, reports filtered in that German infantry units and heavy artillery had broken back into Belgium up and down the line, circling St. Vith north and south. But the details of size and artillery strength were conflicting and dubious. Division brass questioned the whole business anyway, finding it hard to picture the Germans with any significant power at all, much less the numbers they were hearing from every side. All added up, the amounts were staggering.

Word came down that they needed volunteers for a reconnaissance mission to confirm a sighting in the north. They wanted a driver, a man with a radio, and an extra man for the mission to be led by a young lieutenant who was busy studying the maps.

Corbin stepped up without hesitation, then raised a questioning eyebrow at Ragsdale who nodded somewhat easily his consent to drive. John was harder to convince. He responded to the raised eyebrow with a vehement shake of the head, silent gesture met with silent gesture. Corbin leaned in and whispered, "Come on, let's do this one. It might be our only real chance to get in the war." Another vehement shake. "Might give you something to tell Daisy one day." That seemed to do it. John agreed, though not an ounce of him really wanted to go.

It could hardly be thought of as getting in the war since the task was merely to observe the enemy from a safe distance and report back what they saw. Yet they were issued M1 rifles and ammo for the first time, which in Corbin's opinion was incentive enough. "See? This is good," he said to John's doubtful face.

"What's good about it? I have no idea how to load and fire this thing."

They took off thirty minutes later in a northeasterly direction amid patches of fog. Ragsdale attempted to drive the Jeep at a respectable speed without hitting every rut in the road. Beside him sat the lieutenant, head bent over a well-worn map as he followed the route with his finger.

Corbin studied the lieutenant from the back seat he shared with John, a radio and a box of grenades. The officer looked too young and green to be leading this mission, too young to be a lieutenant, though he had to be a year or two older than the rest of them. Didn't seem like the military type. There was a stillness and refinement about him that seemed more fitting for something else – a diplomat maybe or a concert pianist.

A light snow dotted the windshield a few minutes into the ride, melting as it landed. The lieutenant held out a hand to catch some of it. "This mix of snow and fog is a bit odd, isn't it? Don't recall seeing it at home."

"Where's home, Lieutenant?" Ragsdale asked.

"Wilmington, Delaware."

"No foolin', sir? I'm from Dover. Have you been with us since Fort Jackson?"

"I joined the 106th at Camp Atterbury, straight out of West Point. Graduated last June with John Eisenhower, General Eisenhower's son."

"No foolin'? Did you get to see Ike?"

"Afraid not. We graduated on June sixth ... D-Day. Guess he was too busy with the invasion of Normandy."

"Where's the son now? Bet *he* isn't in the line of fire."

"Well, he's over here somewhere."

They approached the road that led to St. Vith, where the convoy had been hit. They didn't take it. "Where we headed, Lieutenant?" Corbin asked.

"Northeast of here about ten miles, judging from the map. German Panzers were sighted heading northwest at the Kaiserbaracke Crossroads, the intersection of this road and a main highway running between St. Vith and Malmedy."

Corbin lifted the lid from the box of grenades. "Sir, have you ever detonated one of these petrified pineapples?

"Only in training and maneuvers".

"Well, I ought to tell ya ... the rest of us haven't even done that."

"There isn't much to it, you just pull the pin and throw."

In a small village made up of a half-dozen houses, an American flag hung from an upstairs window. They watched as the window opened and a bald man stuck out his head. "Die Boche sind zurück!" he yelled in a hoarse voice, then hurriedly pulled in the flag and banged the window shut.

"The Nazis are back?" The lieutenant translated with an incredulous frown. "Not this far west."

Ragsdale instinctively lowered his speed and looked around.

"Let's keep going," the lieutenant waved him on. "These people are just jumpy after living in German occupation for so long."

The pair in the back traded doubtful looks. Corbin plucked two grenades out of the box and attached them to the haversack strap across his chest. "Want one?"

"No," John muttered and glanced away. "Hey, over there!" He pointed ahead on his side of the road.

"What?"

"In those trees. Looks like a Kraut!" John leaned forward. "Lieutenant, I think there's a German up in those trees."

"Shouldn't be any Germans within five miles of here."

"But I saw him. He's ducked down now, probably spotted us."

"Nothing wrong with John's eyesight, Lieutenant," Corbin said.

A single shot rang out.

The lieutenant shifted in his seat. "Okay, pull over. That might have been a warning shot to his unit. This completely conflicts with the reports we received," he said, abandoning the map. "There's a sharp curve ahead. No point driving into an ambush."

John whispered under his breath, "Thank God for that."

"Somebody needs to run through those trees and have a look."

"I'll do it," Corbin said.

"No heroics, just see what you can see and come straight back."

Corbin jumped over the side, adjusted the haversack strap, grabbed his M1 and ammunition bag.

"Private Ragsdale, we need some cover. Back this thing off the road into –" Machine gun fire pelted the ground a few feet away! "MOVE IT! MOVE IT!" the lieutenant yelled above the din.

Corbin froze, not knowing whether to run or hurl himself back in. Ragsdale decided for him by stomping on the gas pedal. The Jeep lurched backward and Corbin dove for a ditch. A second barrage hit the Jeep square on. The men cried out. Tracers followed. One blew a hole in the spare gas can. The vehicle caught fire. Half a minute later the main gas tank exploded in a fearsome ball of black smoke and an earsplitting BOOM!

Corbin stumbled from the ditch. Frantic, he lunged at the Jeep in a desperate attempt to do something but the heat proved too intense. All he could do was dance around it on legs turned to lead. Debris rained down. A grenade landed a few feet off, rolled to the opposite side of the road. He made no attempt to flee. Five seconds ... ten seconds ... nothing. The way he felt at that moment, it could have blown up in his face.

The sight of three bodies in the flames caused him to twist away and be sick on the road. Crushed by horror and unbearable guilt, he fell to his knees from the weight, their surreal outlines to be forever etched on his brain. Up on his feet again, fueled by shame and a tortured heart, he erupted in a fit of raw emotion. He stomped on a piece of radio housing, kicked a chunk of mirror down the road, yanked his helmet off and threw it into the woods, but it wasn't enough. He snatched a grenade from his haversack strap, pulled the pin and hurled it as far as he could for the pleasure of watching it explode. *Come on, let's do this one ... come on, let's do this one ... something to tell Daisy one day.* Those words, his own manipulative, deadly words, taunted him to jump in there where he belonged – back in that seat next to John. He reached under his shirt, grabbed his dog tag chain, and in one fluid motion yanked it over his head and flung it in. Strange comfort came from putting himself back there, even if it were only symbolic.

Over the roar of the flames came the drone of an engine and laughing voices. The enemy! Corbin darted toward the woods the way of his helmet. With seconds to spare he jumped the ditch, grabbed the M1 and lunged behind a bank of spindly trees. Wasn't much of a hiding place; they'd find him with ease if they looked. Oddly, the idea didn't frighten him. Not anymore, not after this.

From the sound of the voices there were six or eight of them. They were laughing. Laughing! What the heck was so funny? He raised his head enough to watch them enjoying their victory. His hatred for them grew as they hovered around the Jeep, picked through debris on the road. With ringing ears and a tremendous headache he did not watch for long. Leaves and sticks made a poor bed for his face, red and tender from the blast. He took a deep breath and let it out gradually in an attempt to quiet a racing heart.

Unable to move or make a sound, he could do nothing but think. No denying it, he was to blame. John would still be safe in Vielsalm if not for him. When this mess was over he'd be stepping off the train alone in Judson – Daisy waiting with John's family, their faces twisted in grief. Pop Ott! Deep emotion bubbled up once more and he stifled a sob as heartache threatened again to take over. He couldn't think now of Pop Ott. Too much to bear and he had to keep his wits. He'd have the rest of his life to be tormented, the rest of his life for his heart to ache. A new thought surfaced, fleeting and uninvited: Daisy was now the free one! What colossal irony! What a preposterous turn of events!

Time rolled on in slow motion. The Germans were still there. Corbin considered breaking from cover to shoot a few of them even knowing it would mean his demise. But it seemed empty and wrong, grossly unfair to his mother, to waste himself so fruitlessly just to quiet the guilt. How many could he eliminate before they mowed him down? Two? Maybe three? He raised his pounding head again to peer through the trees. They seemed to be killing time. Waiting for what? The fire to die down so they could pick through the ruin? It looked like two had been posted to watch down the road, no doubt hoping to pull off another easy ambush. Well, he couldn't just lie there; warning shots might be necessary. He took a real chance and crawled on his belly to another position where he, too, could see down the road. Part of him actually hoped for a reason to fire warning shots, welcomed the chance to make a meaningful sacrifice. And he wouldn't waste those shots, either; with a little luck he'd take out a German with each one.

But nobody, friend or foe, passed on the road. He continued to lie there after they'd gone, fighting the need to move and face it all. A bone-seeping cold was what finally forced him up. Shivering on his feet he made his way to the wreckage, the heat from it a diabolical blessing. The front was pretty much gone. As a sort of punishment he willed himself to move in closer. Most of what was there was blessedly unrecognizable: eyeglasses, twisted and melting; the singed remains of what he supposed were three bodies. It was honestly hard to tell. Anger welled up in him again, white anger at the Germans, which rescued him briefly from the more painful guilt. Well ... they, too, could die. They, too, could lose friends.

One of them must have picked up his ammunition bag. And the unexploded grenade had vanished. Corbin hoped it blew up in the hand of whoever took it. As he retrieved his helmet and placed it on his head, desire for revenge blurred duty and pointed in a clear direction. Without looking back he continued northeast, away from Vielsalm and into the war.

He stayed on the road to make better time, withdrawing into the trees when he rounded a bend or heard the slightest noise. Once, he came upon a family of civilians escaping to the west. They spoke to each other in what sounded to him like French. Running into him so unexpectedly, their first reaction was fear, but they offered tired smiles when he tipped his helmet.

An hour of walking brought him to a decision point. To the left, a dirt road. Straight ahead, an intersection with what appeared to be a substantial highway. Possibly the Kaiserbaracke Crossroads the lieutenant had mentioned. Corbin ventured close enough to read the road sign: arrow to the right – ST. VITH 8 km; arrow to the left – STAVELOT 11 km, MALMEDY 13 km. This had to be the Crossroads, a main thoroughfare fit for tank traffic, enemy and Allied. From where he stood he could see fresh ruts in the mud, deep ruts made by heavy artillery.

Corbin decided against the highway, suicide for a lone man armed with one grenade, a rifle and eight rounds. He set off on the dirt road smoking his last cigarette. The choice proved prudent; he could hear the steady rumble and creak of tank movements on the highway, feel the vibrations underfoot. The dirt road ran parallel for the most part, cutting deep into the evergreens at places and then curving back – close enough at one point that he had to drop on his belly in the underbrush to keep from being seen. It was then that he got a first real look at enemy Panzers with their dreaded 88-millimeter guns. He studied them with fascination. Unlike U.S. Shermans, German tanks ran on diesel fuel instead of gasoline; he could smell it. And the rumble from a Panzer sounded different, a deeper-pitched rumble that reverberated further, signifying greater threat.

The Germans themselves appeared to be of all ranks and ages – formidable black-uniformed officers down to fresh-faced boys too young to be operating such behemoth weapons. Corbin wanted to pick off a few of the Waffen SS riding so haughtily upright with heads and chests exposed, but to give himself away would have been foolish. Another, better time would come for killing. As it was, they didn't even know he was there and he was able to track them for miles, getting almost as much satisfaction from the stealth and spying. Yet, without a radio he couldn't tell anyone. These armor-plated monsters were spreading back into Belgium and nobody was there to stop them.

The sun sank, the temperature with it. Reluctantly, he stopped to look for a place to bivouac while there was still light enough to see. The tanks continued on without him as he disappeared among the evergreens, far enough in to be safe. The deep rumble faded until he heard it no more. He heard nothing, really – no scamper, no rustle, no flutter of wings – all winter life apparently stunned to silence by the intruding metal marauders. Picking his way through the underbrush he, too, felt the need to be quiet. Noise had not been an issue all afternoon; he could have shouted "to hell with Hitler!" and the Germans wouldn't have heard it above their own racket. But ears had a way of sharpening in the dark, and the slightest sound could travel on the night air.

They had camped out often at home, he and John. It had been an adventure then. He told himself it wouldn't be any different here except he'd be going it alone. To survive, according to his boyhood training, a man needed water, food and shelter. Well, there was water enough in the canteen, food in the haversack. For shelter, he cut fresh evergreen branches with his knife and crisscrossed them on the ground as a sort of bed, reserving the fullest two for a blanket.

From the haversack he pulled out a C ration, the Army-issue daily field ration containing bread, pork and beans, and an Accessory Pack. He tore into the pack: water-purification tablets, toilet paper, chewing gum, can opener, matches. And nine Lucky Strikes – what he was searching for. Ah, above anything he needed a smoke. He tucked one between his lips, shielded it with a cupped hand and quickly lit it with his lighter. There wasn't much of a flame because the fluid was low. He slipped it into an inner pocket and thought sadly of John, who'd given him the lighter for Christmas in 1941.

He saved the bread ration for morning and ate the beans cold. A fire would make all the difference here but he dared not. Smoke was easily seen before sunset, and flames afterward. Even lighting a cigarette was risky business once it turned dark, and it was dark enough at this point for the evergreens and the space between them to be indistinguishable.

A few drops of canteen water were sacrificed to soothe his face, still hot to the touch while the rest of him froze. He felt in the haversack for two pairs of extra socks. Grateful they were there, he removed his boots long enough to peel away the damp ones and slide on both fresh pairs. Then he draped the damp socks flat on his chest between field jacket and overcoat. From his own body heat they would be warm and dry as toast by morning – a trick he'd learned from Pappy Dutton.

He arranged his haversack as a sort of pillow and tried to sleep but it was early yet for sleeping and, tired as he felt, he couldn't turn off his ears. In his wilderness bedroom he questioned every sound, and especially the silence. It seemed unnaturally quiet, a sure sign forest life still sensed an intruder. All he heard was the sound of his own breathing, which seemed unnaturally loud. He fed his fears and let them build up until logic pointed to him as the intruder. It had always been John who had listened in the night imagining bears or bobcats or escaped convicts with machetes. And it had always been Corbin putting up a brave front. Well, bravery was easier with somebody watching; it wasn't so easy alone.

Corbin fought hard against images of John. The poor guy had just wanted to go back home, impatient to commence a future with the best girl in the world. It seemed odd to Corbin that he'd been the one to survive since John had always been the lucky one. Though after what happened today, John's twenty years of privilege no longer counted for much – the scale measuring good fortune between them forever tipped the other way. Corbin expected never to overcome the guilt he now felt. In one sense he was glad to be saddled with Velma – grateful for the certainty it brought that he'd never think of John's death as a lucky break.

His thoughts shifted to Ragsdale and the lieutenant, gone as well. Rags had a wife and kid back home; Corbin had seen a snapshot of a chubby dark-haired beauty holding a blond-headed baby. Nothing was known of the lieutenant except that he'd graduated from West Point with Ike's son. What a waste to spend four years in a military academy, only to die. The families would soon be getting telegrams. No bodies to bless and bury, just a rut-pitted Belgium road for a cemetery.

And Pop Ott. How many happy days remained for him before Ezra Knox came knocking to change everything. What would the telegram say? Presumed dead? Dead? Wait. What of his own family? For the first time since the attack, Corbin thought of them. Could his dog tags actually be recovered in that ruin? Did it matter? Either way, they'd peg him a goner. What a dunderhead! The way things were, his mother would be getting a telegram, too. He sat straight up disturbing his evergreen blanket as the scene played out in his mind: Ezra with sad eyes forced to deliver the envelope into his mother's hand while she crumpled to the porch floor. He was such a dunderhead! Well, it didn't need to happen, not to *his* mother anyway. Tomorrow, if he could find a unit with a radio, a simple report of the attack and his survival would fix that.

He considered once again the idea of not going home – even more tempting now with John gone. So tempting to just avoid it all – avoid showing up alone, avoid a life on the farm with Velma, the hurt in his mother's eyes over the foolishness that got him in this mess. But he had to go back. If he made it through this war alive he had to go back, for it was one thing to be foolish and quite another to be a cad.

NINETEEN

I n the surprise German offensive the day before, a column of Hitler's First SS Panzer Division commanded by Regimental Colonel Joachim Peiper had broken through the front at a weak spot north of St. Vith. Since then, Peiper had pressed on in a northwesterly direction, his ultimate goal to cut Allied supply lines by seizing northern Belgium's port of Antwerp. On the way, he captured Honsfeld in east Belgium, plowed north into Bullingen and destroyed an Allied gas supply. South of Malmedy, he attacked a U.S. field observation battalion, took prisoners and gunned them down in a nearby field, killing seventy-some. A few lived to tell about it, those with enough presence-of-mind to fall where they stood and feign death.

All of this Peiper had managed by noon. The column continued north and west the rest of the day, undoubtedly the parade of Panzers Corbin had seen on the highway. By dusk on the 17th the column reached the southern outskirts of Stavelot – a small town through which the Ambleve River flowed. The river was not a particular obstacle for infantry but its steep and craggy banks proved tough-going for vehicles, even tanks. The only way tanks could get to the other side here was to cross the bridge into Stavelot.

As he peered at the town through field glasses, Colonel Peiper saw what looked like hundreds of U.S. trucks parked in the streets. And across the river on the opposite bank, more jammed the muddy road leading north out of town. The scene was misleading: the trucks had gathered to move the U.S. First Army's gasoline supply; few actual troops were there.

But Peiper didn't know that. He halted on the south side of the bridge and stayed put most of the night. Yet precious time was slipping away and one immutable fact must have burned a hole in his mind: to capture Antwerp, this bridge must first be crossed. He attacked at daybreak and drove back a handful of American troops who'd assembled on the other side. Late in the morning the Americans retreated north of town to wait for reinforcements, leaving the door open for Peiper to take the town and roam at will through the streets.

※

Corbin heard the fighting where he'd bedded down for the night. He was in a deep sleep when it started, too deep for distant noise to penetrate. Soon the explosions of heavy artillery broke through, contributing sound effects to a dream of being in bed at home in a thunderstorm. When he awoke enough to isolate the noise, the sun had cleared the horizon, shrouded once again by the incessant fog. He crawled out of his evergreen cocoon, urinated against a tree, pulled the warm pair of socks over the other two. Never had he been so cold.

At mid-morning, not far from where German Colonel Peiper stood the afternoon before, Corbin looked down on Stavelot from the bluffs on the south side of the Ambleve River. He had no field glasses and the fog made it difficult to see. The artillery fire had stopped, no obvious American presence anywhere. The roofs of some buildings were gone. The bridge across the river was still standing; odd that neither side had seen fit to destroy it. And he was certain there were Panzers running the streets.

Corbin dared not cross the bridge. Instead he swung around to the west until he found a shallow point in the river and waded across there. As icy water seeped into his boots he cursed himself for not removing the three pairs of socks first. The bank was steep on the other side, too steep to climb straight up, he discovered. So he angled left to ease the climb using rocks and exposed tree roots as footholds.

Wet to the knees he crept into town, numb feet sloshing in his boots. White dust from the explosions hung in the air and coated every surface. He hugged the wall at the back of a building to listen a moment, get his bearings. What he heard sounded like the cries of humans in distress. Gunfire rang out then, punctuated by more human cries.

Hidden behind a pile of debris Corbin witnessed a horrendous scene: German soldiers posed in a half circle shooting what appeared to be townspeople. Must have been a hundred of them – men, women and children alike – gunned down and falling where they stood, like so many pins in a bowling alley. It was over in a blink – blasts echoing in the ensuing silence, shooters just walking away. Every last victim lay sprawled on the ground, their blackish-red blood pooling out in the dust. The scene so stunned Corbin that he froze, unprepared for such blatant butchery. Murdered for harboring American soldiers, he would later learn. So this was war.

With a fresh rush of hatred he came to his senses enough to get off the streets, ducking into a damaged house with a half-hinged back door. Rifle aimed in front of him, he made his way across the kitchen and halted in a doorway. The air was thick with dust. A young man and woman crouched in a corner, barely visible, each clinging to a child. They looked at him with terror.

He pointed the rifle to the floor and held up a palm. "It's okay, I'm not gonna hurt you," he said, startled by the alien words coming from his own mouth. It was hard to tell whether they understood. They didn't respond but the terror faded a bit, tempered by what seemed like relief at the sight of his uniform. He wondered what language they spoke – whether it was French like the family on the road.

"Where are the Americans?" Corbin patted his chest. Then, dredging up remnants of high school French, he stammered, "Ou … sont … Americains?"

The man nodded at the stairs across the room.

"Up there?"

Another nod.

A cursory glance into rooms on the second floor revealed unmade beds, nightclothes discarded in haste. More stairs led further up. He took them, sidestepping chunks of plaster, roofing and glass to get to the third floor. It was a shambles up there. Part of the front wall and the roof had been blown away. And in all the debris lay a very dead GI.

Corbin turned from what was left of his face to look for anything useful, particularly ammunition. There was a haversack heavy with ammo and food, and the soldier had fallen on his rifle. Corbin tugged gently on the butt to pull it free. The gun had a scope – an M1C! What a find! Well, it made sense

– good vantage point here for a sniper. And better for him to find it than a German.

He reached into the man's shirt and unclipped one of the dog tags to take with him. John Patrick Miller. Another John. *Kill any Germans, John Patrick?* He must have, to draw such enemy fire. Corbin crouched down near the blown-out wall to have a look: damaged buildings across the way; Panzer parked on the corner; intimidating Waffen SS pacing in a boot-length black leather coat; another tank idling below with another black uniform manning it, exposed to the waist; a dozen or more German foot soldiers – the same bunch who'd mowed down the civilians, Corbin was certain.

One good shot was all he wanted. Just one good shot. He raised the rifle and found a target, then another and another, practicing. It was a tough choice who to go for; he wanted to kill them all. But it ought to be an officer. He found the leather coat again, moved the weapon up to zero-in on the man's eye. *This is for you, John Patrick.* He took a deep breath and hesitated like he'd been taught. Then he fired. The leather coat crumpled to the ground. Impulsively, Corbin snatched his last grenade, pulled the pin and hurled the thing into the crowd. At the explosion and cries of alarm he lunged from the window.

That had to be it for this spot; any more would draw further fire to this poor family's house. He draped both rifles (nearly twenty pounds together) over a shoulder. *Well ... I've just committed murder*, he thought as he grabbed all the gear and headed for the stairs. The family hadn't moved an inch from their corner. "Shouldn't you go to the cellar? Uh ... la cave," Corbin said, pointing down.

The man shook his head. "Nous n'avons pas de cave."

No cellar? Seemed a bad thing in a war zone. Reluctantly he left them there and flew out the back door, carrying with him the indelible image of their eyes pleading with him not to go.

It was chaos on the street out front so he must have done some damage. He sprinted away in a northerly direction hugging the backs of buildings to keep from being seen. Every block or so he ducked through a door in search of another good vantage point. From the second-floor window of a crumbling row house he watched an entire truckload of armed infantry rattle down the road and wished he hadn't squandered that first grenade on a fit of emotion. He had to settle for a lone German who stepped alone into a narrow alley to urinate. In an upstairs storage room of what appeared to be a laundry, he got special satisfaction from killing two more who came along in a captured American Jeep. They looked so relaxed – driver smoking a cigarette, the other picking his nose. Corbin shot the nose-picker first, then the driver. Just two quick shots and he was gone.

He spotted a church bell tower ahead, another promising vantage point. The chunky brick tower appeared undamaged from where he stood, though it was hard to really see in the fog. He found a side door that creaked when he opened it. Inside, he paused to assess the danger. The cavernous church echoed with an empty silence. It had a Catholic look: life-sized crucifix, austere confessionals, tables covered with votive candles for offering prayers. The stairs to the bell tower were winding and narrow. He ascended them gradually, hugging a wall and leading with the M1.

It was cold at the top, and windy. The tower *had* been hit. Part of the front was gone, much of it in a pile on the stone floor, and in the rubble he found two more dead GIs. So far, the only Americans he'd seen in this town were dead ones.

On the steps out of the wind, he reclined against the wall and wolfed the bread ration he'd saved, then fished in John Patrick's haversack for something more: an unopened C ration, which meant more food and cigarettes, and two cans of tomato juice. Corbin drank one. He'd never thought much of tomato juice at home; here though, it tasted wonderful. He opened the other and drank it, too, rationalizing it was better to consume it now rather than carry it. Also from the haversack: a mess kit, lighter, pineapple pudding, Hershey bar, photos wrapped in plastic. Two dry pairs of socks!

Little thought had been given to his own poor socks, cold and heavy with river water. He replaced them with just one of the dry pairs and saved the other, imagining how Pappy would lecture him to take better care. Pappy Dutton – if only the man were here right now.

To his own haversack, Corbin added John Patrick's belongings, including for some reason the photos. Then he loaded the sniper rifle with a fresh cartridge and rejoined the lifeless GIs, stepping over the bodies as nonchalantly as the rubble. Odd to be so casually sharing space with the dead. All the bodies he'd seen at home had been tucked into coffins in church clothes to be honored and mourned. They both looked to be about his age. Had they been friends? He hoped so; there were worse things than two friends crossing over together.

He crouched beside what was left of the tower wall. This was the best vista yet; the whole town would have been visible if not for the fog. No civilians anywhere, Stavelot's terrified residents undoubtedly hiding in cellars night and day, if they had cellars. There was a U.S. Army truck on the street just below – a canvas-topped ten-wheeler just like Corbin's, except this one had a German in the driver's seat. He appeared to be alone. Through the scope, Corbin could see every pimple on the corporal's face and he watched the guy nod off every so often, jerk awake again and look guiltily around. Funny. The enemy didn't seem fierce when viewed man by man.

Corbin had planned to keep a tally of the number he killed but he'd already lost count. Hunting at home, when he got the game he came for, he quit. Here, he just kept on killing. It certainly felt right to shoot this one, steal back the truck and speed away.

"Marsch! Schnell, schnell!" A German voice.

A block away, three GIs plodded in his direction, hands in the air. They were shadowed by a rifle-toting foot soldier who seemed nervous and hardly more than a boy, bent over in concentration, white-knuckled hands wrapped around the gun.

Corbin studied the scene with the naked eye, taking stock. There was this German and the one in the truck, and down the road were more buzzing around the Jeep that had crashed into a storefront window. Better to wait, he decided, until the Americans were further from there and closer to here. The foot soldier was probably marching them to the truck. For all Corbin knew there were others tied up in there, rounded up earlier to be driven to some enemy camp. Although, the sleepy corporal seemed too relaxed for that as he stepped from the truck and sauntered toward the captives with a smile, gun aimed at his boots. The smile changed to a sneer as the distance narrowed. He was enjoying this.

Corbin raised the rifle, aligned it to catch the face of the foot soldier in the crosshairs, then over to the corporal, back and forth questioning who Pappy Dutton would shoot first. The one aiming at the GIs. He took a final bead praying the prisoners were ready to run, held his breath and let loose a clean shot. The GIs scattered as if they'd expected it while their captor folded to the ground. The surprised corporal fumbled with his gun. Corbin with a cold calm picked him off next, exhaling as the guy's chest blew apart.

Desire strong to hook up with the Americans, he grabbed his gear, took the stairs three at a time and burst out the side door. He ventured cautiously onto the street in search of friendly uniforms, half-expecting the rush of an angry enemy. Neither appeared. The truck was just sitting there so he took a chance and went for it, grateful to the Army for making them without ignition keys.

A GI came from nowhere and lunged into the other seat. "Jesus, who are you?" he blurted. "Never mind, tell me later. We need to find my friends and get the hell outta here."

"Where'd they go?"

"Cut between those buildings ... probably long gone. No, wait, there they are!" The soldier rolled down the window and whistled.

The breathless two came running and scrambled into the back. Corbin headed north while they all talked at once.

"30th Infantry Division. You?" asked the one in the front.

"106th."

"Were you the one who hosed those Krauts?"

Corbin nodded as he checked the gas gauge, grateful that it wasn't on empty.

"Hey man, thanks. You saved us from some kinda hell. I thought for sure it was John Miller."

"Well, it was in a way. His rifle anyhow."

"What do you mean?"

"I found him in an attic a few blocks south."

"Dead? Aw ... don't tell me that," the GI pleaded, smacking himself in the forehead. "He was practically my best friend." Similar sentiments came from the back.

"I'm sorry," Corbin said, realizing at once how feeble it sounded.

"I can't believe it ... John Miller. He was the best damned shot in the company. Wait'll the lieutenant hears."

"I have his dog tag and his lighter ... and his photos. I'll give them to you," Corbin offered as though it would help. "Lost my best friend yesterday so I know how it feels. Found two more dead in the church tower so you're the first live Americans I've seen. Where'd the rest disappear to?"

"Had to fall back. Outnumbered by those damned 88s. We're up there beyond those bluffs."

"Does anybody have a radio? I need to get a message to my unit."

"A radio we've got but the microphone's busted and nobody knows Morse code."

"I know Morse."

"You do? That's a lucky break. Wait'll the lieutenant hears."

The lieutenant, acting CO for the entrenched 30th Infantry Division Company, set Corbin up in a dugout with a makeshift canvas cover and put him to work as temporary radioman. "You'll be out of danger here," he said.

American reinforcements arrived, launched an attack to retake the town against a growing army of enemy tank formations. Fierce fighting continued into the night. Corbin tried his best to focus on the job while shells from both sides seemed to be bursting just outside. With every hit he braced himself, half-expecting the next one to land on him as the ground quaked and blinding flashes turned night into day. *Out of danger here?* Helpless is what he felt. If he were going to get it he'd rather be giving it back. His forced-fatherhood predicament had been forgotten the last forty-eight hours but it had blended with guilt to color his every move. Disdain for the future had turned him reckless, which could work in a soldier's favor sometimes – freeing him from a fear of dying that often paralyzed the body, stunned the mind.

With the gray morning light came air support and they soon seized control of Stavelot's northern half. When the worst was over, Corbin looked out on the devastated town through the lieutenant's field glasses. Amid pockets of smoke and flames he saw what he knew were corpses – townspeople, beasts of burden, uniformed men from both sides. And it was hard to find a building with a roof and four walls.

He devoured a can of beef stew from a proffered C ration and attempted to contact his own unit to say he was alive. But the crystals in the radio pack were solely for frequencies inside the 30th's network, so he never got through. Exhausted, he pushed the problem aside to worry about later, rested his head in his arms to take a short nap.

He was jolted awake by reports of trouble in St. Vith: Germans attacking on three sides, entire regiments trapped in an ocean of enemy armor and surrendering in droves. Alarming images of Pappy Dutton in a frontline foxhole urged him to rethink duty, and all at once his only thought was to get back to the 106th.

Looking for a way, Corbin discovered he wasn't the only displaced soldier in Stavelot when an officer from a displaced platoon collected him and a hodge-podge of others for a thrown-together contingent to St. Vith. In the afternoon he found himself traveling southeast in the rear of the truck he'd grabbed back from the enemy – part of a three-truck convoy carrying men, weapons and ammunition down the same highway he'd followed in the opposite direction two days before. Two days. Only two days since he'd watched all those Panzers rumble by on their way to Stavelot. He had chosen not to fire on the Germans then. Had it been a mistake? If he'd killed a few, maybe things would be different now – that many less to ravage the poor town, that many less to fight the rest of the war.

Amid jokes hurled around him by nervous GIs, Corbin occupied himself by taking inventory. Things weren't too bad in that department. Nobody had taken the M1C so he still had both rifles and enough ammo to work havoc. Full canteen, four pairs of socks besides the ones on his feet, ten cigarettes, matches (he needed them now, since his lighter had gone dry), eating utensils, Hershey bar, John Miller's entire C ration and part of another. He reached in the haversack for his rosary, fingered the beads without actual prayer. Then, as though moved by a need for protection, he slipped it over his head and tucked it in where the dog tags belonged. He lit a cigarette and offered one to the GI next to him who looked his way at the strike of the match.

The soldier took it. "Thanks. Shapiro ... Solomon Shapiro, 99th Infantry Division," he said in a resonant bass.

"Corbin O'Connell, 106th."

"Was that a rosary?"

Corbin nodded.

"You used it for praying?"

"Well, not just then. It takes a lot longer than that to pray a rosary. But yeah, we offer prayers to God and to the Virgin Mary."

"Can you pray what you want?"

"Uh ... sure."

Shapiro took a deep draw. "I always wondered," he said, leaning back with closed eyes, long legs folded under his chin.

In the shadows of the covered truck Corbin studied him. Everything about the guy was big – big eyes, big mouth, big hands. The cigarette had all but disappeared between his fingers, and his boots looked even bigger than Pappy's size twelves.

As the convoy approached the Kaiserbaracke Crossroads, the driver of the lead truck slowed to a crawl at the sight of a Jeep coming toward them at speed, frantic arms waving. "Germans! Moving south from Malmedy, at the crossroads any minute! Heavy metal and infantry," a voice shouted as the vehicle bolted off.

All the men heard. Somebody yelled, "Take cover!" as the trucks screeched to a halt. They grabbed weapons and ran for it with no time to plan or think or look around. Some dove for the nearest ditch. The luckier ones crossed the road and disappeared into the woods, settling behind trees, under trees, up trees. Corbin was one of them.

A few feet off the ground, balanced on a sturdy branch of an ancient oak, he heard it before he saw it – that unmistakable deep-throated diesel. The enemy came into view through the trees: a Panzer crawling with machine gun-toting troops; a truckload more of armed infantry; an armored vehicle with four men.

Before the column even halted in the road the Americans opened fire. Dodging bullets, the Germans took cover and proceeded to shoot back.

Corbin chose to focus on the tank. As he found its broadside the Panzer seemed to hesitate.

Solomon Shapiro fired a bazooka at it from the ditch and missed, blasting a hole in the side of the truck instead, along with a few Germans.

The tank turret rotated menacingly toward the ditch and the bazookaman.

Corbin zeroed-in on the tank commander. Silver buttons on a gray uniform ... lightning bolts on a collar ... pale neck ... ruddy cheek. He took a breath, hesitated, and fired. The commander's head exploded.

The Germans with their machine guns were ravaging the men in the ditch. With an eye on the Panzer, Corbin started in on the gunners. Target in the crosshairs ... inhale ... hesitate ... fire. Crosshairs ... inhale ... hesitate ... fire. Crosshairs ... inhale ... hesitate ... fire, picking them off one by one like so many metal ducks in the carnival shooting gallery back home. On his side of the road they were pulverizing trees and an occasional man. Corbin heard a grunt and turned to see a GI fall.

Bullets zinging overhead splintered the branch above. Position made! More fire, closer this time, nicked an earlobe, knocked his helmet askew. Time to move! No chance to be choosy! He leapt to a different branch and hugged the trunk, counted his heartbeats as tree fragments rained down.

Above the din, new rumbling. From another direction, muffled and indistinct, but it was there. Corbin listened, confused, trying to pick it out. Then, more distinct, the creaking and clanking of tracks. He jerked his head toward it. Two Panzers burst through tall hedges at the rear, blazing a path where there wasn't one like a pair of King Kongs.

Small-arms weapons proved no match. Men scrambled from cover, yelled warnings, frantically searched for a way to escape. It happened so fast. Corbin watched in a daze as the men soon adopted a posture of resignation, dismantled their guns and hurled the parts afar in prelude to surrender.

He wanted to run for it. He stood a good chance by himself. Wasn't it cowardly to surrender? To escape and keep on fighting seemed the braver thing. He jumped from the tree with seconds to decide. The men, clustering together now, stepped out of the woods with hands in the air. It was all the diversion

Corbin needed to dive into underbrush; now was his chance. Yet it felt wrong to hide. It suddenly felt very wrong to let others forgo freedom alone. To face the enemy with head held high now seemed braver. So he threw his weapons in the brush and came out of the trees with raised hands, stepping over dead soldiers from both sides to join the line forming on the road.

TWENTY

The prisoners captured near Kaiserbaracke Crossroads were searched for weapons and ordered to load the German wounded and dead into the American trucks, which now belonged to the enemy. In a light snow they huddled together while the Germans decided what to do with them. Then, forced to leave their own dead and dying behind, they were marched in an east and south direction toward Germany, some thirty or so men in all, the injured leaning on others for support. Solomon Shapiro, wounded in the thigh, struggled with the aid of a medic half his size until Corbin tapped the medic on the shoulder and said, "Here, let me take over for a while."

As the impotent sun showed signs of setting on this fateful day, the column halted in front of a quaint brick church with a squatty steeple and an arched front door. A sign pointing down a dirt lane beside the church said, *Cimeterie*. A French word ... French for cemetery. *Cemetery?* Corbin sneered at the absurdity. The whole place was a cemetery. Hell, from what he'd seen the last few days the whole country was a cemetery.

Shapiro withdrew his arm and stood on his own. "Thanks for being my leaning post. I was breaking Lep's back." He gestured at the medic tending the injured while he had the chance. "If he were wounded I could carry him all day long, but I'm such a big lug ..."

"He looked at your leg?"

"Yeah, treated it with antiseptic and wrapped a bandage around it."

"How's it feel?"

"Hurts."

"Well, things could be worse."

"How do you mean?"

"At least the snow has stopped, and I can think of worse things than spending the night in there." Corbin nodded at the church.

"Never been in a Christian church before. I'm Jewish ... me and Lep both are," Shapiro said, grimacing. The Jewish GIs had heard enough to harbor a separate fear. "Can't say I've been in a synagogue much either. Lep's the religious one, his father's a rabbi."

"Won't matter that you're Jewish. We'll all be in there together and they don't know one from another." Corbin adjusted his overcoat collar, stuck hands in his pockets against a biting wind and obvious temperature drop. "Wouldn't count on any heat but at least we'll be inside, grab a pew, get some sleep."

But their lodging for the night would be nothing so grand. They were soon led around back to a courtyard with a high stone wall across the way from an ancient graveyard of scattered, snow-dusted tombstones. A few from the 100th Infantry Division were already there, captured trying to escape the Front. Though strangers all, the men seemed heartened. They crowded together under a church overhang to pool their warmth and avoid standing in snow.

The men from the 100th had been stripped of all their personal belongings – food, supplies, cigarettes, extra clothing. Their lieutenant warned that haversacks and everything in them could be taken anytime, so everyone should eat now what food they possessed and stuff into pockets what they wanted to keep.

They had tales to tell of entire platoons, entire companies, even entire regiments of the 106th and 28th, surrounded by the enemy and captured. Corbin imagined a captive Pappy Dutton freezing somewhere similar. It made him feel lonely. All of this would be easier to take if he were with his friends, the men with whom he'd survived basic training and spent the last twenty months. Yet his best friend and his clerk were gone forever, the hope of finding the others, fading.

"For anybody here who's Jewish," the dark-headed lieutenant said, "better get rid of your dog tags now if you haven't already. No telling what the Krauts'll do if they see an H for Hebrew."

"That's you and me, Lep," Shapiro said. They removed their dog tags and, for lack of a better place, jammed them chains and all between the stone wall and the ground.

Corbin wondered whether the guards were Jew haters. They seemed to be hanging around the wrought-iron gate, clustering together for warmth much like their captives. They appeared as cold, fatigued, hungry, nervous and far from home as Corbin felt. Some looked to be about Jimmy's age, sixteen at most, exposed to the elements while their superiors undoubtedly lounged on church pews consuming coffee and sausages in comfort.

In the last shred of daylight Lep swabbed Shapiro's leg wound with an antiseptic. "What you really need Solly, are a few stitches, but the best I can do here is wrap this bandage tight." Lep finished and gave the leg a pat. "I know the ground's cold but you really shouldn't stand. Lying down with your leg propped up would be best, but I'll settle for sitting with it bent." He disinfected Corbin's earlobe and went to tend others.

"How's the leg feel now?" Corbin asked.

"Still hurts."

"He seems to take good care of you."

"Lep takes good care of everybody. His real name's Adam Eisen."

"Then where did Lep come from?"

"Short for Leprechaun. The guys started calling him that on account of his size and the way he looks out for everyone. His father expects him to become a rabbi but he wants to be a doctor."

As they watched, the medic skipped over one wounded man and then a second with a look of deep sadness.

"What's he doing?" Corbin asked.

"I guess they're too far gone. It kills him to do nothing and walk away but he can't waste medical supplies on guys beyond help." A medic's basic principle was to focus on the living, especially in a situation like this. No sending up the line for more supplies, no shipping the wounded off to a medical unit for better treatment. All these men had were Lep and his dwindling bag.

"Known each other long?"

"We go way back," Shapiro said, wincing as he shifted position. "Both from Brooklyn, grew up on the same street, enlisted together ..." His injury didn't stop him from talking. In a few minutes Corbin knew he had studied Agriculture in school, married his high school sweetheart, planned to take over his uncle's farm when the war was over. Now he had a pregnant wife waiting at home and actually seemed happy about it.

Corbin shared some of his story with the soft-eyed Jewish giant. Not so much the farm or Velma, but about the explosion and losing John – even about his dog tags. It felt good to tell somebody and have him understand.

Shapiro did not understand, though, not completely. More than that, he sensed a reluctance in Corbin to talk of home, so he asked no questions. He just said, "Well ... no dog tags for you either. Looks like we're in the same boat."

Corbin nodded, pondering just what boat they might be in. He opened his haversack and pulled out the C rations. "Guess we better eat these."

"Hey, you've got food. I left all my gear on the truck during the scramble."

"Well, I had this thing strapped across my chest and the Kraut who searched me didn't take it away."

Heeding the advice from the lieutenant, Corbin filled his pockets with items from his haversack: spare socks, eating utensils, Daisy's high school picture and one of the family around a Christmas tree. He felt for the empty lighter, ran a thumb over the inscription: *to CO from JO, 1941*. Of little use now, but he buried it deep in an inner pocket as a prized possession, determined to save it forever out of loyalty to John. Discreetly, he wrapped the Hershey bar in an Army-issue handkerchief and found pocket space for it, too.

The captors dished out no brutal treatment unless one counted the withholding of food and water, for the prisoners received neither. They could smell the coffee and sausage served up inside, which was torture enough. The men slept sitting up that night with their backs against each other for warmth and support in groups of two or three. Corbin fell asleep leaning on Solly Shapiro and awoke in the deepest part of night, frozen to the bone and concerned about tomorrow. A day of walking would be hard on the injured, but better that than idling here, exposed to the elements in this frozen jail.

He considered waking Lep and Solly to suggest escape. They could easily evade the careless young guards; all they had to do was scale the wall and slip into the night. But he knew they couldn't go – the wall too high an obstacle for Solly's leg, Lep unable to desert the injured. He considered escaping alone, but only for a moment. Already, after only a few hours of shared trouble, the magnet of camaraderie had grown powerful enough to trump freedom.

At a prisoner count in the morning, the two men Lep skipped over had died during the night, and there were others in questionable condition among the remaining thirty-eight. Injured men were a liability. They were worthy and blameless, but they were a liability nonetheless. The Germans refused to leave them there to be found by the Allies and patched up to fight again, so if they were still breathing they had to go with the group. Not that the others would have left them behind anyway, to trust their fate to the enemy.

Most had gotten over the initial shock of capture. They told each other they were lucky not to have been killed with the rest, lucky it happened so late in the war. Even now, nobody doubted an Allied victory; all they needed to do was hold out until then. But as they moved out with no food and nothing hot to drink, the hungry, stiff and frozen POWs harbored low expectations for the next few days and weeks.

"They've got to feed us sometime," Lep assured them. "The Geneva Convention's rules on the treatment of POWs say they must provide food, clothing and shelter."

The healthy took turns with the wounded as they marched eastward toward Germany on roads slashed by deep ruts of mud frozen solid overnight. Every so often they had to hurry to the side to make room for the enemy. Creaking Panzers, trucks carrying troops, horses pulling cannons, trucks pulling other trucks to conserve fuel – they all struggled in the frozen ruts, polluting the air with insults and diesel fumes for the POWs to hear and inhale. The convoys appeared with so little warning, it was tough to get out of the way without tripping. Other than that, things weren't so bad at first: they trusted their right to eventual food; enough of them had canteens for water; moving helped allay the cold; the guards had yet to be cruel. And they were American citizens, American military, confident in their claim to the greatest nation on earth.

Yet scenes on the roadside dimmed it all. War machines, the pride of U.S. manufacturing, sagged now in the mud like squashed prehistoric bugs – crippled, useless and in the way. Death was everywhere. Dead horses, dead civilians, hundreds of dead Americans, their frozen bodies lying like logs on the side of the road. It was hard not to trample on them.

Solly turned soft. "Those poor guys," he muttered at regular intervals. "Maybe we're lucky to be out of it. At least we're still breathing, at least we've got a chance."

One tall lanky German guard whose name seemed to be Hans, watched with sympathetic eyes, even gave Corbin and Solly an occasional unwitting smile before he caught himself and pursed his lips. They all might have been friends in another place and time.

A sign said, BLEIALF 4 km. "Are we in Germany?" Corbin wondered aloud.

Solly just shrugged, struggling now to keep up.

"I'm pretty sure Bleialf is in Germany."

It soon became clear. From the look of it, the village of Bleialf had been the center of recent large-scale fighting. Demolished military vehicles and armor from both sides clogged the roadways, stuck in the mud and abandoned in such numbers it made one doubt either side had anything left. The village itself was a snowy graveyard – the bodies of soldiers and civilians lying in doorways, hanging out windows, often piled two and three deep.

Solly forgot his pain at the sight of them. "Those poor people," he kept saying, "those poor, poor people."

But the scene only angered Corbin. All this death and dismemberment in the midst of winter's fury. Why not add a plague, an earthquake, a dam breaking nearby to produce another Johnstown flood. Wait … who's fault *was* this? God's?

No! Definitely not God's! How many horrors would disappear if man's part in it dissolved? Deep-rutted impassable roads, frigid foxholes, blown-apart bodies, bombed-out villages like this one, frostbite for lack of shelter, hunger for lack of food, and the indiscriminate fear from villagers for the destructive, pillaging, single-minded intruders in uniform. And what would remain? Just pristine villages of fireplace-heated cottages, people gazing out in relative warmth at the frozen winter landscape where silent smoke curled from chimneys into the sky. "This sure as hell isn't God's doing, none of it," Corbin mumbled under his breath.

"What?" a suffering Solly asked.

"Never mind."

As the column tramped through the battered street, villagers paused from their grisly clean-up to form an unexpected gauntlet on the road. To punish these men for what the war had dumped on their thresholds they delivered punches unfettered, shouted words the astonished GIs did not understand but took as hate-filled profanities. Hostile children spat. Then they followed the POWs into the square and dished out more of the same. The guards allowed it for a little while, then waved the civilians away like pesky picnic flies, permitting the captives to gather in peace around an armless, headless statue. The men scraped the grayish topcrust from a mound of old snow and ate handfuls of the cleaner middle. It did nothing good for body heat but there seemed no other option for water. Corbin attempted to conserve some of it for later, painstakingly pushing snow into the mouth of his dry canteen.

More POWs staggered through the gauntlet, this group larger in number, as many as fifty. Most seemed to be from the 28th. They were like the others – hungry, thirsty, fatigued from carrying their wounded. But their captors appeared to be of a different order. One in particular, a slovenly low-ranking officer, joyfully assisted the townspeople by beating his captives with what looked like a peace officer's nightstick.

The two groups merged, swapping quips as they looked for friends. Hot drink and food were on every mind, though where it would come from in all this ruin nobody knew. They soon set off again, buoyed somewhat by their increased numbers and shared situation. Many from the second group were wounded, some supported between two men, a few on stretchers carried by four.

In the gray mid-afternoon the route became hilly and slower-going. At the high point they could see far across the valley and what they saw made them queasy. Thousands more just like them stretched out on a web of roads below – line upon line of uniformed men, five and six abreast, marching east on German soil. From the look of it, half the U.S. Army must have been captured by the Nazis. The men just stood in their tracks and gawked, hopes of a round-the-corner Allied victory blasted with a glance. This unscheduled halt was fine with the jubilant guards who celebrated the scene with slaps on the back. They took it as a sign of renewed German superiority, which expanded even further the slovenly officer's imagined right to be cruel.

His name was Lance Corporal Wetzel but he was Weasel to the men. "Schwein! Faule Schweine!", he'd bellow in banal repetition, flogging with the nightstick whoever was near. Corbin had a run-in himself with that nightstick merely for stepping out of line to urinate on the side of the road

– sobering evidence that even the most basic of life's choices were no longer his.

They marched for hours without a break, feet screaming at them to be let out of their boots. Anyone who slowed too much felt the point of a gun. As the sun sank low, every step became a struggle for Solly, dragging heavily on Corbin in order to keep up.

Near Prum, Germany they were corralled for the night with other POWs in a warehouse with a cold cement floor and high broken windows. It was too dark to look for familiar faces. All they wanted to do anyway was eat, drink, and rest. But nothing was offered, not even water. Corbin traded his wet socks for dry – the one positive thing he could still do for his health.

Weasel hung around, evidently preferring to harass the prisoners rather than rest with the other guards. Armed with nightstick and flashlight he weaved through groups of men, barking, "Stille, du Schwein! Den Mund halten!" (Silence, you pigs! No talking!), whether they were talking or not. As he aimed the harsh light into sleepy faces he chose to torment some and bypass others, advertising to the world that he liked to pick on Jews.

At dawn the next day, December 21, while Lep hurried to change Solly's bandage, a gray-uniformed German lieutenant stood on an overturned crate, clapped his hands to grab attention and spoke in accented English. "There are many hours of walking ahead. You are to leave your wounded here. They will be well-treated." That was all – no mention of food or drink.

"You can't stay here," Lep whispered to Solly. "No telling what'll happen to you if you do."

"Yeah, you need to walk outta this place without any help," Corbin said. "And they might be watching, so try not to limp. Once we're on the road it won't matter so much."

They were soon rousted out and ordered to march further east, doing so with burdens lighter and hearts heavier from leaving behind the stretchered men. As a fresh snow fell they joined more POWs, and more after that. Led by stolen American Jeeps and trailed by creaking German trucks, their column seemed to stretch for a mile.

"Look how many there are of us," Corbin whispered, assessing what appeared to be hundreds behind and as many ahead. "Must be close to a thousand. Why don't we do something?"

"Because they've got the guns," Solly said. "Be patient. They might have the upper hand now but not for long. We just need to hang on til it's over."

"We could rush them."

"Somebody would get shot."

"Yeah, but then others could grab the weapons."

"Are you volunteering to be the one that gets shot?"

"Well ..."

"Forget it. A revolt like that would take planning."

"That's why they don't want us to talk."

The snow soon stopped and a veiled sun raised the temperature. Ahead, on the abutment of a bridge, water flowed down in a steady stream from melting snow. Thirsty men were bunching up to gather some of it in canteens and cupped hands. Many succeeded before Weasel noticed, but the timing was bad for Corbin and Solly who had just stepped in with their canteens.

Giddy with power, Weasel jumped from a Jeep and hurled himself into the knot, screaming, "Schwein! Faule Schweine!" With swings of the nightstick he flogged every man in reach – first Solly, then Corbin, then Solly, then another man, then Solly and so on until he was out of breath. Chest heaving, eyes cold as steel and wanting more, he snatched every canteen in sight, tossed his spoils in the Jeep and rode away.

"Are you okay? I can't believe what I just saw!" Lep croaked in a loud whisper. "That man just broke every rule of the Geneva Convention!"

"I doubt a guy like Weasel cares about the Geneva Convention," said the placid Solly who walked away with a myriad of upper-body contusions. Corbin was in better shape, just an aching head and fat lip, but his mind was plagued by gloomy images of a future with no canteen.

They marched all day without food, water or rest – footing it at the pace of the better-fed guards who climbed in vehicles every two hours to ride. There was a noticeable difference now in Hans whenever Weasel was around. "Stille! Den Mund halten!" he'd say, parroting the older, meaner man as he swung the butt of his rifle like a club. But he never touched them.

Constant motion had the one advantage of keeping away the cold, yet as the winter sun slipped behind a distant tree line and disappeared below the horizon, it abandoned the men to plunging temperatures and set them adrift in the dark. Some tucked icy hands into armpits and walked that way for miles. If they'd wanted to revolt they should have done so earlier. Now all they could do was stumble along, each trying to ignore the bone-chilling cold and condition of his feet as he blindly followed the man in front of him – as empty of any other purpose as a line of Gil O'Connell's cows trailing to the barn.

It was late when they arrived near the railhead in Gerolstein, Germany. There would be no food or water and they were to spend the night out in the elements, yet they almost did not care. They were all so tired ... so very, very tired. Lep managed to change the bandage on Solly's thigh but he was waved away when he tried to check Solly's back and shoulders for lacerations and treat Corbin's throbbing lip with a dab of antiseptic. Rest was what mattered most. The three pooled their overcoats in order to sleep, spreading one on the frozen ground to lie on, with the other two draped over them against the cold.

Sometime during the night the fog yielded. The sun rose in the morning amid scant puffs of cloud and wintry blue sky. Food was finally handed out – a chunk of bread and portion of foul-smelling cheese. They were given water, too. Though, without canteens, they had to collect it in their helmets.

At the rail station, Germans with snarling police dogs guarded a thousand or more frowsy Americans with three-day beards – men from the 28th, the 42nd, the 100th, the 106th and more. Long trains waited in the sunshine but they didn't look like passenger trains. These were reddish-brown boxcars, more for cattle or freight. Corbin eyed them warily. He searched in a sea of Golden Lions for Pappy or any familiar face, trying to find them for his sake but hoping he didn't for theirs.

When boarding began he might have seen Pappy climb into a car down the tracks, but he couldn't be sure. The captives from Kaiserbaracke Crossroads were forming into a tight bunch in an effort to stay together, stepping up three and four at a time into boxcar number 5531. They all fit in there, and many more besides, ignorant of the impending ordeal. Relief was what they felt at that moment; wherever they were going, it would be such a comfort to ride.

But the reality surfaced when the doors rumbled shut and the heavy steel latch slammed home, and they knew they'd be locked in there until somebody let them out, and they saw they were packed like cattle with no room for all to lie down at the same time, or even to sit at the same time. The reality surfaced as the steam locomotive chugged out of the station piercing the relative silence with a shrill whistle, and they wondered where they were going, and they hoped the trip would not take long. And the reality surfaced when they realized they could not control the where, the how long, or anything else anymore.

TWENTY-ONE

The boxcar smelled like cattle. For an aching moment it carried Corbin back to the farm. He never expected to be sentimental about manure, but all of a sudden he wanted to be shoveling it at home. Tiny wire-covered windows sat high on each corner, too small to escape through but big enough to let in light and air. An empty five-gallon lard bucket had been placed in the middle of the car for what they presumed was the latrine. The dung-caked floor had been spread over with a layer of fresh straw; that was something at least.

They recovered enough after the initial shock to try and make the best of things. The odor brought ribald remarks about the shitty Krauts, shitty trip, shitty accommodations, shitty Army, shitty predicament, and what would soon be a shitty latrine. Crude jokes emerged about their captors in general and Weasel in particular, their substandard breakfast, the war, the lousy weather, each other. Crude jokes – the oft-used antidote for fear.

Suggestions were made to improve things: *we should move the latrine; yeah, move it under a window; no, the corner by the door so it can be emptied easier; let's do it now before it gets full.* Options were limited but it helped to take some action, even in this severely restricted world, or perhaps especially. Lep said the wounded should be given a little extra room and be put together so he could keep a watchful eye. It took further shuffling but they did it.

Cramped quarters required the worn-out men to sleep in shifts, lying against each other like spoons in a drawer to conserve space and warmth. But by nightfall the boxcar was freezing. The only guys who felt any warmth were the ones in the middle. By this time the smell of cow manure had vanished under the reek of human waste from the steaming lard bucket. Arguments erupted among the sleepy men about where and how to urinate and defecate, and how often. Somebody desperately suggested they pee out a window but the windows were too high. A rule was then set to do it on the floor of the latrine corner and use the brimming lard bucket exclusively for the other.

By morning, December 23, the odor was beyond imagining and by afternoon they had run out of adjectives to describe the stench. As the hours ticked by it clung to clothes and hands, penetrated every pore until it could be felt on the skin, invaded dry mouths and nasal passages until it could be tasted. Yet they had no water to wash it away. Men with canteens had long since drained them dry.

In the afternoon the train pulled into a rail station and stopped. The change waked those asleep. They all grew quiet and stared at the door, waiting. These men, pride of their nation, well-fed and cocky just four days before, now merely hoped for the door to open, hoped to be let out, hoped at least for water and an empty lard bucket.

The men by the windows saw guards run from the train into an adjacent field. They all heard the sound then – the drone of low-flying aircraft in the distance.

"Is it us or them?"

Then the wail of air-raid sirens.

"Looks like a pack of P-47s! It's us! It's us!" There was jubilation in the heart of every man. Americans right above them! Fighting Americans, powerful Americans here with them in Germany!

But then machine-gun fire.

More machine-gun fire.

"God, they're attacking the train! Our guys are attacking the train!"

More firing, then an explosion – a bone-shaking, ear-splitting explosion as the strafing hit something big like a locomotive or boxcar full of munitions.

"Wave something, wave something! Get their attention!"

Frantically they ripped the wire from the windows and waved anything at hand – arms, gloves, handkerchiefs.

They were animals in a trap.

"An SOS! We need to send an SOS!"

Corbin tripped over men to get to a window. "I need something to reflect light!" he screamed. He unbuckled his watchband, held the watch out the window, angled its face to catch the sun. Then he rocked the watchface back and forth, flashing the light in the familiar Morse pattern for SOS – three fast, three slow, three fast.

Ground shooting added to the din as German anti-aircraft fired back. The men could do nothing but cower against each other.

Another explosion. This one rattled the boxcar so much it seemed ready to fall apart. Another one, further away.

Then it was over.

One boxcar had been hit, half the GIs in it wounded or dead. Those in boxcar 5531 were only shaken, left to wonder if the P-47s had been chased away by ground fire or whether their desperate signals had been seen from the air. They counted themselves lucky to have survived this time and knew it could happen again. The Allies bombed and strafed all forms of German transportation in an attempt to immobilize the enemy, and these boxcars had not been marked in any way to signify human cargo rather than freight. Odd to be the inadvertent target of one's own side – cheering them on in principle while screaming, "No! Not us! Not us!"

The need for water, food, and fresh air had been momentarily forgotten in the chaos, but as the train rumbled again through the winter-barren countryside the need returned with a vengeance. The best the men could do was try to sleep. Corbin kept seeing images of his trip to Washington on the eve of Pearl Harbor – sweet ones of John and Pop Ott that made his heart ache; shining ones, more like a fantasy now, of cushiony coach seats, white-tableclothed dining car, happy GIs he'd watched and envied. A lifetime ago.

They had a second scare after dark. High-altitude planes dropped bombs on another rail station while the train sat there. Probably the British this time; Americans bombed and strafed in the daytime, the Brits at night. The bursts lit up the place enough to show faces full of fear. Nobody said anything. They just stared at each other in the bomb flashes and prayed.

Falling snow blew in the windows of the boxcar that night and gathered on top. The next day it melted in the sun, dripped for hours between the roof boards at a brutally slow pace, but steady. Lep claimed one of the more fruitful drips for the wounded and caught the water in a mess-kit cup. Icicles forming at the windows caused squabbles over how long to let them get before breaking them off like popsicles. As a source of water they didn't add up to much, just enough to soothe lips, relieve cesspool mouths for a little while.

In the afternoon the train stopped at a rail hub and the Germans actually opened the doors. Beams of bright light hurt every pair of eyes. Two POWs were ordered to empty the reeking lard bucket, and an aging couple brought two pails of clean water and a sack of coarse black bread! Whether they'd been directed to do so by the Germans or risked punishment to perform a kindness on Christmas Eve, the men would never know. But they thanked the man and woman again and again. "Danke, Danke, Danke," they chorused, some with tears in their eyes. Per man, the amount of bread and water was small, but it was something.

No bombing that night or the next day. The men wondered if a deliberate cease-fire had been called for the twenty-four hour period. In honor of the day they sang Christmas carols. A few offered prayers. In the spirit of the moment, though it wasn't a Friday night and he had no candles, Lep recited in English the Shabbas prayer he had heard his mother say in Hebrew a thousand times:

"Blessed are You, Lord our God, King of the universe, Who has made us holy through His commandments and commanded us to kindle the Sabbath light."

They reminisced and longed for home. They guessed at the probable packages waiting in an Army mail depot somewhere. They talked of family and the feasts they'd shared before the war, before rationing, when tables sagged with meat, side dishes and every delicacy. Despite their hunger they enjoyed discussing the food, topping each other with vivid descriptions of favorite dishes from recipes handed down.

Corbin wondered whether Jimmy had bagged the turkey this year, and how big it was. He pictured his father carving a perfect bird from his place at the table. He saw mashed potatoes, corn pudding, yeast rolls and pumpkin pie, a table so crowded with platters and bowls that they bumped against each other hiding his mother's best linen tablecloth.

In musings of home he tried not to think about the woman he wanted and couldn't have, or the woman he had and didn't want. He suddenly remembered the unsent reply to Velma buried in his duffle bag in Vielsalm, and knew among his mail would be worried letters from her. *Ye gods, what must she think of me?* He guessed at the contents of the Christmas box from his mother and, with deep concern, wondered what the family had heard – whether they'd gotten a telegram, what it said if one had come.

He felt for the chocolate bar. It had softened from the warmth of his body and rehardened a few times in the cold until it had become flat and misshapen. Part of him wanted to keep on hoarding it for a more desperate time, yet what could be more desperate than being trapped in this rolling hell on Christmas Day. He removed it from an overcoat pocket and cradled it lovingly in his hands. The Hershey paper was intact, the whole thing still wrapped in the clean handkerchief that had, in itself, become precious. He banged the bar against the splintery wood wall until it broke into tiny pieces, smoothed the handkerchief out on his lap and gently opened the bar onto it, careful not to let even one beautiful morsel fall on the filthy floor. There wasn't enough for every man but Corbin handed it out as far as it would go, saving the last sliver for himself. He placed it in his mouth and let it melt slowly on his tongue to relish the sweetness of it, the creaminess of it in a moment of ease and luxury. Then, to prolong this brief escape from entrapment, he brought the paper wrapper carefully to his lips and licked off every trace of chocolate dust.

The day after Christmas, all of a sudden, they were there. The train pulled into a station and the doors rumbled open to guards standing watch. "Raus! Raus! Schnell!" they ordered, in such a big hurry to get them out after cooping them up for days. The men from boxcar 5531 had to shield their eyes as they stumbled down to the platform. Blending in with the other dry-mouthed, hungry POWs they stood in the cold while guards took a count and organized them in loose groups of a hundred.

The sign on the station building said BAD ORB.

"Bad Orb? What kind of name is that?" Solly asked.

"Bad means bath," Lep said. "Must be some sort of hot springs here."

There was a Coca-Cola sign. Corbin stared at it with eyes narrowed in resentment. Considering what was happening here, considering that the Germans had started this war in the first place, it riled him to see so prominently displayed on a German building a sign so very American.

In a light snow they tramped wearily east through Bad Orb, a small mountain village decorated with Christmas wreaths and garland. Civilians stopped what they were doing and drifted into groups to watch. The prison camp sat high on a hill three miles or so from the rail station. A climb that would have been nothing a few days ago, now seemed like Mt. Everest. Up ahead, Corbin was certain he saw Pappy in a cluster of men from the 106th. He let out a weak laugh and pointed. "Hey, I see a guy I know up there."

"Yeah? Where?" Solly asked.

"On the curve. I'm sorry as hell he was captured but I gotta admit ... it'll be good to be with him again. Wait'll you meet Pappy Dutton," Corbin said with as much enthusiasm as he could manage. "Best damned soldier in this man's Army ... a cracker-jack shot with a rifle."

"You're not bad yourself."

"Yeah, but nothing like him. They finally wised up and made him a sniper."

On the entrance of an imposing barbed-wire enclosure, a sign in bold white letters said "M. Stammlager IX-B."

"Stammlager. What the hell does that mean?" Solly asked.

"I don't think it means 'welcome,'" Corbin said.

"I'm guessing POW camp," Lep said.

They shuffled through the heavily guarded gate, then another gate, and another. The in-processing took hours while thirst and hunger raged. The men ate snow and stamped frozen feet waiting in line in front of tables where other POWs served as clerks. Corbin searched unsuccessfully for Pappy in the crush of nearby men. When it was Solly's turn a young GI with blond hair and red eyes recorded his name, rank, serial number and hometown address on a ledger. Then he asked, "What's your religion?" and Solly hesitated.

Corbin whispered, "You don't have to answer that."

"No sense denying it. With a name like Shapiro everybody knows I'm Jewish."

The clerk put up a hand. "Never mind, I'm gonna put Protestant. I'm putting down Protestant for Jews."

"Thanks," Solly said. "How's the chow here? We haven't eaten in days."

"Just like home," the clerk said, rolling watery eyes, "but don't study it too much."

When it was his turn Corbin asked, "Why do they want the home address?"

"They send postcards telling our families we're POWs."

"Boy, that's a relief. Better for them to know we're in here than to think we're dead. Why the *religion* question?"

The clerk nodded at a pair of guards and dropped his voice. "Beats me. They just told us we had to get it."

Corbin shrugged. "Okay then, I got nothing to hide. I'm Catholic."

The clerk rubbed at his eyes and pretended to study the ledger until the guards moved on. "Well, I'm gonna put Protestant for you, too. The Germans don't seem to like Catholics much either."

Their first meal would have been dinner for the pigs on the O'Connell farm, but there was nothing for the hungry men to do but eat what Corbin guessed was a conglomeration of turnip tops, carrots and sugar beets. At least it was something; at least it was hot. And the mealtime assembly produced a brief reunion that began with a rush from behind, a pull at his elbow and a hearty, "Hey, Spuds!" There was no mistaking Pappy's voice.

"Damn, it's good to see you!" Corbin crowed with more genuine joy than he'd felt since the ocean voyage.

"How'd *you* get here?" Pappy said. "I thought you'd be safe and sound in Vielsalm."

"That's a story for another day."

"What about John?"

"John's dead." The words landed with a thud.

"Oh," Pappy said with a dispassionate nod.

Corbin assumed, since they were both imprisoned here, that he could see all he wanted of Pappy Dutton. But there was a basic truth he had yet to fully grasp: nothing was likely to go his way until after the war. Just a day after finding Pappy, Corbin lost him again when Commissioned Officers and Non-Coms were rounded up and moved to a section of camp on the other side of a barbed-wire fence. Lep was taken away to work at the Krankenhaus (hospital) and assigned to barracks 23, the nearest housing.

The prison camp itself was cut into heavy woods as if the location had been purposely chosen to isolate occupants from the outside world and hide from view what went on there. Inside the compound a collection of one-story buildings sprawled, each divided into two barracks with a latrine in the middle. Some actually had bunks, others just straw on the floor.

Corbin and Solly were placed in Barracks 26. At first glance they judged it as not too bad: rows of three-tier bunks, wood-burning stove in the center. A longer analysis revealed not enough bunks to go around; the daily wood ration only enough for an hour of heat; the latrine a cold water tap and a hole emptying into a stinking cesspool. Still, anything was improvement over the train.

They often got to see Lep at meal time. The kitchen was down the hill and they all walked down there carrying little pots they were given. Not everybody got a pot, but Corbin and Solly and Lep each had one, and they learned to eat without analysis whatever the kitchen help put in there.

Bread groups were soon formed – six men to a group – each group given a loaf of bread a day to share. Corbin was the official bread cutter in his group because everybody trusted him, and he owned a mess-kit knife. While the others watched, he would spread out his handkerchief, set the bread on it and try his best to cut the thing into six equal shares.

The POWs got organized and elected a fellow soldier to be spokesman, one who spoke good German and knew as well as Lep the Geneva Convention's *Rules and Rights Regarding the Treatment of Prisoners of War*. Everyone hoped the spokesman would improve conditions by standing up for their rights with Camp Commandant Seiber – a remote shadowy figure with a thin mustache seen walking through camp trailed by an entourage of guards. But the Germans here seemed as ignorant of the Geneva Convention as Weasel had been; it might as well have been written in the snow for all the weight it carried. Harsh reprisals, insufficient food and heat, no toilet paper, no change of clothing, no way to keep clean, no letters or packages from home.

And the Germans appeared unduly preoccupied with counting. Morning and night, despite the cold, no matter how deep the snow, the men stood outside in the square to be counted and recounted in a ritual the captors called "Appell". Sometimes it took hours when the count came out wrong, or when junior guards with clubs got carried away delivering blows for infractions minor and imaginary. All the POWs could do was stand there and take it, though the guards' delight in their own power soon became pitifully transparent. It seemed, the lower their mentality the greater their delight, rendering them less fearsome in the captives' eyes.

The cold and lack of food were the biggest threats, spurring the men to inventiveness in order to survive. Bunks and blankets were scarce so Corbin and Solly doubled-up. Their mattress was simple ticking stuffed with straw and lice and bedbugs, but at least it was off the floor, which was better than some. The two slept in overcoats and combat boots for the extra warmth and to keep them from being stolen. On a walk to the kitchen they found a cluster of dead oak leaves with four acorns on it. They stuffed the leaves in the mattress and ate the acorns after roasting them on the wood stove. They saved the twigs for ... they weren't sure what. Then a day or two later Corbin found himself chewing on one of the twigs and ended up using it to clean his teeth. Solly told him he was gritting his teeth at night. Had he always done that?

Corbin had managed to hang onto five pairs of socks and continued to rotate them regularly, so his feet were in decent shape. Solly on the other hand was limping a good bit and, as far as Corbin knew, had not removed his boots since the capture. "How are your feet?" he asked. "You got any extra socks?"

"Nope."

Corbin dug in the pocket of his overcoat for his cleanest pair and tossed them to Solly. They were both shocked to see how bad his feet looked.

"They're in the early stages of frostbite," Lep said later. "It's important to stay off them as much as possible and keep 'em warm. Wear double socks if you can manage."

Staying off them was no problem. Except for the hated Appells and getting stuck occasionally with cleaning the latrine cesspool, they just huddled in the bunk all day with the blanket wrapped around their shoulders trying to keep warm. Corbin gave Solly another pair of socks so they each had three.

They had time to talk and dream of better days. They talked most about eating. They talked of home, or at least Solly did. They talked of women, cars, football. They talked of the latest Allied invasion rumor and what they'd do at the end of the war. To pass the time, any subject was fair game. Out of the blue one day, Solly said, "So ... tell me again what made you throw your dog tags back in the burning Jeep."

Corbin gave him a frowning stare and then shrugged. "Well, it wasn't planned. I just did it without thinking. A knee-jerk reaction, I guess, to seeing John get it like that. Ought to have been me instead of him." He laid out the details in a vapid voice, loading himself down with all the blame. "John was the one with all the reasons to go home, and now he never will."

"What do you mean, 'the one with all the reasons'? You've got reasons to go home." Solly hesitated and added doubtfully, "don't you?"

"Yeah, I've got reasons, all of them bad."

"Hmm, I can't let a remark like that go unexplained."

Corbin held a phantom cigarette between thumb and finger, resisted the urge to take a pretend puff by rubbing his hands together. At that moment, above everything, he longed for a smoke.

"Come on, what did you mean?" Solly persisted, having sensed numerous times Corbin's reluctance to talk of home.

"Only if you find us some cigarettes."

"You're kidding, right?"

"Nope."

Solly sighed, crawled off the bunk and hobbled out of the barracks. He came back ten minutes later with two.

"How the hell did you manage that?"

"Never mind."

Corbin held the treasure to his nose just to smell it, then lit it and inhaled. "Ah, that's good."

"So tell me."

Required now to open up, Corbin tilted his head in resignation. "Well, for one thing, it'll be rough going back without John."

"Yeah."

"Pop expects me to work the family farm. And more than that ... I have a girlfriend waiting to drag me to the altar, and since she's pregnant with my kid I can't say *No* anymore." He held up a hand to Solly's confused face. "I know, I know ... you don't understand since you *want* to work your uncle's farm and you love your wife. But you asked and I'm just telling you."

"I take it you don't love this girlfriend."

"It's worse than that. I love somebody else."

"The one in the photograph?" Solly had seen Corbin gazing at pictures from home – one of his family and the other of a knockout, dark-haired girl he'd never been willing to discuss.

Corbin nodded.

"Boy that's rough. I can't imagine having to marry somebody besides Helen."

It had been days since Corbin had given serious thought to any of it. He stared at Solly through cigarette smoke. "Well, count yourself lucky," he said, eyes turning sad and dull as he faced it afresh.

A heavy silence developed between them that made Solly squirm. It took him a few uncomfortable seconds to fill it with something. "Uh ... how many acres does your family own?"

"Changing the subject ... wise move," Corbin said, scratching his jaw. "Four hundred, give or take. Don't look so surprised, we don't farm all of it. Half of it's in forest."

"And you're going to inherit all that?"

"Yeah, me and my brother."

"Boy, count *yourself* lucky on that score. I'm happy to get Uncle Jeb's eighty. Your father must own a tractor with all that land."

"Sure he does. He bought a new Harvester in '39, paid six hundred dollars for it."

"A Harvester's what I want some day, and a cultivator. Uncle Jeb wrote and said the new ones are dandies, except they don't have rubber wheels because of the war. He's getting greater yield per acre with the new fertilizers. And the new feed formulas are something to behold – hens lay more eggs, cows make more milk. Hell, Corbin, with all this modern stuff it's a great time to be a farmer."

"If you say so. I gotta admit ... the idea doesn't seem so horrible right now. I guess I just miss home like everybody else."

Cigarettes could be had in a trade for anyone willing to sacrifice something of value. After fighting the urge for days, Corbin gave in and traded his mess-kit spoon to a fast-talking Italian New Yorker for nine Lucky Strikes. Then he regretted it when the cigarettes were gone and he had no spoon. He still had the lighter. Zippos were American-made, reliable, and desired by the Germans, so he could have traded it to a guard for several packs of cigarettes or something equally good. But he knew the regret he'd feel would be ten times worse than regret over the spoon.

As bad as things were, at least the POWs knew the routine; it was the not knowing that had been the worst. Most were resigned now to accept their fate and simply wait out the war. Looking at it that way, things weren't really so bad. And Corbin was content in the belief that, no matter what the Army had concluded when they found the Jeep, his mother would get the postcard and know he was in here.

TWENTY-TWO

B ut it would take months for the countless POW postcards from all over Germany to weave through enemy
channels, travel through enemy land, and cross the
ocean to the United States. Veneered over the devastation of
war was the confusion of war – the delayed, lost and wrong
information that was, in its own way, nearly as damaging as
bullets flying at the front.

The people in Judson had carried on with cheerless celebrations through the end of 1944, prayed the next year would be
better while they sang *Auld Lang Syne.* The rush of military
production continued into 1945. For the folks at home idle
time was the enemy, making room for worry and doubt.

In the O'Connell household Jimmy was persistently optimistic by himself. Opal immersed herself in winter chores,
finished a new quilt for her older son's bed and kept his room
dusted for the day he came home. She never let on but the
worry was always there: Corbin in a foxhole, in a hospital
wounded, lying dead in a frozen field. The family never spoke
of such things; to do so would only give them substance.
When they did mention Corbin it was generally about what
they'd do when he got home. Yet Opal saw her worry reflected
in Gil's eyes and picked up on his melancholy moods – vex-
ation that his son had enlisted, regret that they'd parted on
uneasy terms.

George Ottinger, seeing an end to war-time contracts, was busily planning a transition of his existing factories back to peacetime, as well as a plunge into the new territory of plastics production and molding – an area considered speculative by some.

Daisy buried herself in work to keep busy, spending such long hours at the market that her father relinquished to her much of the responsibility for the accounts and the ordering. She filled her calendar with USO duty, first-aid training at the Red Cross, and practiced the piano with a frenzy at home. She tried her best to ignore the goings-on of Ezra Knox but her office above the market looked right down into the street, so his every movement caught her eye.

Unlike Daisy, Velma had made a clean break of her worries. Her romantic focus had recently shifted to a handsome Army Air Corps flight instructor she'd met at the USO on New Year's Eve.

The morning of the telegrams brought snow, a heavy wet blanket that collected on sidewalks, turned quickly to slush on the streets. Ezra had already been out once to deliver cables, all of them innocuous, all a short walk. By noon it looked like the snow had ended so he went out to shovel the front sidewalk, propping the door open to stay within earshot of the teleprinter. It buzzed halfway through the job. When it buzzed again five minutes later he leaned the shovel against the building and went inside. He stretched out the dangling coil and gave it a cursory glance. Two, both from the War Department. His heart pounded as it always did getting anything from WD.

Ottinger! The pounding spread to his brain as the name jumped out:

MR & MRS G OTTINGER: WE REGRET TO INFORM
YOU THAT YOUR SON, JOHN JAMES OTTINGER,
HAS BEEN MISSING IN BELGIUM SINCE 18 DEC
1944 AND IS PRESUMED DEAD ....

He felt sick. He invariably felt sick reading something like
this. By now he should have acquired a healthy professional
detachment but his had never quite developed. Nor would
it, functioning as human intermediary between disaster and
his friends. With a deep breath he tore off the message and
steeled himself to read the second:

MR & MRS G O'CONNELL: WE REGRET TO INFORM
YOU THAT YOUR SON, CORBIN LEE O'CONNELL,
HAS BEEN MISSING IN BELGIUM SINCE 18 DEC
1944 AND IS PRESUMED DEAD ....

Both of them! Paralyzed with sadness he sank down on
a chair. In his experience *presumed dead* meant *dead*. He sat
with his head in his hands for a full ten minutes, in no hurry
to move. One thing he'd learned on this job: when it came to
bad tidings there was always plenty of time. Delay in fact was
often merciful. Let the parents have another thirty minutes of
ignorance, even another hour. They'd be forced to deal with it
the rest of their lives, so the extra time was a gift.

But, Daisy! She showed up at all hours. She could pop in
right now with a can of something and here he'd be – unable
to tell her and ill-equipped to hide the truth. All thumbs, he
hurriedly prepared the telegrams, donned his black hat and
coat and whisked out to the car.

He decided on Ottinger Industries rather than the Ottinger estate so he could hand the telegram to George. As hard as
it was to tell fathers, telling mothers was so much worse. Well,

he never actually told anybody anything. All he ever did was hand over the envelope, let his eyes say everything and walk away. People needed space and privacy; Ezra could at least give them that. Plus, he so disliked intruding on grief. George Ottinger had to be called to his office from somewhere deep in the factory to accept his envelope, which he did with stoic dignity for the few seconds it took Ezra to leave.

The O'Connell delivery was another matter. The sun had drifted far enough into the western sky to aggravate him through the windshield. He lowered the visor to block the glare. At the farm it glistened on the snowy fields, bounced off rooftops, melted buildup on the fences into steady drips and nearly blinded him as he bumped up the half-mile road.

He had hoped to hand the telegram to Gilford but it was Opal who stepped out on the porch. She stood there without a coat, arms hugging her body for warmth while he got out of the car. The situation could not have been worse – Gil nowhere in sight, Opal with a heart-wrenchingly unaware smile. As he climbed the steps, black hat in hand, the smile disappeared. She searched his face with fearful eyes. When he reached in a pocket for the envelope and held it out, she sank to her knees and yelled, "Gil! Gil!"

There'd be no gentle exit here. The only thing to do was help her into the house, point out the "presumed" part and wait there with her for Gil.

Ezra returned to town visibly more stoop-shouldered than when he left, beat down emotionally, giving serious thought to retirement. Though it was hardly fair and made no real sense, every bad piece of news he delivered seemed to chip away at his humanity. He parked the car hoping to escape to the sanctuary of his apartment, at least for a few minutes, but there was to be no reprieve. From the corner of an eye he watched Daisy exit the store and angle across the street toward him carrying a can. When enough distance closed between them she studied his face with dark wary eyes. "You've just come from the west," she said.

The words hung there for a moment, then he nodded with an anguish he made no attempt to hide.

"Who was it for?"

He placed an arm on her shoulders. "Let's go inside."

"Oh, no!" She dropped the can and let it roll into the street.

Ezra opened the door and ushered her in.

"Oh God, just tell me," she said with mounting fear. "It was one of them?" Her voice was meek and childlike.

He hesitated, taking a few seconds to convey preparatory sympathy with a look.

She probably thought his hesitation cruel, unaware that the reality was worse than any imagined. "Please Ezra, just tell me," she said with heavy, exaggerated calm.

He grabbed her shoulders with firm hands. "It's not definite yet, do you hear me? It is *not* definite." Then he wrapped both arms around her and said, "But it was both of them, my dearest girl. It was both of them."

The whole town reeled at the news. Things were predictably bleak on the Ottinger estate. At the farm, Gil cried for the first time in his adult life, shoulders shaking in silent grief. Opal took to her bed for a full twenty-four hours leaving the farmhands to fend for themselves in the kitchen. Jimmy simply refused to believe.

Daisy retreated into herself, inconsolable.

A few days later on the Mutual Broadcasting System, national news analyst Cedric Foster devoted his entire program to the 106th – how the inexperienced division had been in Europe a month and Belgium only a week before being struck by "an avalanche of German steel and fire." Out of the twelve-thousand-man division, he reported, seven thousand were missing and presumed to be prisoners of war.

Seven thousand missing! This created hope. The telegrams said *presumed* dead. Maybe the boys hadn't been killed after all but were merely prisoners of war. *Merely prisoners of war*, what a phrase. But when faced with the alternative ....

"Isn't it possible that it's just a big mix-up?" Daisy asked her father.

"Sure it's possible, sure it is."

But then the two letters came. The one to the O'Connells read:

Dear Mr. and Mrs. O'Connell,
    This letter is to confirm a recent telegram informing you that your son, Corbin Lee O'Connell, 34548410, was reported missing and presumed dead in Belgium since 18 December, 1944.
    When the phrase "missing in action and presumed dead" is used, it means the status is not precisely known but in all likelihood he is dead. In your son's case, here is what we know: Corbin was one of four men who

were part of a reconnaissance mission out of Vielsalm Belgium on 17 December. They were not heard from again. On 18 December, the wreckage of their Jeep was found. It had been destroyed by enemy fire and a resultant explosion, the occupants beyond recognition or recovery. We have no reason to hope for survivors.

It is with deep regret that I have nothing more optimistic to report. I can at least assure you that his death was instantaneous; he would not have suffered or even been aware. Corbin had volunteered for the mission, and was in every way a credit to his unit. I sincerely hope you are able to find some comfort in these things. It is only because of brave men like your son that we are finally seeing an end to this horrible war against tyranny.

I extend to you my heartfelt sympathy.
Sincerely Yours,
J. A. Ulio, Major General
The Adjutant General

It was hard for anyone to be hopeful after that. Daisy drooped through each day with lackluster interest and picked at her food, reacting the way everyone expected, grateful nobody could read her mind. She felt truly bad that John had lost his life, truly sick for his parents, so truly thankful she hadn't written him about backing out of the marriage. But the other's death spawned her real grief. With Corbin, went the best part of her. She felt terribly alone.

Worse than that was the belief she was being punished. She bore her guilt silently a few days and then shared it with her father on a frigid afternoon. He was in the market storeroom putting prices on canned fruit while he consumed a hurried lunch of bologna wrapped in bread. Resting his hands on the top of the work table he listened without comment until she finished, then gave her a look of confusion and asked, "What has my Petunia done that's so terrible?"

"Isn't it obvious? Engaged to one man for two years and loving another?"

"Pretty hard on yourself, aren't you? For one thing, you had some help in that department if I recall." He shot a deliberate look into the store toward his wife. "If you learned to care more about Corbin, well ... feelings are hard to control. We can suppress them, try to talk ourselves out of them, but feelings are feelings."

"It's worse than that, Dad. I knew I was destined to make one of them unhappy. It was a terrible feeling on one hand, but I wonder now if a selfish part of me actually *enjoyed* having them both on a string."

"I see, so you think God punished you by taking them away."

She nodded, dabbing at wet cheeks with the sleeve of her sweater.

He slid a handkerchief from a pocket and handed it to her. "Let me get this straight. You believe your personal punishment was so important to God that he sacrificed the lives of two young men?"

At that, she had to smile through her tears. He chuckled and patted her on the back as she retreated into his arms, guilt tamed for the moment by his blame-releasing words.

TWENTY-THREE

January, 1945
Stammlager IX-B
Bad Orb, Germany

A t Appell on Thursday January 18, a stiff German officer made a jaw-dropping announcement: all Jewish
prisoners must be prepared the following morning to
step forward and move to separate barracks.

The men stood stunned. Nobody said a word for fear of
reprisal but the Jews were quaking inside. What could this
possibly mean? They'd heard about the corralling into ghettos
of the European Jews but it had no relevance here. They were
American citizens, American military. Whatever was happening to civilians in Europe had naught to do with them. They
hovered in groups the rest of the day and talked of little else.
The real question was: should the Jewish soldiers comply?
Everybody had an opinion:

"I was born a Jew and I'll die a Jew. It wouldn't feel right to
deny who I am."

"I'm sure as hell going to deny it. To admit it might be
suicide."

"That's ridiculous. The Germans wouldn't dare treat American soldiers that way. The Geneva Convention—"

"Enough with the sonofabitching Geneva Convention! Who's gonna stop them?"

"Yeah, who's gonna stop them?"

"They'll be afraid the news will get out. Maybe not right away but after the war ... the world will certainly hear about it after the war."

"They'll know some of us are Jews. With a name like Shapiro I don't stand a chance."

"What if they shoot us if we don't step forward?"

"What if they shoot us if we do?"

"I think we should all stick together. Either nobody steps forward or we all step forward." This from Corbin.

"They might decide to punish everybody if nobody steps forward."

"Then so be it. Let's don't make it easy for them."

That night the American spokesman spread the word that no Jew was to step forward. So at Appell the next morning when the officer gave the order, everybody stayed where they were. The Germans got angry, ordered the spokesman to Headquarters, promised harsh punishment for everyone if the Jews did not comply. Tension grew across the compound. Corbin and a few others still believed they should all stick together and be treated the same, but how was such solidarity to be orchestrated among thousands? The Jews had no choice in the end.

When the POWs filed out of the barracks into the cold gray dawn, troops with machine guns awaited them on the Appell square. After formation, the officer, considerably more intimidating now, positioned himself in front. "Alle Juden! Vortreten!" (All Jews! Step forward!) A few seconds went by in which nobody moved. "Vortreten!" The officer punctuated his words with a forward jerk of his arms. The troops aimed their guns.

Harry from Chicago and Harry from Cleveland stepped forward. Then Lep. Solly saw him do it so he stepped forward. Then two more, and more, and more. They were led away. A deep pall formed over the compound, and in the afternoon, word spread that they'd been isolated together in Barracks 32 or 33, beyond another barbed-wire wall. The Germans justified the action as nothing more than a simple policy to segregate Jews, much like America's policy to segregate Negroes. Corbin felt picked-on. Was he to lose *every* friend in this life?

In early February, Camp Commandant Seiber received orders from on-high to ship 350 prisoners by rail some 125 miles east. He was told they had to be fit for hard labor so he took it for granted they ought to be Jews, but only eighty had stepped forward in the recent attempt at segregation. The extensive pool of officers had not been tapped, nor would it ever be. Soon there would no officers left in camp. The commissioned officers had just been transferred to a POW camp in Hammelburg, and it was already in the plan to move the non-coms north within the week. Not that it mattered. Officers were not to be used to build a slave labor force like this one, not even if they were Jews.

So, only about eighty. Seemed a small number out of thousands; there had to be other Jews lurking in the ranks. A hurried campaign ensued to find them: if the name sounded Jewish it probably was; if the man looked Jewish he probably was. Don't forget the dog tags (religious affiliation was stamped there). And if a man did not have dog tags it was because he'd thrown them away, which had to mean he was either a Jew or a spy.

The POWs knew nothing of the commandant's orders, never once imagined the perilous tomorrow for 350 men. Yet the segregation of Jews had been unsettling, and when the Germans began their further separating-out, it set the whole camp on edge again.

In Barracks 26 a guard with rotting teeth singled out as Jewish the Italian New Yorker who had talked Corbin out of his spoon. Then the malodorous guard continued his stroll down the line of nervous prisoners and paused in front of Corbin. "Name?" he asked, eyes narrowed at the dark hair and stubbly beard.

"O'Connell."

The guard jabbed him with an accusing finger. "You Jude," he sneered in a rush of vile breath.

"No, I am not a Jew."

"You tags," the guard demanded, reaching in with a hand.

"No. No tags." Corbin shoved the hand away.

And just that fast, he found himself part of a growing line of other singled-out men force-marched down the hill through the snow to Headquarters.

After hours of waiting, Corbin stood in front of a moon-faced German officer behind a desk. The officer took a great yawning breath and let it out with a sigh. "Are you a Jew?" he asked, weary of covering the same ground again and again.

"No."

"You are dark enough. Maybe you are lying."

"I am not lying. A Jew with blue eyes?" Corbin tried not to show how idiotic he thought it all was.

The restless officer rapped his fingers on the desk. "Your name is O'Connell, yes?"

"Yes."

"Your mother is a Jew."

"No."

"You are Irish, yes?

"Yes."

"Then you are Catholic," the officer said with a touch of mockery. "And you have no dog tags."

"That's right."

"Perhaps you are a spy."

"I am not a spy."

"You say you are not a Jew. You say you are not a spy." The rapping on the desk speeded up. "Then you disposed of your dog tags for what reason?"

How could he answer? It had been hard enough to understand it himself, harder still to justify to a friend. To explain in a few words to this impatient German officer seemed impossible. Corbin settled for a prideful, unblinking stare in lieu of a weak reply.

Perhaps it didn't really matter. The decision had been made; it was out of his hands. Now that he was snagged in the net they would not throw him back– not when he was Catholic, not when they needed 350 men. The Germans kept at it and kept at it, adding supposed Jews, rule-breakers, known dissenters, troublemakers who'd mouthed off, and a few more Catholics, until they had enough.

They said the camp had become too crowded. They said they were resettling them to a new camp – a far-superior camp with better food and better quarters. The Germans had successfully relocated, from ghetto to death camp, millions of European Jews by offering just such soothing lies.

Thus, on February 9, after forty-five days at IX-B, Corbin, Solly and Lep trudged back down the hill to the rail station with 347 others to board a train headed they knew not where, all of them clinging to a flimsy hope that their captors told the truth. Their only real choice in any of this was between believing and not believing. Corbin's view that they should all be treated the same was finally coming to pass: from that point on, as far as the Germans were concerned, they were all to be treated as Jews.

At the site of the cattle cars lined up on the tracks they remembered with dread the journey here. This time they managed to leave space in the far corners and bunch up near the door so the yawning guards would think the car was full. It all had a pitiful familiarity – dung-caked floor, musty straw, bucket latrine. As the door rumbled shut and the train rattled east, the men thought they knew how the trip would be, but they were ignorant of much. The door would remain locked – no breaks for fresh water, bucket emptying or bread from a kindly couple. And it would take even longer to reach journey's end.

It was a hellish trip, worse than the first one, weak as they already were in body and spirit, and hungrier. At least the magnitude of the hell came gradually. They were okay at first, grateful for the extra room that required nobody to stand. If only the human body could at times like this suspend the need to eat, drink, and excrete. But hunger proved vicious by the second day and, though hunger was bad, it paled compared to thirst.

The inevitable *Ifs* began to pile up for Corbin: if he'd kept his dog tags; if he'd stayed in Vielsalm; if he hadn't been demoted; if he hadn't lost his canteen. And, oh ... if only he had stayed on the farm.

On the third day, to separate himself from the other thirst-crazed inmates and the creek of urine weaving its way across the floor, Corbin escaped to the window and peered out through rusty barbed-wire at fields of pristine snow, heavy stands of white-tipped evergreens, fresh air, freedom. With an almost unbearable longing he devoured the scene with his eyes, knowing the farm at home looked just like that in February. Such a place of wonder to find right out there, just a few feet beyond his world of horror, separated only by a collection of nailed-together boards set down on wheels.

Yet all was not wonderful out the window. Hidden behind thick trees in the distance beyond his line of sight, beyond his imagination, a larger world of horror thrived. As the train steamed further east it cut just south of the sprawling Buchenwald Concentration Camp where people from all across Europe were starved and worked to death in a stone quarry the size of a small Grand Canyon. They were dying by the hundreds every month – had been since before Corbin entered high school. Even as the forlorn GIs rumbled by, piled-up corpses awaited incineration in a crematorium.

If the men had seen it all they would have felt pity, unaware that their own destination was shockingly similar. Sub-camps had spread out from Buchenwald like leprosy and they were headed to one of them – a slave-labor sub-camp in Berga Germany, some fifty miles southeast. But they were too over-whelmed by their current horror to fathom another. All they could do was endure and pray the journey would end, fooled once more into a belief that what came next had to be better.

It was February 13 when the train pushed into the Berga Rail Station. The unloading was the same as before: the bark-ing dogs, the orders by armed guards to "Schnell! Schnell!" While the Germans conducted yet another headcount, the POWs, tongues swollen from lack of water, fell like madmen on banks of snow, shoveling handfuls into their mouths with little concern for commands.

A portion of the sub-camp became visible immediately – an ominous enclosure where hundreds of gaunt men had packed themselves against the wire fence, dressed alike in filthy blue-and-white striped uniforms that hung loosely over coat-hanger shoulders, toothpick arms. Bony hands clutching wire, pinched faces blank of expression except in the sunken eyes. It was a nightmare assembly that unnerved the pass-ers-by. Corbin gawked at them. He tried to look away but couldn't help himself. They were living cadavers, deathly-qui-et living cadavers. All they did was stare with those enormous unblinking eyes – the saddest eyes Corbin had ever seen, con-veying a depth of misery that had no limit. He did not know who they were or why they were there. He knew only that he was relieved to be marching past them, prayed their dreadful situation had nothing to do with him.

They were political prisoners – mostly from Europe, mostly Jewish – the Americans would later hear, trapped in the barbed-wire prison known unofficially as Berga One. The wretched souls watched the POWs with something akin to fascination, or as close to it as one could muster drained of all emotion, curious about these men in unrecognizable uniforms who, in spite of their exhaustion, marched with an air of pride and precision completely foreign here. The question was whether they could keep it up after a few days where they were going – their own barbed-wire prison known unofficially as Berga Two.

The bedraggled POWs were marched up a hill to a compound of five wood and tar-paper buildings, and endured another Appell standing in a frigid wind. Their first meal was hot tea and thick potato soup – the tea ersatz and bitter, the potatoes predominately rotten. But at least they were something, at least they were hot. The camp appeared to have advantages their old one lacked. It seemed to be a new compound – the smell of fresh-cut lumber from triple-decker bunks, a new outdoor sheltered latrine with a clean cold-water tap. They even got a spoon that appeared unused. "So far, this is better," Lep said and the others agreed.

They desperately craved hot showers but that was a fantasy. Corbin ran icy water into his helmet from the tap and scrubbed a pair of socks. He tried washing up with one after removing his overcoat and field jacket, but went no further than his face and neck. "To hell with this," he muttered, buttoning back into his outer garments. "It's just too damn cold."

Sleeping two to a bunk that night on mattresses of straw-filled burlap bags, they huddled together to keep warm while wind whistled through gaps in the walls. They listened to a fly-over of planes that seemed to go on and on. The British Royal Air Force Bomber Command, they would later find out, on the way to attack Dresden, Germany. And the following day it would be the U.S. Eighth Army flying over in a three-day raid that would reduce the major city to rubble.

But for all the Allied power in the skies, it was of little value in Berga. The commandant, Captain Ludwig Merz, had been ordered to provide slave labor to dig seventeen tunnels into Stone Mountain on the bank of the White Elster River. Specific orders were to dig these tunnels into the mountain about fifty meters and then spread each laterally to create an underground cavern. Nobody in Berga seemed to know what the cavern was for, but speculation pointed to an armaments factory or other war-related project the Germans were trying to hide.

A few tunnels had already been dug by slave labor from Berga One, of which there was an endless supply. This current sad collection was nearly depleted after just a short period of *Tod durch Arbeit* (death through work), a widely-practiced basic principle of "the master race". Now they had additional labor, a fresh supply from a surprising source – 350 POWs from the United States. Though it was late in the war, though the Germans knew it was lost, they were still proceeding. And one had to assume the project had priority since ultimate control of it fell with the powerful SS, under pressure to complete whatever it was by October, 1945.

The POWs' first full day at Berga began with an abrupt "Raus! Raus!", when guards opened the barracks doors and charged in with guns before the sun came up. Corbin and Solly dropped numbly from either side of the upper bunk they shared and lumbered outside with the others. All this rushing only to stand groggy and freezing for a morning Appell.

After that, tea and a slice of hard black bread.

After that, the assignment of jobs. Lep and eight other medics were singled out and set aside. No hospital here, no medical supplies, but the medics had just been freed from other work to do whatever they could with whatever they already had.

The rest were marched out of camp and across the Elster Bridge in a cutting wind. They got to the tunnels in time to watch a line of Berga One inmates stagger away after working all night. It was an unsettling notion at the very least, to be taking over for these men who were obviously driven so hard and fed so little it appeared they might not make it back to camp before they died.

Old men who spoke little or no English were foremen for the tunnel operations. One of them handed Corbin a jackhammer. It was the biggest drill he'd ever seen; the bit must have been at least six feet long. The idea seemed to be to drill holes in the tunnel's rock face where the foreman pointed. As the drill came alive, Corbin held the thing in place and pushed. It vibrated like crazy; he could feel it up and down his arms for long minutes after it stopped. When the men with jackhammers had drilled numerous holes, the foremen filled each with a sausage-shaped explosive and chased everybody out. Then the explosions, which blew chunks of rock from the wall.

Before the noise stopped echoing, before the dust had begun to settle, they were forced back in to pick up the rocks. No masks or protection for the eyes. It was impossible to see. They had to feel their way around at first, stooping down to load them by hand into a mining car until it was full. Choking on rock dust, they forced the creaking car out of the tunnel along a track to the edge of the river. The foremen demonstrated how to release a lever, which tipped the car sideways, which dumped the load into the flow. Then the men pushed the car upright again, shoved it back to the tunnel to start over. And over, and over.

It was a miserable twelve-hour shift. They trudged away coughing and covered in dust, heads down against an icy wind that slapped them in the face on the bridge. Back at camp, in desperate need of food and rest, they first had to endure the evening Appell before bread and turnip-green soup.

In the barracks the outrage began: *why are we here, we're American soldiers; this is not the right place, not the right treatment; the work is too hazardous, the work is unhealthy; it's slave labor; the Germans are breaking every rule of the Geneva Convention; do they actually expect us to share the same fate as the poor wretches in Berga One?*

They whipped themselves into a lather that night and refused to leave the barracks in the morning. But such rebellion must have been foreseen. Guards barged in with rifles to roust the men out while more guards restraining vicious German Shepherds waited outside.

TWENTY-FOUR

T he first full day in Berga proved representative of the days to follow: "Raus! Raus!", morning Appell, ersatz tea and bread, long march across the river, grueling twelve-hour shift, long march back, evening Appell, soup and bread. Dark when they left, dark when they returned, and achingly cold.

The guards marched them to the worksite each morning and then disappeared for the day, leaving them in the hands of the foremen who charged around ready to strike with a billy club or pick-axe handle any man not working fast enough or well enough, which happened often. The last thing the POWs wanted to do was *help* the Germans. Inventing ways to impede progress was their one real way to fight back, and therefore worth a few moments of pain.

Corbin's favorite form of sabotage was to occasionally break the drill bit by suddenly jerking the drill to an angle when the foreman wasn't looking. The benefits were twofold: it slowed down production while they fetched a replacement, and gave Corbin time to rest.

Sometimes at the river's edge an entire mining car filled with rock would suddenly plunge into the water and need to be fished out and placed back on the track before work could resume. And sometimes an explosive charge assembled by a POW would prove defective, go off unevenly to produce a harmless and amusing fizzle instead of a boom.

The foremen hollered every time and pounded heads. After a few days, they complained that the Americans were *idioten;* this kind of trouble started only after they arrived. But it could be said that the foremen were *idioten* to have Americans make the explosives in the first place, where every so often one could be assembled with a glob of mud mixed in.

The POWs rarely saw the camp commandant. Daily operation of Berga Two seemed to be in the hands of a Sergeant Kunz, whose normal tone of voice was a threatening growl. But that seemed to be the worst of him. Kunz supervised the guards, older men mostly, who could be almost human alone. Yet two or more together became a menace, and they obviously feared the SS because they became crude and abusive when one was around.

The main danger though was not cruel captors. It was hard labor combined with lack of food. A slice of bread and cup of something twice a day was nothing to these men, already thin and weak from two months in captivity. The evening soup was not substantial, more like a watery broth with turnip greens and unidentified lumps floating in it. They ate the evening ration in the dark with little chance to analyze it, which was probably just as well. Many were plagued with diarrhea and, in some cases, dysentery – no doubt from the sawdust in the bread and those lumps of whatever was in the soup.

Simply put, they were expending energy by the truckload without replenishing; the loss of weight and energy was daily and noticeable. When Corbin caught another GI stealing mattress straw to use for toilet paper, he ran at the guy with all his strength intending to pound him into the wall, but they both just fell exhausted on the floor.

Lep and the other medics were dropping weight as well, though without the burden of slave labor their situations weren't so dire. Survival was all coming down to calories burned and calories consumed. At home in the summer, Corbin had put in just as hard a day in the fields but he'd eaten at his mother's table three times that day, too.

On occasion, sympathetic local women slipped turnips, potatoes or apples to the GIs. So long as the SS weren't around, the guards looked the other way. Twice, Corbin had been in the right place when a kerchiefed woman in a frayed brown coat ventured near the fence with her three-wheeled cart. Both times he'd gotten a turnip and was grateful; an old turnip was better than nothing. But he ate the tough-skinned peppery root vegetable with watering eyes and a wistful heart, hoping the next time a woman reached out a hand to him there'd be a potato in it.

Eating was a constant preoccupation. Corbin soon traded his GI wristwatch to a guard for a whole loaf of bread. Back in the barracks at night the men tried to make the evening rations last as long as possible, isolating themselves to linger over them within the confines of their bunks – the closest thing they had to privacy. Waiting for sleep to come they talked of nothing but food. One soldier and then another described the first meal he intended to have when he got home. And they dreamed up fantasy recipes to try at the first opportunity, most involving some sort of pie. Solly described a kind of meat pie – a typically-male, double-crusted concoction heavy in beef and gravy, which caused all the fellows to sigh.

"Yeah, we'll have your dish for dinner," Corbin said. "And for dessert we'll have this ..." He gazed dreamfully toward the ceiling. "First, I'm gonna line a pie-plate with a ... with vanilla wafers. Then I'm gonna add a thick layer of chocolate pudding. After that some sliced bananas, then vanilla custard, blueberries, and I'll top the whole thing off with whipped-cream and chocolate shavings." And all the fellows sighed.

There were other hardships as well, and frustrations. No change of clothing for one thing. The GIs were still wearing the same uniforms, same underwear they were captured in – laboring in them, sleeping in them, even at times excreting in them. And the lice! It was hard for the men to sleep, despite their exhaustion, scratching like hounds in summer until they reached into their clothes and crushed the worst offenders one by one between thumb and finger.

But the Berga One inmates had it worse. Whenever Corbin and Solly had food detail they saw them. Food detail involved wheeling wagons filled with large empty cans down the hill morning and night to the kitchen inside Berga One, waiting for the cans to be filled, then wheeling the wagons back up. It was a frightening sight every time they went there – black-uni-formed SS troops guarding the gate with German Shepherds tugging on leashes, emaciated kitchen-workers scurrying to fill the cans fast enough to avoid punishment, foundering inmates shivering in their prison-issue pajamas at an endless Appell. Once there were lynchings! Right in front of them, right out in the open! Bodies hanging like laundry from ropes thrown over a beam in the courtyard as the GIs stood in the kitchen waiting area. Like the rest, Corbin turned away. He didn't want to see, feared what the SS would do if they caught him looking. All he wanted to do was separate himself from that horrible place, get back up the hill, back to the relative safety of Berga Two.

The whole scene was so upsetting that nobody spoke as they pulled the heavy wagons up the muddy hill, and for hours afterward they lodged few complaints, grateful for their own situation. One thing was clear: that agonizing train ride to get here had been a fitting trip to this man-made hell – vacation spot for the devil himself.

Sometimes the POWs saw the Berga One inmates at the worksite latrine. The two groups were easy to differentiate even from a distance: Berga One identical in their stripes and shaved-heads; Berga Two in military field jackets, overcoats and helmets, each with a giant white K painted on his back – K for "Kriegsgefangener", German for "prisoner of war". The difference was more than clothing at first, the average political prisoner a shivering scarecrow with eyes to the ground, shuffling hurriedly to take care of business while he had the chance. The GI by comparison was rosy-skinned, more sure-footed and alert.

Among the Berga One prisoners on a cloudy noonday were a group of new arrivals. Not yet cadaverous, not yet shuffling, they stared with open curiosity at the GIs. An eager one actually dared to angle over to Solly and speak. "Italien?" he asked.

Solly shook his head.

"Englan?"

"American."

"Amerika!" the man said, astonished. He grabbed the arm of a young inmate and dragged him over. "Englan," he said by way of introduction. "Amerika!" he said, touching Solly's arm.

"You chaps are from America?" asked the blue-eyed teenager with a bandage on his head. "What the bloody hell are you doing here?"

"You're from England?" Corbin asked with his mouth agape. "Are you military?"

England nodded. "RAF, captured in France with members of the Resistance. They think I'm a spy. It's some of my friends you've been hearing at night, flying over on their way to bomb the hell out of Dresden and elsewhere in this bloody godforsaken country. Only thing that keeps me going."

"And what about him?" Solly nodded at the other man.

"German baker from Dusseldorf."

"A German baker? What did he do to get in here?"

"Same as the rest." England waved an expansive arm. "He was born a bloody Jew."

Corbin and Solly neglected to get the names of the two men before they were chased back to the tunnel, but they would see them again. Political prisoners had an amazing grapevine despite their desperate situation, somehow getting news of what was happening on the outside: German cities bombed, the depth of Allied troop penetration – American and British from the west, Russian from the east.

The marked difference between political prisoner and POW faded noticeably every day. Soon the Americans had the same unhealthy pallor, dragged their feet, sometimes even collapsed. And after only two weeks in the tunnels they began to die. Sometimes a man was found dead in his bunk after quietly passing in his sleep. Sometimes he dropped dead at the worksite and had to be carried to the compound. And sometimes he dropped during Appell after an entire day's labor and the long march back. Wherever it happened the body was unceremoniously taken behind the barracks and dumped in a pile until the next burial detail.

Burial detail. The men dreaded it more than food detail. Everybody got stuck sooner or later with transporting a wagonload of corpses to a field outside the cemetery to bury them in the frozen ground. Callousness had begun for Corbin as early as the Stavelot bell-tower, but burial detail was grim business even with that protective shell – the stiff bodies nearly naked, stripped of their clothing by others in desperate need. The holes dug by the reluctant gravediggers were pitifully shallow, and one big hole for all the bodies was often the best they could do. With some degree of solemnity they marked the spot with dog tags on sticks and stood there a moment out of respect. Sometimes there were prayers; Corbin's Catholic sensibility required him to present his rosary and pray over the grave. Then on the walk back with rosary still in hand he continued to pray, pleading with God to allow the rest of them to live so they wouldn't be treated in such a way.

Harry from Chicago got up one morning and announced in a monotone that Harry from Cleveland was dead. The others responded with empty nods as they stumbled outside for Appell. There was no color in Berga. Death seemed everywhere in this dead of winter – no sign of life from nature for the eyes or ears, men turning withered and crushed like the leaves on the ground. Corbin ached for home and willed himself to think of it no more. But then he had nothing and that was worse.

The medics felt helpless. They had run out of supplies and it was not in their power to provide food and rest. Lep applied his own emollient in a calming hand on a shoulder, cool cloth on a feverish forehead; at least of that effective treatment he had a liberal supply. On Friday nights he led prayers to usher in the Jewish Sabbath. There were no candles to light or challah loaves to break. No chicken soup, Gefilte fish or buttered potatoes. And he recited the opening prayer long after sunset. But the men who'd practiced religion at home – not only Jews but Catholics and Protestants, too – found it comforting. Especially his closing words, which were the same every time, and his own: "Even the darkest night has an end."

Cinching his belt tighter each morning to hold up his pants, Corbin began to think of escape. If the Germans were going to work him to death he might as well run now while he still had the strength. He studied the barbed wire, questioning how he could get through it without wire-cutters. He pondered ways to get around the floodlights, calculated how long it might take to dig a tunnel under the barbed wire from the closest barracks. And he puzzled over what to do about the K on his back – whether to discard his overcoat and freeze, or risk being turned in by hostile civilians. In hushed whispers he suggested it to Solly, trusting nobody else.

"I can't go on a long walk with these feet," Solly said. "Besides, we'd be in unfamiliar territory surrounded by Germans. Just where would we go?"

Conditions were causing everybody to at least think about escape. A few actually tried it only to be captured and returned within a day or two, their bullet-ridden bodies put on display as a lesson to the rest. Then in early March, three escaped and did not return. This angered the SS lieutenant in charge, causing him to sack the innocuous Sergeant Kunz and replace him with Corporal Erwin Metz – the World War I veteran under-officer who'd been operating with spirited brutality the compound down the hill.

Corporal Metz made an instant and lasting impression in Berga Two: tall and fleshy, wire-framed glasses on a pointy nose, nasty and not very bright. The first time they saw him he bludgeoned the face of a Jewish GI with a rubber truncheon while screeching at the poor guy in German. His voice was a big surprise – a distinctive garbly voice that sounded a bit like Donald Duck, which colored the scene with an unsettling mix of amusing and macabre. In front of hundreds of men craving cigarettes, Metz pulled one from a new pack with a knowing grin, lit it with an American lighter and made an elaborate display of puffing smoke.

Things worsened with Metz in charge and the simple passage of days. At the end of a long workday when every man wanted only to return across the river to food, barracks and bunks, the guards assigned to march them back took a long time to show up. And the infernal Appells grew longer. Disguised as punishment for contrived infractions, they were nothing more than occasions for Metz to torment Jews. He seemed to love it, willing to stand in freezing rain for hours himself during ceaseless counts and recounts.

He especially liked to pick on Solly. Corbin suspected that Metz the child had been the sissy in the play yard, harassed by all the big kids. Was he now enjoying this chance to beat up the biggest kid in the Berga play yard? He had the guards to shield him; he had the gun. Maybe he wanted Solly to retaliate so he could kill him. But that was never going to happen, not with the gentle giant. Solly seemed able to tolerate any amount of pounding, and take it all with a serene face. He had a weakness, though. It was his feet, fragile since the first frostbite. The one thing that could break him was standing sixteen hours a day.

Lep soon built up the nerve to protest, telling Metz his actions violated the Geneva Convention. Metz nodded and said, "Ja, Geneva Convention." Then he struck Lep across the cheek with the truncheon and sneered, "I am Geneva Convention."

Lately, Corbin had done his own sneering about the Geneva Convention – this gentlemen's agreement on the rules of civilized conduct for war. What an absurd oxymoron – civilized conduct for war. "Why didn't those gentlemen, while they were together," he inquired of Lep, "just agree not to have a war at all?"

After Appell each night, when they were finally given food and ordered to barracks, the stench in the closed-in space was almost too much to bear – bodies gone for months without a proper wash, neglected teeth, festering sores, uniforms suffused with urine and feces. They never spoke anymore of women or sex; to do so would have been too painful. What would a woman want with any of them in this filthy, emaciated state? And where would they get the energy to perform? Perhaps this would be the most frightening thought of all, had they the mental strength to dwell on it.

In long days at the worksite the GIs moved like robots, eyes to the ground, scarcely reacting to the foremen's blows. They no longer attempted deliberate sabotage; there were screw-ups enough without trying.

A few hours into a miserable day, one of the older foremen edged over and handed Corbin something wrapped in brown paper. It felt like a sandwich. The man pointed to his pocket and put a shaky finger to his lips not to say anything. Corbin was stunned, nearly cried from the unexpected kindness. He wanted to devour whatever it was right then but he dared not. Quickly, he slid it away for fear someone would snatch it. Luxury enough just to anticipate eating it, to feel it in his pocket – something he did a dozen times to be sure it was still there.

He waited for the evening's rations before allowing himself to unwrap what turned out to be a cheese sandwich. It was smelly German cheese but it was thick, nestled between two pieces of decent black bread. He tore the sandwich in two and gave half to a surprised Solly. Relative to the offered fare (not much more that night than sawdust bread and brown water) it was a feast. And he now had the brown wrapper, a valuable extra, which he folded neatly and tucked inside his shirt.

Corbin fell asleep that night feeling almost full but awoke an hour later dreaming of home. He wasn't quite sure what awakened him. Whether it was an Allied flyover, lice running up his neck into his hair, or the usual late-hour sounds of the barracks – choking coughs, night-terror screams, soft and muffled sobs, or the sudden urgent strides of someone with a diarrhea attack bolting to the latrine to keep from further befouling himself and his bunkmate.

Sometimes waking up seemed more than Corbin could bear – escaping in his dreams to the safety of the farm only to be yanked back here. Often after waking he thought he was still at home, but just for a moment. The smell was usually the first thing to remind him. Was it possible to remember a smell? If it were, the stench of Berga would be forever etched in his memory. He'd been dreaming of the farm a lot recently, longing for those few days he'd so foolishly traded for New York City. It wouldn't have to be a few days; he'd settle for one day at home, one hour. He'd settle for an hour in the barn. It would be nice and warm in the barn, all those cows giving off so much heat that he wouldn't need a coat.

Corbin hoped the necessity for coats here in Berga would soon end. He could ditch the overcoat grafittied with the giant K – a big advantage for a man wanting to run. And the Germans had been shutting off the compound floodlights after dark because of the ever-closer Allied flyovers. Both these things together would give escape a much better chance. Solly's foot problem, though, was still tremendous, along with wandering in enemy territory without a clue where to go.

But the situation in Berga had become so precarious it was almost a choice of whether to die here or risk death trying to escape. The result would be the same. And getting killed in an escape would show *some* form of resistance instead of dying like a worm in this devil's gristmill. Corbin decided to take a chance involving England in the plan; the flyer knew the over-all territory, might actually have ideas where Solly could hide until rescue. The Allies sounded so close!

The following day while clouds built on the horizon, Corbin managed to cross paths with England at the worksite latrine. But his heart sank when he saw him. He hadn't seen England in a week, and a week was an eternity. Even a day could bring ruin with decline happening so fast. England had the look of the others now – the gray pallor, the eyes set deep and shadowed in their sockets, nose startlingly prominent in an angular face. The flyer wouldn't have the strength now to escape, which wrecked any hopes Corbin had. He grieved the rest of the day over the man's declining state, unaware he looked about the same.

His plans were dealt a final blow by vivid evidence that each man's escape made life harder for the others. A GI managed to slip away during food detail only to be captured in a nearby town. Metz shot him in the back, dumped his body outside the barracks and left it there to decompose. That night the rest of the compound paid with a brutal Appell in a sleety rain – hours and hours of standing on throbbing feet while guards ran countless counts. Bellowing threats to shoot others, Metz wielded the rubber truncheon on the heads and shoulders of unarmed starving men who, preoccupied with hunger and weariness, were nearly beyond pain as they slid into despair. The extra hours were almost too much for Solly but he never let on, knowing Metz would just exploit the foot problem through some new form of torture.

Corbin would have killed Metz given the chance, even if it meant his own end. As it was though, he simply sank with the others to that place of giving up. After carrying his lighter all this time he finally gave in and traded it to a guard for extra bread and two sausages. It occurred to him that John had gotten the best of things again after all; he was lucky to be dead.

On the morning trek across the bridge, Corbin considered a dive into the river. Not to escape but to drown. Drowning seemed such a peaceful and happy end. He couldn't quite ready himself fast enough to do it, dragged along with the tide of feeble men to the halfway point, the three-quarter point, and the step off on the other side. He satisfied himself with a soothing delay: *maybe I'll do it on the way back ... I'll see about it tonight.*

But the POWs did not cross back over the bridge twelve hours later. They were marched instead to different quarters, a filthy tumbledown warehouse on the same side of the river. As Corbin waited for sleep to come that night after making it through the day, his thoughts ran on a similar track: *maybe I'll die tomorrow ... I'll see about it then.*

TWENTY-FIVE

Sickness struck Corbin after the move to the warehouse. Lep said he had a high fever. Boyhood memories washed over him of trifling illnesses soothed by his mother with lemon tea and hot bricks. During violent bouts of vomiting and diarrhea he ached for her like a little boy. He knew how concerned she'd be. She was not a woman prone to sappy displays of emotion, but she would certainly cry if she saw him now. In repetitive, temperature-induced nightmares he hailed a taxi in New York City on the corner of 52nd and Broadway and ended up in Berga no matter what he told the driver. Vicious men that plagued him during the day followed him into his dreams, or vicious men he conjured in his dreams followed him into the day. In his fitful stupor Corbin wasn't entirely sure. Corporal Metz was there for every moment, every terrible moment dreamed and real. As the yellow taxi pulled up to the Berga warehouse, Metz was there every time to drag him out.

When a raging attack raced Corbin to the latrine to erupt into the makeshift toilet and retch on the floor, Metz was there. Corbin wanted desperately for this one to be a dream but it wasn't. He sat on the toilet with his eyes squeezed shut, praying for that bit of privacy even the basest form of humanity guaranteed.

But Metz just stood there grinning, degrading, humiliating. He nudged Corbin roughly on the shoulder. "Innen," he barked, motioning back to the warehouse.

"Nein," Corbin said. "Not until I'm finished."

"Innen." Metz pulled out his Luger and cocked it.

"Go ahead and shoot me you bastard. I don't give a damn."

With threatening eyes Metz pushed the point of the gun against Corbin's temple.

Corbin held his breath. All he wanted was for the awful man to shoot and get it over with.

But the corporal just slid the Luger back in its holster and walked away.

At daybreak, Corbin didn't rise. He felt no pain, no hunger. He hardly felt the lice anymore. Solly shook him until his eyes opened. They were vacant, as if Corbin had already moved out. The desire for peace and death – a sign of giving up.

"No you don't," Solly said, "you're not leaving me and Lep here alone." He pulled Corbin into a sitting position, swung his legs around and forced him to begin another day.

Allied bombers were flying over almost daily now, but no liberators had yet appeared to storm the gates of Berga. Each man knew the liberators would come; it was more a question of which would happen first – liberation or his own day of death. Desperate men with no pre-war religion sought refuge in Lep's Friday night prayers, driven to their knees by the overwhelming truth of having no place else to turn.

In a sudden display of altruism, born no doubt from the increasing number of overhead planes, the Germans sent eight sick GIs to another POW camp for hospital treatment. It must have been a random selection since most of the camp, including Corbin, could have qualified. It was a lucky reprieve for Lep, chosen to go as one of four medics. Even the two German guards selected as escorts were happy to escape Berga, adopting agreeable and festive moods as if going on holiday.

The POWs at Stammlager IX-C were British soldiers – non-coms as well as privates – well-fed, wearing clean uniforms. It was a revelation to the four Berga medics that a POW camp could be like that. They were deloused; their uniforms were deloused; they were permitted to shave and take hot showers. And most important, they were given Red Cross packages filled with food, wonderful food – two to share among the four of them. The British said it was in the Rules of the Geneva Convention to distribute these packages to supplement an otherwise restrictive diet. Of course, Lep already knew this. He told them the Geneva Convention rules did not exist at Berga, that no Berga inmate had ever seen a Red Cross package until now.

On a spring day that seemed to crowd out winter overnight, the medics returned to Berga strengthened, renewed, refreshed. They declared the trip a life-saving divine intervention, and not just for them. A British officer at IX-C had promised to send a load of Red Cross packages and medical supplies. Lep got Corbin and Solly alone and handed them two cigarettes each, plus a meat roll, package of biscuits, and a chocolate bar to share. "See, I told you," he said, "we're supposed to be getting these Red Cross packages."

Early the next morning Corbin heard a bird. Without the adjacent coughs and moans he might have imagined himself in bed at home listening to the same bird through an open window. It was a sign of warmer weather, greening fields, budding trees. A sign of life. Coupled with the food from Lep, it was enough to pull him from the depths.

That same morning, as if the bird call had been a foretelling, they got an unexpected reprieve. Instead of a march to the tunnels they were taken into a forest to begin a work detail hauling logs out to the side of the road. Another divine intervention – it had to be. The work was back-breaking for the shape they were in, but glorious. It was worth any labor to trade the alien tunnels for fresh air and flocks of birds. Corbin stole calming moments to focus on their pleasant racket high in the treetops, to study the trees themselves and the quiet space between the trees. He managed to take a piece of that restorative calm with him by smuggling back to the warehouse a branch he'd broken from a budding River Birch.

Near the end of March the promised Red Cross packages arrived from IX-C. As word spread, they became every man's obsession. But the day ended, the next morning came and went, with no distribution. True to character, Corporal Metz was dangling the packages over them, giddy with his own authority as any of the mediocre in positions of power in wartime. He announced at evening Appell in bumbling English, "You will not receive the box until you clean yourself, shave and appear orderly."

Clean yourself? Shave? Appear orderly? Such colossal absurdity! What a demand after depriving them of the very things needed to stay clean and orderly. It was just another form of torment; Metz knew they could not comply. No razors, no soap, nothing to clean with – not even toilet paper. No change of clothes, and it was hard to appear orderly dressed in rags.

In an attempt at hygiene Corbin scrubbed his face and neck with cold water and a sock, scraped the crud from his gum line with a dirty fingernail, polished his teeth with a small section of the brown wrapper he'd saved. He tried washing his hair but it hardly made a difference. The hair was just too filthy and such an alarming amount came out that he decided not to do it anymore.

A day or so later after he'd had his fun, Metz begrudgingly issued some of the Red Cross packages, kept a few for himself and gave the rest to the guards. One box for every four men was all the POWs got. Lep said it should have been one for every two men, once a week, but starving men tend to be grateful for anything.

The Allies were getting closer. Their bombs produced tremblings that threatened to shatter Berga windows, rip hinges off doors. Any day now the brute force of the American military would surely crash through the barbed-wire prison walls.

April 1, Easter Sunday, brought a big surprise when the Germans gave the POWs the day off. Their first break since they got there. Amidst all the bombings the worried captors must have suddenly gotten religion, as if one act of decency could make up for it all. From a local woman with a basketful of vegetables, Corbin and Solly got potatoes – old and shriveled, eyes spread over them like albino spiders, but still potatoes. The day brought sunshine and a breeze from the south, gifts in themselves to men needing to soak up warmth.

"I had a birthday last month," Corbin remembered with surprise. "I actually made it to twenty-one."

"Yeah?"

"To tell you the truth, I didn't expect to make it."

"I turned twenty-one on the train."

"Geez, what a time. So we both made it."

"What would you have done at home? To celebrate, I mean."

"I don't know. Something really life-threatening ... like switching from pop to beer."

"Well, one thing we've got going ... we can't die any younger," Solly said. "Wonder what time it is?" He, too, had traded his watch to a guard for bread.

"Around noon, I'd say ... sun-up at home. Breakfast time."

"My kid must be born by now. Hope I get to see him someday."

"That's no way to talk, of course you'll get to see him. Wait a minute, you said *him*."

"Yeah, I've been hoping for a boy. I mean ... if it's a boy I can teach him to fish and throw a ball. Make sure he grows up to be strong and decent and unafraid."

"And never go to war."

"Right. If it's the only thing I do, I'll make sure of that. How about you? What are you hoping for?"

Hoping for? Corbin hadn't thought much about the child except as part of a trap. Certainly not as a little kid who'd call him Daddy. That line of thought was simply too underdeveloped to say whether he wanted a girl or boy. Later, he pondered what it might be like to have a child; he pondered it a lot. If it were a girl, well ... he still didn't know. But if it were a boy he could teach him to hunt and play the trumpet. Maybe the son would find a place in the music world; at least there'd be no war to stop him. Or maybe he'd want to work the farm.

It was a prospect Corbin himself was warming up to, which raised again the question of what he'd really want to do if he survived the war. Well, it wasn't a question anymore. He had abandoned the need to break the ties of his youth and actually wanted to go home. Any other notion seemed ridiculous. Somehow he would rise to all the occasions; somehow he'd learn to be more than just half a husband and distant dad.

He saw his father's point now about the importance of land, rich sustaining land that would last forever and nobody could take away. It didn't seem such a bad thing anymore to spend one's life on it growing food, storing food. Not such a bad thing to look out on one's own green fields. With acres of crops and a dairy full of food he would never starve again, nor any of his family, nor anyone he knew. No matter what happened – another Depression, another war – nobody around him would ever go hungry like he and his friends here.

That night in a rainstorm he put a phantom trumpet to his lips, rested stiff fingers on the keys and played the entire Sousa March from memory. Then he drifted off to sleep mouthing the Lord's Prayer.

On April 2 they were back on the job, not in the forest but the tunnels. More and more, the planes came, and these were American planes. At one point that day the sky was dark with them for almost an hour because of the astonishing numbers. The GIs stood a little taller as they watched those marvels of American industry keep coming and coming.

The foremen moved around with fear in their eyes that they tried to conceal. Corbin locked eyes with the one who'd given him the sandwich and gave him a look of sympathy. The man nodded, made the sign of the cross and muttered, "Gott erbarme dich unser." (God have mercy on us.)

On April 3 the soldiers were rousted out of barracks for what they assumed was another wretched day. But this one would be different. Commandant Ludwig Merz had received orders to evacuate the POWs from Berga and march them south, away from the encroaching Allied armies. For weeks the Germans had been emptying their death camps all over occupied Europe in an attempt to hide their atrocities from the world.

The soldiers stood at Appell that morning as usual. But afterward, instead of being marched to the worksite, they were led out of town by a handful of aging guards under the command of Corporal Metz. No warning, no time to pack, yet it hardly mattered since there was little to bring. All Corbin had left were the cracked and faded pictures in his shirt, the threadbare extra socks crammed in his pockets.

They did not know where they were going, but sensed the truth of their sudden departure: the Americans were getting close! There was little apprehension among them. Wherever they were headed had to be better than Berga, and no matter where, the Americans would find them. And they were walking. That was all, only walking. Out on the open road after being penned up so long. If they'd been stronger it might have been pleasant, for it was a world of the living out there – yellowing forsythia, birds nesting in trees, farmers planting seeds in recently-harrowed fields.

The White Elster River was running fast, high and vibrant from melted snow as they followed it south. Their line soon strung out a quarter of a mile. Escape from the token guard force might have been easy for anyone with the strength to try, but it was challenge enough just to walk without a fall. And the risk wasn't worth it; at their present crawl it couldn't be long before the liberators caught up.

"It'll be that crazy Patton who'll come for us," Solly said in a hopeful tone amid painful steps. "The Krauts can't stop him. Wait and see ... it'll be guys from Patton's Third Army who'll come."

Somewhere, Corbin found ironclad will. He envisioned every step as taking him closer to Judson and promised God that when he got back home, he'd value the blessings there and no longer want for something else. The worst had to be over. No quitting now. And no matter what, he'd see to it that Solly did not quit either. He refused to leave another friend to rot on a foreign road. They would all keep going as long as it took – if necessary for days, if necessary without food.

Yet the miles ahead would test his endurance; the days ahead, his tenacity. The column would struggle endlessly south, prodded by their captors, spurred again and again by assurance that they were just going as far as the next town ... the next town ... the next town. But there was no real destination, no planned end to what would become a death march. These American soldiers, captured in Belgium fifteen weeks before, had merely joined thousands of other captives – overwhelmingly European, overwhelmingly Jews – forced out on a strange road and driven south to hinder their liberation.

TWENTY-SIX

S ome of the energy had drained out of George Ottinger with the loss of his only son. Much of the delight
in building his empire had come from knowing John
would one day carry on. He had proceeded with his plans for
a new plastics factory near Philadelphia but not with the same
joy or drive. And he depended more and more on Mitch Kenny, bumping him into a management position and an office
in the Ott Building with his name on the door, almost like a
replacement son.

On April 12 radios blared that President Roosevelt was
dead, the most devastating news since the Japanese attack on
Pearl Harbor. It put the whole town in a blue funk. Roosevelt
had been president since 1933, twelve years. Most young people couldn't remember a time when he was not in the White
House. And who was this man named Harry Truman?

The only happy person in town seemed to be Velma, who
had recently married her Army Air Corps flight instructor.
It was done in the typical wartime rush – proposal one week
and a wedding the next – to squeeze in a three-day honeymoon before his transfer to Maxwell Field in Montgomery,
Alabama. Even now she was hurriedly packing to join him.

Opal and Gil were trying their best to cope. It helped that
it was spring and they still had a farm to run. In memory of
Corbin, they bravely replaced the blue star on the door with

a gold one. And they prayed the conflict across both oceans would be over before Jimmy reached eighteen, his gentle nature being so terribly unsuited for war. They feared trips to the mailbox and the sight of Ezra's black car – irrational fears since they'd already heard the worst.

Mealtimes were somber and silent with their son's chair so obviously empty. Rufus continually whined there and at the vacant bedroom door, giving voice to the family pain. The dog had whined for Corbin like that for two years, but now it meant something different to those who had to listen.

With Rufus at her heels Opal finally found the courage to enter Corbin's room. The dog sighed and flopped down on the rug between the beds, his sleeping place when Corbin was home. She fluffed up the bed pillows and dusted the dresser, idly lifted the lid on the box of trumpet mouthpieces and stared with curiosity at the gum wrapper. She encased his trumpet tenderly in a length of flannel and went to place it in the cedar chest at the foot of his bed. When she opened the chest, all those years of boyhood accumulation produced a flood of memories that only brought more tears. It was all too soon, too much to face. She coaxed Rufus into the hall and closed the bedroom door.

Daisy spent much of her free time these days with the Ottingers as though she were trying to fill the void. On Friday nights she drove Anna and Jimmy O'Connell to a movie at the Monarch and picked them up afterwards, amused at their dreamy-eyed looks. Daisy was showing up at the O'Connell farm, as well, to help Opal can rhubarb and set out onions. Her insufficient sorrow about John continued to weigh heavy as she cried into the night missing Corbin.

Meanwhile, Julia Hall had shifted her focus to Mitch Kenny as the ideal son-in-law. She'd observed with interest his sudden rise and remarked on it incessantly. At the kitchen table on a balmy evening in April, when she tried to start again, her husband cut her off by saying, "Petunia, play me something on the piano while I finish my coffee." Daisy got up from her chair, tossed her father a smile for his timing and went to the living room. Thumbing through a stack of sheet music she chose Chopin's Lullaby in D flat major, a favorite of his. Her mother allowed her to play in peace for a few minutes – a pleasant few minutes to get lost in the melody.

Then she followed. "That's lovely dear," she said, patting her daughter's arm. She sank into an armchair beside the piano and crossed her long legs, still shapely at the age of forty-four. From the side table she picked up a magazine and idly flipped through it. Finally, she said, "Mitch seems a good man." She raised her eyebrows expecting a response. "Don't you think so?"

Daisy gave an obligatory nod.

"I mean ... he must be. George obviously thinks so." Julia got up from her seat as if to heighten her words. "Dear, I know it's too soon for you to think again of marriage but–"

"I'm glad to hear you say that."

"On the other hand, decent men are scarce, and that situation is never going to improve for women of your generation."

Abruptly, Daisy stopped playing, thumbed through the stack again and pulled out a funeral march. After a few notes she could almost hear her father smile over his coffee.

"It will be doubly hard," her mother went on, oblivious, "to find a man with a bright financial future. They've all been so busy fighting the war, the poor dears, they haven't had time to build a future or get an education. Lucky for Wally that he'll have a ready-made future when he comes out. There might be two stores by then."

"How *are* Daddy's plans coming for a second store?" Daisy already knew but asked anyway, aiming the question toward the kitchen in hope of rescue.

"Hasn't your father told you? He got wind yesterday of one in Doylestown coming up for sale next month. Good frontage on Main Street and a raised loading dock off the alley." Julia dropped to the edge of the chair and leaned forward. "But back to Mitch ... it looks like George has latched onto him like a son. You don't want to put him off so long that he tires of waiting and finds somebody else ..."

Charlie Hall stood in the doorway with his arms spread, hands resting on either side of the frame. "Leave her alone, Julia. She already knows all that."

But her mother's words resonated. What *should* she do about the future? Marrying now was out of the question, but to never marry? Despite her mother's off-putting insistence, Daisy liked Mitch Kenny. He seemed the one person lately who could make her laugh. It was Mitch in fact who propelled her through the days – his gusto balancing out her numb lack of interest. Once, she'd even let him kiss her, a quick gentle kiss she found unobjectionable. But the relationship lacked any spark, at least for Daisy anyway, and though there was lit-tle about Mitch to remind her of John, the bond they were forming seemed similar – more somebody else's idea than her own.

Soon a goodnight kiss became a regular thing. Daisy took part; she couldn't deny that. Yet she feared Mitch was wasting his time if he wanted love in return. She even told him so as a kind of warning. He could kiss her a million times and never blot out the one with Corbin. In a sense, Daisy had traded her whole heart for that one perfect kiss in the cold armory storeroom in 1943.

But Mitch summed it up his own way. "It's just too soon for you, that's all," he said. "I can wait. I'm a very patient man when it comes to getting what I want. One of these days, though, I'm going to propose." In truth, she could do worse than Mitch Kenny. There'd been talk of him moving back to Philadelphia to manage the new plastics factory – a notion Daisy found appealing. A move to a big city like Philadelphia might be the only real way to escape memories. Marriage to Mitch would be second best, but marriage to any man would.

TWENTY-SEVEN

The POWs shuffle along a road somewhere in Bavaria, absent of any thought beyond self-preservation. Death has shrunken the column by some number. Corbin has lost count but it's close to forty. Harry from Chicago is dead, and Sy from Newark – both captured with them at Kaiserbaracke Crossroads. Corbin has lost count of the days, too. The last time it rained, Metz told them Roosevelt was dead. How long ago was that? "Your Jew president is dead," he told them. But the men don't believe it.

Solly's feet are barely useable; he might as well have nubs at his ankles for all the good they are. His two friends must support him now – Lep on one side and Corbin on the other, yoked together like a trio of oxen.

They struggle to keep going as the road rises. The fields are green and lush on both sides. There are odd little gray bundles everywhere on the hillside ahead, on the road, scattered in the fields. The soldiers' eyes are weak from hunger; they must wait until they get closer to understand. They are trespassing through a graveyard for hundreds of Jews – shot in the head, skulls blown to pieces, masses of red pulp jutting out from striped collars, oozing blood in an uneven circle on the ground.

Why here, why now? the soldiers question. Couldn't make it up the hill? That has to be the reason ... shot because they couldn't make it up the hill. *What about us?* is the next question. *Is this how it will end for us?* The ghoulish landscape is too much for Solly. His friends are practically dragging him now, determined not to leave him. But it is a lot for two walking skeletons to demand of themselves.

Corbin wonders whether there will ever again be a time when they aren't in mortal danger, ever again be a time when they aren't on this march to nowhere. Blurry days of trudging up hills and slogging through rain, relieved by comatose nights spent in fields and barns only to face the horror anew with every dawn.

They hear booms in the distance. *Is it thunder? Cannon fire?*

Corporal Metz has disappeared. It will be the last they ever see of him. By nightfall word has spread that he is gone. Some say he's been replaced, some say he just got on a bicycle and rode off.

Hours of walking seem like days, days like weeks. Solly can't wear his boots anymore. They wrap his swollen feet in discarded winter clothing and keep moving. He says his feet don't hurt so much now. Lep thinks it's a worrisome sign.

There's a dying dog on the side of the road, panting its last breath, another casualty of the war. The sight is beyond endurance for Corbin. He weeps unashamedly, tears running into the hollows of his cheeks, too fragile of spirit to be governed by male pride.

A signpost with a bold arrow pointing ahead says ROTZ in heavy Gothic lettering. The booms are nearer now. Definitely cannon fire. This should inspire renewed energy but all reserves are dry. They can manage only to drag themselves along, one foot and then the other, each fearful of falling lest he won't get up again.

At sunset they struggle up a hill to a large rambling barn and collapse there on the straw, spirits at the lowest ebb. Solly says he's finished, too consumed with pain and despair to continue. The liberators may very well be near, but so is the insatiable angel of death.

In the morning the guards are standing at the barn door. "Raus, Raus." They give the familiar order with little enthusiasm, almost as weary of wandering as the POWs.

Word buzzes through the men, *Don't move ... nobody move.* The men lie there. If the guards want to shoot all of them then so be it. They are finished marching.

Yet the guards just walk away.

———— ∞∞ ————

The 11th Armored Division, assigned to General George Patton's Third Army, has been battling German Panzers since the enemy's surprise December offensive in Belgium. Most of that battling is finished; the Germans are in full retreat. The American forces, no longer met by flying bullets from village windows, are greeted with white flags of surrender in the form of billowing tablecloths and bedsheets.

The war is not yet over, but it's mostly a mercy mission now for the 11th. They have blazed their way south through Germany the last few days rescuing over four thousand Allied soldiers from POW camps. And they have encountered many thousands more victims of concentration camps – a wretched population all dressed alike in dingy blue and white stripes, pushed out on the road and force-marched south. The fields and roadsides are littered with the dead; the living are left to wander aimlessly through the countryside. They are pitiable beyond words, shuffling up to the tank convoy with arms outstretched begging for food, kissing the hands of tearful soldiers who give them everything they have. The convoy is receiving a steady flow of supplies but never enough to feed such a multitude.

On the morning of April 23 a long line of Sherman tanks from the 11th Armored rattles through eastern Bavaria near the village of Rotz. The scents of spring – early-blooming flowers and manure-laced fields – clash with gunpowder, tank fumes, the decomposing bodies of humans and blown-apart farm animals – the stench of war.

From the convoy's lead vehicle the tank commander sees movement in his peripheral vision. Across a greening field, people are lurching down a hill toward him waving their arms. "More concentration camp victims, sir," his driver says. The commander nods, his face heavy with sympathy. He can tell the poor creatures are trying to hurry but they are bone-weary and starving like the rest.

And yet ... he holds up a hand for the driver to halt, lifts his binoculars for a better look. "Peculiar," he says. What he sees is most peculiar: long-haired, bearded, cadaverous men, staggering in groups of two and three in Army uniforms. Tattered and stained to be sure, but definitely Army uniforms. Combat boots, some with helmets, and wait ... on one is a distinct Golden Lion insignia of the 106th.

Even then, Solly did not want to move. "It's the Americans, Solly!" Corbin could barely contain himself. "It really is, I saw them with my own eyes! And Lep, too. Shermans, Solly, a whole line of them!" They pulled him up bodily, practically carrying him out of the barn.

There it was! A convoy of Sherman tanks on the road below, better than they'd ever imagined it. Giant white stars on the sides. And an American flag! What a sight! Nothing on God's green earth could ever be as beautiful as that American flag fluttering on a breeze. The convoy had clearly stopped in its tracks but the POWs careened down the hill anyway, tears flowing, fearful of missing their chance.

Soldiers from the 11th grabbed food and scrambled from the tanks. They didn't know what to make of these brothers they've never met, uniformed apparitions who carried with them a horrible smell, their faces an odd blend of death pallor and joy.

The first soldier to reach Corbin handed him a canteen and two Milky Way bars from his haversack. Corbin took a long drink first and then fumbled with shaky hands to get a wrapper off. The soldier, cigarette slanting from a corner of his mouth, watched for a moment before he peeled the paper back. Corbin wolfed one bar, then the other. He immediately got sick on the grass, his body rebelling against such rich food after months of starvation. It kept coming and kept coming, more than he ever imagined could still be in him. It was the same for all the POWs – eating too much too fast. C rations were too rich; everything the soldiers had was too much and too rich. One died in his liberator's arms. The rest were quickly loaded up and whisked away.

At an Army mobile hospital, uniforms were taken and burned, the men themselves deloused with DDT. A few men, the ones in the worst shape, were transported out immediately. The rest were put on an immediate regimen of diluted paregoric to stop the dangerous diarrhea rich food had exacerbated, sapping strength and impeding weight gain just when they desperately needed to put on pounds. Corbin had lost half his body weight – captured at 180 and liberated at 90.

Lep feared Solly would lose both his feet. Early stages of gangrene had set in, which usually meant amputation. But because an eager young Army doctor insisted on first trying Penicillin, a potent new wonder drug, Solly lost three toes and kept his feet. Corbin's feet weren't too bad thanks to his dedicated sock-changing, but he was plagued with lice bites – dozens of angry oozing lice bites the doctor described as serious.

Six or seven times a day the Berga survivors consumed salubrious cereals, puddings, applesauce and the like until they improved beyond peril. They gradually found themselves transferred out in groups. Corbin, Solly and Lep were flown on a DC-3 to Camp Lucky Strike, an Army hospital in LeHavre, France. Nurses there were exactly what nurses ought to be: clinical and unseeing at embarrassing moments; bossy as drill sergeants about the important stuff; gentle as mothers caressing with cool hands; playful as sisters giving pats on the butt. And pats on the butt always helped. One of the nurses had Daisy's way of walking, which Corbin found both a comfort and a haunt.

They heard Hitler was dead, the war over, so life was good. The Red Cross brought cigarettes, chewing gum, other sundries. Corbin got a new razor, which would be good to have once his beard grew back. When he was strong enough they let him take a shower – his first real shower in five months. It was heaven to be clean again, heaven to sleep in a real bed with clean sheets and enough blankets. He tended to lie there and fight off sleep just to feel how good it felt.

Plus, as much as he needed sleep, he feared it. The lice returned to plague him in his dreams. Corporal Metz was there, too. And countless corpses – corpses hanging, corpses piled in shallow graves, corpses cluttering an endless bloody hill to impede his progress on the only road home. At least once a night he awoke from such a nightmare, perhaps rescued from it by the screams of another trapped in a similar scene. Each time, it was the feel of the sheets and the pillow under his head that first assured him this particular nightmare wasn't real.

As soon as Corbin could think straight and steady a pen, he wrote a letter home in a shaky scrawl. He knew nothing of the anguish going on there, still under the delusion the POW postcard had arrived from Stammlager IX-B. After that he wrote more letters. In fact he did little more than eat, sleep and write. Each letter came hard and often drained him. The one to Pop Ott was all sympathy and apology, written with watery eyes. Velma's he had to do twice, the first nothing more than an antiseptic repentance, acceptance of his fate. So he wrote it over, infusing it with the warmth he tried his best to feel. After all, he was probably a father by now.

His carefully-worded letter to Daisy took him an entire morning to compose as he struggled to keep from saying what he had no right to say.

The easiest was Jimmy's. It was a breezy letter – nothing apologetic or sensitive, nothing heavy. Corbin ribbed him about Anna Ottinger, asked if he were driving the truck yet and razzed him about changing the oil. Corbin could only guess at what might be up with his 16-year-old brother, which pointed out just how little he knew of home.

TWENTY-EIGHT

May, 1945

Much of the world had reason to rejoice on May 7, the day the Germans surrendered. The following day, May 8, was marked as VE-Day – the official day to celebrate the Allied victory in Europe. But it was on the 7th, when the surrender actually took place and was first announced, that such spontaneous rejoicing occurred. In London, Paris, and coast to coast in America, people bumped against each other in the swarming streets, drifting along in a wave controlled by a common pulse. No words were too flowery, crying too maudlin, displays of affection too effusive on such a day.

For the O'Connells and Daisy Hall there would never be a greater one since it was also the day the good-news telegram arrived. The Western Union teleprinter had been buzzing all afternoon because the phone lines were jammed and nobody could get a call through. They were continually spilling in the open door from celebrations in the streets to send cables, nearly all of them jubilant. Daisy had been hiding there for hours, grateful for the surrender but in no mood for gaiety. To be useful to Ezra she had made a convenient seat out of the back counter, on hand to prepare incoming cables for delivery, stack the envelopes in the cigar box for the high school messenger boy.

Amongst all the happy missives, Ezra cringed at the sight of another one from the War Department. *Oh please, not now, not today.* He didn't say anything but Daisy saw his face. Concerned for her brother, she jumped from the counter as he stretched out the tape:

```
MR & MRS G O'CONNELL: ARMY CHIEF OF STAFF
DIRECTS ME TO INFORM YOU YOUR SON CORBIN
LEE O'CONNELL, PREVIOUSLY PRESUMED
DEAD, WAS LIBERATED FROM POW STATUS ON
23 APRIL 1945 AND RETURNED TO U.S. ARMY
CONTROL. DETAILS FOLLOW IN LETTER.
J.A. ULIO, ADJUTANT GENERAL
```

What a glorious day for Ezra, charged for a change with carrying such joyful news! It could never make up for all the others, but it helped, it surely helped.

Opal and Gil, though desperately happy, half-feared taking it as fact. What if this telegram were the false one and the previous one true? Then a very satisfying pair of communications appeared at the same time among the mail. The postman had dumped a sizeable stack in the box that day but an official-looking envelope from the War Department commanded all the attention. Opal tore into with shaky hands:

```
Dear Mr. and Mrs. O'Connell,
    This letter is to confirm a recent telegram
stating your son, Corbin Lee O'Connell, was
liberated from POW status on 23 April, 1945
and returned to U.S. Army control. I am happy
to report that he is currently at an Army
hospital in Le Havre France, recovering from
```

```
malnutrition, but with no serious injuries.
    He cannot receive mail there but he can
write to you of his progress. I am confident
you will hear from him soon. Be assured he is
getting the best of care and will be returned
home as soon as he is able.
Sincerely Yours,
J. A. Ulio, Major General
Adjutant General
```

Apart from the words "malnutrition" and "as soon as he is able" it was glorious assurance, yet they continued to react cautiously; that horrible first telegram had been followed by a confirmation letter, too. The rest of the mail had been tossed aside and an hour went by before anybody remembered it. Sandwiched between the monthly utility bill and a letter from Opal's sister lurked the POW postcard – all travel-worn, unassuming and tardy: KRIEGSGEFANGENEN SEND-UNG across the top in bold letters; a faded date sometime in January; "O'Connell Corbin PFC in German captivity and all right."

What a thing to find in one's mailbox! What a thing to so joyfully receive! But they did receive it joyfully, for it increased a hundredfold their trust in all of it. Opal treated these dispatches like treasures, placing them in a drawer of the china cabinet atop the good silver. Now, trips to the mailbox became an adventure. Two days after the POW postcard, Opal found a small tan envelope edged in red, with a red air-mail stamp. Holding her breath she opened it carefully, so as not to damage the envelope or the single sheet inside:

Dear Folks,

 I'm writing to you from a GI hospital in France. It's sure good to be back in friendly territory. So sorry John isn't here with me. He was killed in an explosion that I managed to escape from. Every day I wonder why. I can't receive mail here but at least I can write to you until I get back on U.S. soil. Don't know yet when that will be.

 Now, about Velma. I know you're disappointed in me for getting into such a jam. You warned me, Momma. When Velma wrote to me with her news, I wanted to escape from being a father and never come home. That's the sad truth. But I'm ready to face my responsibility now. I guess the last few months have changed me.

 Please don't worry. Getting good chow every day and gaining some weight back. Did you save me any Easter dinner? I'm expecting some when I get home. Tell Jimmy to look for separate letter.

Love always,
Corbin

They read it over and over, crying over it, puzzling over it. He hadn't said much about his health, his handwriting a bit shaky. Was he hiding something? And the part about Velma was most confusing. Lovingly, Opal placed the envelope and letter in the silver drawer with the others. She opened his bedroom door and left it open, bringing some light once again into that end of the hall. She took his trumpet out of the cedar chest and unwrapped it, opened the windows to air out the room, freshened the bed linens by hanging them outside.

Daisy scoured the mail every day for her own letter from Corbin while languishing in a prison of guilt. Her father observed her by the hour and finally said, "You seem so sad. I know there's still reason to be sad, but there's reason to be happy now, too."

"I don't deserve to be happy."

"Why not?"

She hesitated. "Well ... John's death makes it so convenient for Corbin and me."

"My poor Petunia, part of an impossible triangle."

"I prayed for them both equally when they went overseas, I really did. At least in terms of time. But I'm sure my prayers for Corbin were more ... truly meant. Now it turns out that he's alive and John is dead."

"There you go again, taking too much on yourself," he said, rubbing her cheek with a gentle hand. "Do you actually believe your prayers have that much power? I'm your father and you're my perfect little girl, and even I don't think *that* much of you."

She smiled a little. It sounded absurd when he put it that way.

"John is gone. It wasn't your fault, or Corbin's, or any-body's. It just happened. Do you still love Corbin?"

"Yes, I'll always love Corbin."

"Does he still care?"

"I don't know."

"Well, when he gets home you can find out. There's no tri-angle anymore ... only the two of you." He put an arm around her and sighed. "I sure hope you don't put John in the way of your happiness because I don't think he would like that."

She felt better after her father's words, as always. But the real question was Corbin. She found herself clinging to the words he spoke in the storeroom that night when he said, *It will always be you*. That was two years ago, though. So much had happened since then. Still, she broke things off with Mitch before getting in any deeper. With Corbin still in the world it changed everything, no matter how it turned out.

When her own tan envelope edged in red showed up in the mailbox she opened it with high hopes but it left her confused and shaken:

Dear Daisy,
    There's so much I want to say to you, yet so little I can say. I'm truly sorry about John. I didn't protect him the way I promised. The truth is, he died because of me. He didn't want to go on that recon mission. He only went because I coaxed him. Now he's dead and I'm alive. I'll never forgive myself for that. Though I'm longing to get home, it's going to be hard without him, hard to face you and Pop Ott.
    I have such good memories of you, the family and the farm. It was those memories that got me through the ordeal of the last few months.

Please forgive me.
Corbin

When she showed the letter to her father, he said, "Well, I see your problem. Isn't much here to feel good about, is there? Corbin is filled with his own guilt about John, that's for sure. But look ... don't go reading anymore into it than that. You'll just have to wait and see. Frankly, it wouldn't hurt either of you to cut down on the soul-searching. And like I said before, I really hope you don't make that poor boy a stumbling block to happiness."

The next morning Daisy took the letter to Opal who nearly cried at her son's tortured words. Then Opal went to the silver drawer for her own letter from Corbin, handed it to Daisy and watched her saucer-eyed reaction to the part about Velma.

TWENTY-NINE

August, 1945

J apan surrendered on August 15, ending the Second World War and any fears the Berga survivors had of going to the Pacific. Two days later their distinction was blurred as they became part of the uniformed masses boarding the RMS Queen Mary at Southampton – fourteen thousand soldiers headed for home.

On August 21 the "Grey Ghost" docked in New York while the elated travel-weary troops stood on deck gazing at the Statue of Liberty like a shipload of awe-struck immigrants. The New York skyline had *home* written all over it – the Empire State, the tallest building in the world, poking a hole in a cloud as it soared twice as high as the rest.

Before the end of the day they found themselves in Halloran Army Hospital on Staten Island. A doctor released Lep and sent him home to Brooklyn to convalesce. Since liberation, bit by bit and without much ceremony, the Berga survivors had been splintering off. Corbin and Solly got beds in a crowded ward full of recovering GIs, a long narrow room with two-tier bunks on both sides forming a middle aisle barely wide enough for a doctor, nurse and pushcart.

Now that they were home, all they could think about was a telephone. They collected a few dimes and stood in line for an hour. It was hard for Solly to stand for long so they found him a chair to sit on to wait his turn. Then Corbin got to watch him holler and limp around at the news he had a baby boy.

At his turn, Corbin first put a call through to Velma hoping her dad wouldn't answer. He did, though. It was a short, astonishing conversation. Expecting a rebuke from an irate father, Corbin gingerly identified himself and asked to speak with Velma.

The man hesitated a moment, cleared his throat and said, "Well Corbin, afraid I have some bad news. Velma got married a few weeks ago. She just moved to Alabama to be with her husband. Sorry to have to tell you ... I know how close you were."

Corbin was speechless.

"I never gave her the letter you sent. Thought it was best to throw it away ... I hope you understand." He paused a moment. "Corbin, are you still there?"

"Yes, sir."

"Oh, okay. Well, I just want to tell you how relieved we both were to hear you made it through."

"Uh, thank you, sir."

That was it. No angry words, nothing about a baby. *Married?*

Solly stared at his stunned face. "Well, what happened?"

"That was her father ...."

"Yeah, what'd he say?"

"She got married! He said she got married!" Corbin whacked himself in the forehead. "Didn't say anything about a baby. He only said ... Velma got married." Keeping a lid on his emotions he put a dime in the slot, dialed zero for the operator, gave her his hometown and phone number and asked to reverse the charges.

"Hello?" It was his father's voice.

"This is the New Jersey operator," the woman said in an accent decidedly New Jersey, decidedly American, decidedly beautiful. "I have a collect call from Corbin O'Connell. Will you accept the charges?"

"Of course I will! Opal, get in here! It's Corbin on the phone!"

"Go ahead please," the beautiful accent said.

"Pops! Boy, it's good to hear your voice!"

"Oh, it's good to hear you too, son! You gave us quite a scare the last few months." They talked for a minute or so – a jubilant exchange but surprisingly stilted, each with so many important things to say that neither knew what to say first. Corbin heard his mother in the background, itching to get on the phone before the call ran too long. His eyes filled hearing her voice.

"Corbin! It's really you! I can't believe it's really you!"

"It's really me, Momma."

"Where are you?"

"Army hospital on Staten Island."

"Staten Island! Lord love a duck, you're so close! Tell me the truth, son. How are you?"

"Well, I was in pretty bad shape at first, but I'm doing okay now."

"Then, why are you in a hospital?"

"I hope it won't be for long, once the doctors here see I'm okay."

"Then what?"

"Soon as they release me I can come home. The Army still owns me but I'll be furloughed for at least a few weeks of convalescence."

"Want us to come and get you?"

"Naah, I think I can get there okay."

"I can't wait! I'll be sure to have all your favorite foods. We'll get that weight back on you fast enough. What do you want the most?"

"Biscuits and apple butter. And mashed potatoes. And and ... fried chicken. And and and ... bacon. And Momma, there's a recipe for a new pie I want you to make."

Opal laughed at the list and then got teary-eyed. "Anything you want, son, anything. Promise you're okay?"

"I promise. Look, Momma .... I got quite a shock earlier. I called Velma, and her dad said she got married."

"That's right son. I've been worried how you'd take it. And I have to ask ...what was all that in your first letter about being a father?"

"Velma wrote and told me she was pregnant."

"She did? When?"

"Back in November. I've been thinking this whole time that she was pregnant with my kid."

"The little trickster! She was never pregnant! Well, this explains a lot. So, how *are* you taking it? You upset?"

"Upset? Gosh no! I've just been liberated for a second time."

He slept the sleep of the truly emancipated that night until the light of dawn lit up a window at the end of the room. His first thought was of Daisy. Not Daisy the untouchable but Daisy the attainable, as if his mind had carried out the conversion overnight. He sweated through another letter, worked on it off and on all day, felt right about it one minute and doubted the next. In the end it was Solly who grabbed it from him, sealed the envelope and buried it in a mounting pile of outgoing mail:

Dear Daisy,

I guess you've heard by now about the trick Velma played on me. I suppose I deserved it. I feel like a fool, but a happy one, I confess. You need to know that I have changed. What I've done, what I've seen has changed me. I guess the war has changed us all. I'm more settled now I think, with simpler goals. I once thought the only way I could be happy was to move to a big city and play the trumpet. (Part of my motivation there, I believe, was to get away from you and John).

Now, after witnessing so much starvation and death, and nearly starving to death myself, the prospect of growing food, food and more food seems like the best idea to me, and I feel darned lucky that I can come right home and do it because of what already belongs to me.

That last night in the storeroom seems like a lifetime ago. Maybe it happened to two different people, I don't know. I remember promising not to pressure you. I said if we ever speak of us again, it will be because you start it. I plan to keep that promise even now.

I'm trying not to have any expectations. This war has caused so much death and gloom and loss. Is there too much guilt and damage between us? Can we possibly shake it all off and begin again? I don't know the answers but I owe it to myself to find out.

Yours forever,
Corbin

Corbin and Solly were released from the hospital at the same time with just a few hours' notice. Both had their sights set for home but dreaded the moment of parting. What they'd been through together, what they'd endured, could never be conveyed to family and friends. Where was the language? Words could never make anybody else understand, so going home would mean a special kind of isolation.

Each owed his life to the other. It felt inadequate to break away so abruptly with simple bear hugs and slaps on the back, yet other than promising frequent reunions there was nothing more to do. The bonds formed in such life-changing trials could never be broken anyway, not by miles or time or separate paths. They shook hands (something they hadn't really done before) and walked backwards away from each other, holding a gaze until they were too far apart.

Going home meant a short ferry ride for Solly, across the Verrazano Narrows into Brooklyn. For Corbin it was a trip by rail. If the New Jersey depot were any indication, transportation systems in the United States continued to be overrun by the military. As he waited for the train to Philadelphia, Corbin found a seat and watched the swarm. Army tans abounded, some with the pressed and polished look of state-side duty, others battered and fatigued, propped on crutches or wheelchaired, dazed looks marking them as coming from the war.

When the announcer barked his train number, Corbin joined the horde exiting the station into the humid night. This was to be his first train trip since that endless misery to Berga. He tensed up on the platform until the balmy temperature and gold Pennsylvania Railroad logo relaxed him. He might have panicked entering the passenger coach if not for other marks of civilized travel so absent in his last trip: the effortless one step up, the carpeted floor and plush seats, the relaxed laughter, the occasional female, and the wide windows giving a view of the lit-up station.

He discovered though, once the train rolled out, the importance of open eyes. Closed, with the uneven rocking and clickety-clack, it was February again and he was on his way to hell. Once, he fell asleep and awoke with a start. Maybe he even cried out, he wasn't sure. He locked eyes with another gaunt GI across the aisle who conveyed in a companionable look his own fight with inner demons.

In Philadelphia he waited in the station an hour and caught the 614 home. He tried to stay awake peering out the window, yet with the exception of sporadic flashes from distant towns there was nothing to stare at in the blackness but his own reflection.

He felt pretty good about what his mother would see. There'd been enough of a stubble that morning to shave. His hair was coming back nice and thick – thick enough to warrant a comb in his back pocket again. And just before he left the hospital, when a pretty nurse gave him a pat on the butt, he felt that familiar old desire pulse through his loins and knew he'd be okay. For the first time in a long time physical need had ventured beyond food, the stirrings of youthfulness not destroyed as he'd feared but merely buried under months of deprivation.

Maybe his father had been right about staying home to work the farm. John certainly would not have gone if Corbin hadn't, and heaven knows he could have done without the horrors of the last few months. Yet, with all the others forced to go, would it have been right to stay behind? The simple event of being born had doomed him to suffer the scars of war – the physical scars for going or the mental scars for taking a lawful dodge.

The war had carried him thousands of miles and a long way in his thinking. It had made him both villain and victim – the villain had killed, the victim paid the debt. At least he hoped the debt had been paid with that four-month prison sentence because a man had to live with himself and his deeds a long time. The son his parents knew was gone and a different one, hopefully a better one, stood in his place.

He'd spent so much of the last few years not wanting to be home, and now he couldn't wait to get there. Yet shame overshadowed it with the inevitable question, *Why was I spared?* Corbin knew there was no answer, at least not one the human mind was privy to, but it would be a long time before he stopped asking. About Daisy though, he bore no shame or guilt. The truth was, he never felt John deserved exclusive claim. The truth was, he always believed the match a mistake.

The lights on the Judson Rail Station platform appeared as tiny pinpoints growing to bright beacons in the night – his single form of welcome. He had agonized over this moment fearing brass bands and flag-waving while he stepped off the train without John, but the whole town was asleep at this hour. It was too late to be greeted by anyone, too late to call home for a ride, which suited him just fine. His parents had gone to bed hours ago, ignorant of his arrival.

He headed up Main Street, strolling through stretches of dark into pools of lamp light, and out again. It was more than five miles from here to the farm. *Five miles*, he laughed to himself; five miles was nothing. A breeze from the west had chased away the humidity and imposed a touch of cool air on an otherwise warm night. Everything was closed up and dark – service station, drug store, movie house – but even in the shadows Corbin could see how much Judson had grown. A bank on the ground floor of the Ott Building hadn't been there before. On the corner of Fairview and Main, a block from Velma's Star Diner, sat a new restaurant. And he could see what looked like the sign for another around the corner and a few doors down.

Ah, it felt good to be back. This was his town, his home. He found himself comparing it to bombed-out Europe. At least this hadn't been a war zone; at least while over there he hadn't needed to worry about over here.

With pride of place he stood in front of Western Union and looked across Main to Hall's Market. Soon, he'd see Daisy. Soon, he'd find out. His heart beat faster at the prospect. He peered through the telegraph office windows at a faint glow from Ezra's back apartment, and decided to tap on the glass.

Ezra popped his head around the kitchen doorframe to have a look and then strode to the front, curious. For a moment in the dim light he saw a stranger in an Army uniform. It wasn't until Corbin said something, that Ezra recognized who he was. Then Corbin got his first happy greeting, as well as a ride home.

Time and again Corbin had imagined this moment, pictured the family crowding around when he opened the door. But they were all upstairs in bed, the house dark except for the amber front light spilling onto the porch. Suddenly it seemed a fine idea to just sneak in, go to bed and have his mother find him in the morning as if he'd never left. He circled around to the back of the house and thought of Rufus, half-expecting the dog to bark and wake up the entire farm.

Meanwhile on the second floor the animal lifted his head, shot up from his current place beside Jimmy, thumped down the stairs and around to the back door, ready to wag not only his tail but his entire back half when the long-lost master slipped into the house. Corbin dumped his duffel bag on the floor and stooped down to rub the dog's head with both hands, rewarded with a melodious whine that had to be the canine version of gladsome tears.

Gil arose as always before the sun appeared. Rufus raised up a moment and listened to the stairs creak, then sank back down on the rug beside a sleeping Corbin, perhaps fearing his favorite might disappear again if left alone.

Opal heard Gil's stair creaks too, expecting them to be followed by Rufus's four-legged galumphing. When it didn't come she frowned in her sleepiness but nothing else, rolling over to a cool part of the bed to give herself five minutes more. The dog's failure to follow should have been a solid clue, but even Gil didn't catch on that his son was home until he tripped over the duffel bag left by the kitchen door.

Gil rubbed his wife's arm and kissed her cheek. "Opal, wake up."

"Hmm?"

He kissed her again. "Get up, Opal. I've got something to show you."

She rolled over to face him. "What is it?"

"Just put on your bathrobe and come with me."

"It's nothing bad is it?" she asked. The question was more a sign of the times than anything, for she could see by her husband's face that whatever it was must be good.

He held out the robe for her to feed her arms through, then steered her down the hall and positioned her in the doorway to see her eldest son, sound asleep.

THIRTY

Opal kept touching Corbin all day long, running a hand down his angular face at regular intervals to be sure he was real. She could barely contain her happiness at the entire family around the table once more, all of them watching Corbin wolf her breakfast of bacon, eggs, biscuits, gravy. She cried as her boys roughhoused again, more evenly matched now with Jimmy older and Corbin in his weakened state. She kept providing and Corbin kept consuming little meals of his favorite foods: more biscuits with apple butter mid-morning, pork chops and apples at noonday, an early supper of fried chicken and mashed potatoes.

Corbin had expected his father to be ready with a dozen varieties of "I told you so", but to the man's credit he offered nary a one. Gil just sat back with smiling eyes and watched his son's every move as if he couldn't get enough.

After supper, Opal served the pie Corbin had dreamed of for months, prepared the way he described except for the blueberries, which were out of season and therefore unavailable at any price. She cut half the pie in pieces and served them out on plates. Corbin took the other half and ate it from the pan with a spoon, then carried it empty to the sink where his mother stood with her hands in the suds. "Momma, have you seen Daisy?" he whispered with a touch of concern.

"Lordy son, I clean forgot!" Opal dried her hands on a towel, grabbed an envelope wedged between the flour and sugar canisters and handed it to him. "Daisy brought this by earlier in the week and asked me to give to you." Their eyes locked in curiosity as Corbin felt the soft and lumpy sealed envelope. "She said you'd know what it meant."

Corbin tucked it in a pocket and made a show of stretching. "I need to walk off some of this dinner," he said with pretended casualness. "I'm going up to Rocky Knob."

"Want us to go with you?" Gil asked.

"Naah, I think I'll just ... go alone." He left through the back door and skirted the vegetable garden in the late-afternoon sun, determined to wait until he got there to open it. *She said you'd know what it meant.* It was a struggle to keep his mind a blank; whatever it was would seal his fate. He crossed the creek on the log footbridge and climbed the hill where a half-dozen cows nosed for grass. The nearest looked up as he reached out a hand.

The rock felt good on his legs and buttocks after baking all day in the heat. Corbin loved the sun's warmth these days, doubted he'd ever again complain of it. He broke the seal of the envelope carefully, out of respect for whatever was inside. Waves of Daisy came out of it – the scent of her, the look of her, the feel of her. Folded inside was the handkerchief, the one he'd returned that night in the storeroom. But embroidered all over it now was *Us...Us...Us...Us...Us...Us...Us....* He draped it across a palm and stared at it, trying to understand. Then it hit him, his own words in his letter: *if we ever speak of us again, it will be because you start it.*

His first reaction was laughter, a spontaneous burst of it. As he held the handkerchief to his face and breathed, he changed to downright crying and back to laughter as the true implication took hold. He jumped off the rock and danced around it like a child. Then he was up on the rock again, standing. From this height he could see the farm over the maples and he spread his arms as if to embrace the scene – the whitewashed buildings etched perfectly against trees of green and sky of blue. He could not remember ever being so happy.

Daisy showed up at the house about then. Jimmy answered her knock.

"Momma, Daisy's here," he whispered, nodding toward the living room.

"Well, tell her to come in here."

"But, what should we do?"

"Do? What do you mean?"

"Corbin is still up on the Knob and ... he said he wanted to be alone."

A bright-faced Opal patted his cheek. "I'm fairly certain he won't mind her," she said, chuckling.

Daisy crossed the footbridge and climbed the meadow hill. She saw him before he saw her, studied him in profile there in his open-collared blue shirt. She'd always loved Corbin in a blue shirt. The sight of him brought back that adolescent thrill she'd expected never again to feel.

Youthful vigor pulsed through Corbin as he watched her circle the cows. He slid from the rock and moved toward her slowly, as if to savor a new beginning. She understood and aligned her pace with his, content with the mere sight of him. As the distance closed he held out his arms and she went into them. Neither said a word. She rested her head on his chest, closed her eyes, blocked out everything but the feel of his body and his arms.

He lifted her chin, kissed one cheek, and the other, and her nose. She responded with a little frown of need that made his sensuality soar. He held her face in his hands and kissed her with urgency, a deep penetrating kiss they both got lost in. As though fate were still against them they clung to each other a long time, doing nothing more than a subtle sway among the disinterested cows.

With a sober expression he held out the handkerchief still clutched in his hand. "Daisy, I've been reading a lot into this clever message of yours. I pray it means you think we have a chance. Does it?"

"Yes, Corbin, I think we have a chance. I'd say we have an excellent chance ... if you still love me. "

"If I still love you. If I still love you? Daisy, you're everything to me. I need you more than air." He swooped her up in his arms, spun her round and round until all the cows scattered and they were both dizzy. Then he set her down and they laughed from joy until they were weak.

As they strolled to the rock she rubbed a hand across his shoulder blades and leaned away to look at him. "How are you? You're still so thin."

"This isn't thin. You should have seen me a couple months ago."

"You're really okay?

"Okay? I'm more than okay. I was strong enough to twirl you around back there and I'm strong enough now to put you on this rock." He placed his hands on her waist and lifted her up in one fluid motion.

She could easily have hopped up there herself but she'd always loved it when he did stuff like that. Her heart ached remembering the good and bad of the past. They sat there together, legs dangling over the side. "At first ... I felt so guilty about John," she said. "But my father said his death was nobody's fault and John wouldn't like it if we made him a stumbling block to happiness. Do you believe he's right?"

"John is in a place of all understanding now ... at least that's what I think. We know he loved us both and he'd want us to be happy. I spent months feeling guilty about him but it didn't bring him back. I could feel guilty about other things too, Daisy. I killed people. With cold and casual hatred I killed a lot of men in the name of war. I could carry guilt around the rest of my life, but I'm finished with it. It's poison. There's been enough separation and tragedy. Now we have to hold onto what we know and love, grab happiness when we can find it and be grateful. Nothing about the future is guaranteed, the war taught me that much. If we have a chance at happiness and we don't take it ...."

"Maybe the trick is simply to recognize reasons to be happy when they're already there."

"That's for sure. And right now, I have a lot of reasons." He stared pointedly at her and then gazed around.

"It's wonderful on this hill," Daisy said, watching him revel in his surroundings.

Corbin hugged her close. "You're wonderful, this handkerchief is wonderful, this hill is wonderful, and it belongs to me." He jumped to his feet on the rock. "Stand up, I want to show you something. Come on ... I've got you, I won't let you fall."

"Wow," she said, "I can see the entire farm from here!"

"Everything in sight and more besides will one day belong to me. Well, to Jimmy and me ... there's plenty for both of us. This is my birthright, Daisy. It's been here all along and I was too stupid to appreciate it."

They stood together taking it all in – the fertile fields, the wandering creek at the ravine bottom, the scent of apples traveling on a breeze from the orchard.

It was the beginning of another September in Judson. At last, a September of peace. The world had somehow endured another war, required now to begin numbering them. Released from their bondage of misery the dead warned from yesterday, while the youth begged for a future of peace on a whispering wind from tomorrow. If the world were perfect, tyrants would wage war only against themselves. No, in a perfect world there would be no tyrants.

The farm looked perfect from up on Rocky Knob – no visible weeds in the tomatoes or worms in the corn, no fences in need of repair. Corbin pictured the unseen abundance – woods full of wildlife, the dairy stocked with this year's harvest. As he gazed out on his own green fields, it seemed a perfect world. "Right now, I feel like the luckiest man alive. I don't think I could count all my blessings if I had fifty years." He folded her tighter against him as though afraid she'd slip away. "Daisy ... if I build a house on this hill, will you live with me here?"

She turned to search his face. "Corbin, is this a proposal?"

His eyes flickered affirmation. "Will you stay with me always?"

"Yes Corbin, I'll stay with you always."

"All the summers?"

"All the summers."

"Even the cold winters?"

"Especially the cold winters." She nuzzled her head against his chest in wonder. Being with him felt so easy, so natural. Was the rest of her life really to be filled with moments like this? A flock of birds moving as one looped low in front of them while the sinking sun set the western sky ablaze. She sucked in her breath and pointed. "Oh, look how beautiful!"

As Corbin gazed across the great expanse, the birds and the sun, the very clouds in the sky seemed to be his. "I know we're not supposed to bargain with God, but I did and ... here I am. You'll never catch me blind to happiness again, Daisy," he said. "With you by my side, everything I'm ever going to need is right here. Just think of it. We have each other now and this beautiful place is home."

HISTORICAL NOTES

*E*ighteen in 1942 is an historical novel. Fictitious characters play out imagined dramas against an historical backdrop, drawing attention to critical times by bringing them back to life.

The following separates
fiction from fact:

Judson, Pennsylvania is fictitious, its inhabitants imaginary, intended to represent the wartime home front. Movie house newsreels, shortages of gas, sugar, and coffee, ration stamps, draft registrations, and telegrams from the War Department all took place across the nation as described.

In Washington, D.C., the Carlton Hotel (now the St. Regis) and the Carlton Night Club, are real. Tommy Dorsey and Frank Sinatra did appear there, though not on the night of Dec 6, 1941.

America on Sunday, December 7 is an accurate depiction. The Washington Redskins did play the Philadelphia Eagles that day, and the description of what went on at Griffith Stadium, though partly imagined, is based on fact. John Daly's announcement of the attack on Pearl Harbor is actual, as is the reaction of the country in the following days.

The short summaries of the war throughout are true. Any dates related to real events are as accurate as possible, within the constraints of contradictions that have developed over time.

It is recognized here that the language used in dialogue among the men is mild compared to the actual flying profanity of GIs in World War II.

The 106th Infantry Division is real – its creation, general activities and movements. Basic training in Fort Jackson, maneuvers in Tennessee, Camp Atterbury, Camp Miles Standish, crossing the Atlantic, and the dates associated with same are all true. As are their short stay in England, arrival in St. Vith, take-over of the "quiet sector" on Schnee Eifel, and ultimate surrender.

The surprise German offensive along the Schnee Eifel in December, 1944 is the famous Battle of the Bulge where forty-two thousand Americans, including large chunks of the 106th, were captured or killed.

The military track of the main character, Corbin O'Connell, is inspired by the actual life in uniform of a member of the 106th HQ Artillery Battery who generously shared his experiences (which did not include, by the way, a demotion). Though not at Stalag (abbreviation for Stammlager) IX-B or Berga, he was captured in a similar way on December 17, endured a similar torturous train ride, and bore similar deprivation until Palm Sunday, March 25, 1945.

The men Corbin meets in the Army – Pappy Dutton, Vinne Cartuzzo, Charlie Ragsdale, Major Stewart Shiller, Solly Shapiro and Lep Eisen are all fictitious.

General Eisenhower's son, John, did attend the U.S. Military Academy at West Point and graduated on D-Day, June 6, 1944.

German Regimental Colonel Joachim Peiper's panzer march to Stavelot really happened. Though Corbin's exploits in Stavelot are an invention from beginning to end, the other goings-on – the American vs. German battle, the gunning down of civilians for harboring Americans – are factual.

Corbin's capture at Kaiserbaracke Crossing is a fabrication, but a similar event could certainly have taken place near that spot. The march to Gerolstein and the people mentioned therein are contrived, although thousands of GIs were marched to Gerolstein in much the same manner. The Gerolstein Rail Station itself, and the nightmare train rides, are real.

The description of Stalag IX-B, including the segregation of American Jews, is taken from real accounts.

Berga is unfortunately real, along with that second train ride to get there. Commandant Ludwig Merz, Sergeant Kunz, and Corporal Edwin Metz are real people. The events at Berga, though happening to fictitious characters, actually did happen to men that were there.

The death march in early April, 1945 really took place. The survivors of that march were rescued by General George Patton's 11th Armored Division, and the description of their conditions is not exaggerated.

Camp Lucky Strike in Le Havre, France is real – one of several U.S. Army hospitals set up in Europe to handle the overwhelming numbers of wounded and ailing GIs. Many did return to the United States on the Queen Mary, and many were admitted to Halloran Army Hospital on Staten Island.

A little more about Berga: From arrival on February 13, 1945 until liberation on April 23, an estimated 73 men from the original 350 died. Berga's main villains, Merz and Metz, were tried in Dachau by an American court in September, 1946. They claimed to be simply obeying orders, which was probably true. Both were found guilty and sentenced to death. Their sentences, however, were commuted to life in prison, then later reduced. Merz was freed in 1951; Metz, in 1954.

It is hoped that any survivors of World War II POW camps, nightmare train rides, nightmare marches, and especially Berga, will view *Eighteen in 1942* as an honest effort to paint an accurate picture of their ordeal.

RESOURCES

Books:

Time Life Books: *World War II – The Home Front*, 1978

St. Vith – U.S. 106th Infantry Division, 1999 by Michael Tolhurst

Given Up for Dead – American GIs in the Nazi Concentration Camp at Berga, 2005 by Flint Whitlock

Publications:

War Department Pamphlet No. 21-7 *"If You Should Be Captured, These Are Your Rights"*

Life Magazine December 25, 1944 *"Life Visits a GI Phone Center"*

Sports Illustrated November 29, 1999 *"The Second World War Kicks Off"* by S.L. Price

The Bulge Bugle May, 2003 *Captured in the Bulge"* by Joseph M. Elek

New York Times February 27, 2005 *"The Lost Soldiers of Stalag IX-B"* by Roger Cohen

World War II Magazine 2007 *"The Fuhrer's Final Hurrah"* by Stephen Ambrose

Military History March/April, 2008 *"Sniper"* by Geoffrey
  Norman

Documentaries:

"Berga: Soldiers of Another War", 2003 by Charles Guggenheim

"The War", 2007 by Ken Burns

"World War II in HD", 2009 by Lou Reda Productions

Websites:

PBS.org Berga: Soldiers of Another War

PBS.org American Experience: Battle of the Bulge

OralHistory.Rutgers.edu: Battle of the Bulge

IndianaMilitary.org: 106th Infantry Division Golden Lions

LoneSentry.com: 106th Infantry Division

JewishVirtualLibrary.org: The Soldiers of Berga

World War II Troop Ships / Troop Crossings

MilitaryRanks.US

Wikipedia.org

ACKNOWLEDGEMENTS

Three particular members of the World War II generation deserve my sincere thanks: Donald "Dusty" Rhodes for spending hours and hours with me and generously allowing portions of his personal history to be used as foundation for this book; William L. Freienmuth for answering my incessant questions and letting me claim him as a friend; Flora Bolling Adams for being my first reader, grammar coach, encourager, mother.

For their time and interest I am grateful to my other readers, all precious to me in their own way: Rebecca Green, Jordan Green, Debbie McGeogh, and Judy Welterlen. Each offered keen advice, which I acted on. Special thanks to my editor, Craig Welterlen, who attempted to set a higher standard through substantial amounts of unvarnished critical advice softened by the occasional tidbit of approval. No doubt, the book is better because of him, and I would still be making changes if he hadn't insisted I stop.

Although the contributions of those acknowledged here have been substantial toward any strengths this book might have, all errors and omissions are mine alone.

ACKNOWLEDGMENTS